THE THEGN'S CREED

❡ This book is dedicated to all those loved ones who made my childhood such a happy one and encouraged my imagination to roam free

The Thegn's Creed

SUE BODDINGTON

Privately printed for
Sue Boddington
Dacia, 99 Poulshot Road, Poulshot, Devizes, Wilts SN10 1RX
sue.boddington@virgin.net

by The Hobnob Press
8 Lock Warehouse, Severn Road, Gloucester GL1 2GA

Design and typesetting by John Chandler. The text is set in 14 point Doves Type, leaded 2 points. Doves Type is a digital facsimile, created by Robert Green, of the celebrated face made by Edward Prince in 1899 for the Doves Press, based on Jenson's 15th-century Venetian type.

Born and bred in Wiltshire Sue Boddington graduated from Bristol University in History, English, Theology and Philosophy. After flirting with teaching, acting and singing, she joined Wiltshire Library Service, holding the posts of Senior Librarian Adult Learning for the county and Community Librarian for the Calne area. Now retired, she still lives in Wiltshire and is the voluntary curator of Calne Heritage Centre.

Front cover design by Freda Jackson.

CHAPTER ONE

There were flashes of light, aggressive, darting flashes. The noise that accompanied them was aggressive too. It was the disciplined zip of the scythe as it cleaved the air and struck at the stalks of barley. It was mid- August and Dunstan had begun to harvest the ripe crops. Colour and movement blended together. The silver sheen as the sun caught the blade of the scythe; the backdrop of the blue sky as the horizon seemed to touch the very tips of the barley ears; the strain and knot of the sinew down the long arm that swung the scythe; the amber of the trembling barley stalks and the flaxen hair of the reaper were all united so that it was hard to imagine that any one element of the scene could exist without the other.

The reaper was alone in the large field, but he had worked his way through more than a quarter of it. His pale complexion was tinged pink with exertion. A bout of coughing interrupted his work. For a second or two it bent him double. Perhaps a barley moat had lodged in his throat, but it was more likely that the exercise was irritating the cough that had dogged him all through the year. He took a deep breath and began to reap again. He was proud of that barley. It was a splendid crop this season and glancing beyond the barley to the wheat field beyond it, he could see that too was maturing well. The contrast with the meagre yields of the past two years was something to warm the heart.

His eyes were still on the wheat, when he noticed a figure moving along the narrow path that ran as straight as a plumb line between the crop fields and pasture land. It was a small figure and as it drew nearer Dunstan could see that the man was lame. The young reaper could now identify his cousin Cerdic. He smiled to himself and continued to reap.

Cerdic was soon picking his way through the barley that had fallen before the scythe. He had taken very little time to reach the field, for he walked briskly despite his disability. He stood watching Dunstan for a while, following the rise and fall of the blade, trying to stare into the flashes of reflected light without blinking, then he murmured, 'I love watching you work. It does as much for my soul as Augustine or Boethius. The fathers are quite right; toil is a cornerstone of the soul. I always realise it much more when I'm watching someone else work than when I am working myself.'

Dunstan turned around, laughing, well acquainted with his cousin's dry sense of humour. Cerdic's face was perfectly serious. He had his hands folded demurely in front of him, head to one side, clearly intending to give the impression of complacent piety. His cousin's answer was to offer him the scythe. 'Well then, benefit my soul.'

Cerdic's mock self-righteous look dissolved into a broad grin, as he waved the tool away from him as if it had been infected with the plague. Now he looked himself. Cerdic always gave a general impression of mischief, elf-like. He was small and neat; the compact little body looked full of energy. His features were small too, finely made; a firm pointed chin, cheek bones that were high-ridged and light blue eyes whose expression alternated between a shrewd perceptiveness and sheer mischief.

'That was a perfect answer Dunstan- the very thing to uncover my vicious sloth.'

'Oh I do not think I have ever noticed that you had the time to be lazy,' Dunstan said, knowing just how little time his cousin had for leisure.

Dunstan and his brother Edmund were both strong, easily capable of managing their farm. Their Uncle Cenred however was growing old; battle wounds and cares had aged him before his time. He could not work as hard as he was wont to and his farm was almost as big as theirs. This placed much responsibility on Cerdic's shoulders and sometimes Dunstan felt that it was too much. He was agile, despite his twisted leg. He could work as hard as anyone and he never complained, but at the end of a long day, Dunstan, who knew him so well, could sense his exhaustion. If anyone appeared to be self-sufficient, it was Cerdic, but he had long learned that he needed Dunstan. They had grown up together. Cerdic was four years the senior, but if the elder boy ever needed reassurance or understanding he came to his cousin. Dunstan had always been compassionate, sensitive to the needs of others.

They had not seen each other for three days, for Dunstan had been to Bath Market, selling vegetables and six fine piglets. Edmund had reckoned that they would get a better return in the market of that expanding town than locally. But Bath was fifteen miles away and once Dunstan had paid for over-night lodgings the profits had been much slimmer than Edmund had hoped. The Norman Conquest and the years of unrest that followed meant lean times for the towns. Although the markets of Normandy were opened to English traders, King William's relations with France and Flanders were not on a good footing. So instead of trade with the Continent increasing, it had diminished in volume. The King of Denmark was still hoping to take the English crown and the constant threat of invasion from that quarter hindered trade in the north and east of England. The traders in Bath market were quick to point out that they could no longer afford to pay the generous prices for goods that they had in King Edward's day.

'How was Bath?' Cerdic asked, running his finger along the blade of the scythe to test its sharpness. He winced to find it sharper than he imagined.

A thin stream of blood appeared on his finger, which rapidly filled the intricate channels of lines so that they stood out like a mosaic. He began to suck the cut as Dunstan replied, 'Much the same as ever, except that it grows so swiftly. They have taken the fortifications down on the west side and built houses. Houses are creeping up the sides of the valleys too. It is a beautiful sight at dusk, if you are travelling down into the town. All the rush lights in the houses shine and beckon you.'

He had met an Irish ascetic on the road, an ancient brown man, steeped in the traditions of Iona and Lindisfarne. He had shared some bread with him and he told Dunstan stories of the heroic days, of the devotion of great men like Columba and Aidan. The Irishman, despite his wrinkled face and bent back, gave off the kind of zeal that had fired the early champions of Christianity and Dunstan was spellbound. The young man loved God with an unshakeable devotion. The stories of those great missionaries of the faith thrilled him. The Irishman's words and those distant lights, as they moved down into the wooded slopes that led to Bath, produced an exquisite emotion in him that he could never put into words. In his effort to recapture just the smallest part of that feeling he had almost forgotten Cerdic until he heard, 'Don't look through me like that Dunstan. You look as if you are about to have a vision.'

'Sorry. I was just thinking of my journey.'

'So I gathered. Well, did you get our Edmund's top prices?'

Cerdic emphasised the last two words as if they had become a catch phrase with Edmund. Dunstan sighed.

'No I did not. Once the expenses were paid out, we made little more than we would have done in Melksham or Calne market. Poor Edmund was not happy.'

He remembered the disappointed look on his brother's face when he had returned home and revealed the results of his marketing. He knew that their financial position was declining, particularly after a series of bad harvests and it was Edmund who felt responsible for the continuing prosperity of the farm. Dunstan felt guilty because he did not share the worry. They had always managed in the past. This year the harvest was good.

They would recover.

Cerdic ran his hand briskly over his close-cropped brown hair, the smile on his face fading away. He might joke about Edmund's concern, but he did not take it lightly. He was less optimistic than Dunstan. His father too had troubles. Cenred was less secure economically than his nephews. Life was not easy for the Saxon freeman in Anglo-Norman England. Cerdic had sought out his cousin that hot August morning for that very reason.

'Dunstan, I came here on father's orders with very serious intent and I waste time playing the fool as always. We called over to see you early this morning. Father is back at the house with Edmund. He has made an important decision and he wants you both to hear it. You know what he is like, chronically ceremonious. He will not utter a word until we are all assembled. To stall for time he is probably discussing every individual vegetable in the plots.'

This conjured up a picture of Cenred and Edmund measuring beans with precision. Both men acknowledged it, but neither laughed.

Cerdic now looked agitated and Dunstan felt a wave of fear pass through him.

'Are you bound to secrecy until we get back?'

'No.'

'Then what is the matter?'

Cerdic stared at him thoughtfully, and then said, 'Father has decided to sell out to De Tosny.'

Dunstan did not know what to say. He gnawed his bottom lip, considering the repercussions of this decision.

Edmund would be mortified. He looked helplessly at Cerdic, who was silent.

The two farms lay adjoining each other on either side of a strip of woodland. The land had been in the possession of the family for many generations. Eadberht, the four times great grandfather of Dunstan and Cerdic was a thegn, a gesith of King Athelstan. In 927, Athelstan had granted a large area of land to Eadberht in his home county of Wiltshire, to be held by his descendants in perpetuity. The land was freed from all public burdens except the three fundamental services of supporting the cost of the repair of fortifications and bridges and bearing some of the expense of recruiting local men to serve in the militia when needed. The King had taken the land from one of his own royal estates and it was a fine reward for his faithful Eadberht.

The thegn had died the death which all thegns from the early days of the war band and the joys of hall would wish to die. He had died in battle, during King Eadred's Northumbrian campaign and tales of his daring courage grew up, which were jealously preserved in his family.

His son Osbert settled down on the land and built himself a handsome house of wood and became a gentleman farmer. Lucrative economic intercourse with the villages of the royal estate assured him of prosperity. The descendants of Eadberht the thegn of King Athelstan became important in this particular hundred of Wiltshire. The head of the family attended the shire court.

But Osbert's descendants lived in an age that saw the gradual extension of territorial over-lordship. Peasant and thegn alike, faced with bad harvests and hardship were commending themselves to lords, surrendering up certain of their rights as freeholders in exchange for the security of protection. The tenurial rights were manifold and loose. Some paid rent, others rendered labour services. The Danish invasions of the 9th and 10th centuries accelerated this process. It became increasingly difficult to maintain a free status, but the family of Eadberht held out.

In 1049 Wulfstan, the fourth direct descendant in the male line, died and left a provision in his will that the land be divided between his two sons, Edgar and Cenred. Conveniently, a strip of woodland divided the land almost in half. Edgar, as the elder son took the slightly larger acreage and helped his brother to build a house on the other side of the wood. Seventeen years later England was hammered by the Norman invasion. The family could not forget its thegnly traditions. Edgar and his eldest son, Edmund, who was then almost twenty, accompanied King Harold on his march up country to meet Harold Hardrada at Stamford Bridge. They also took part in the hectic scramble back south again, in a desperate effort to oppose William of Normandy's landing at Pevensey. Edgar fell at Hastings; he was cut down by a superbly accoutred Norman knight who distained the army of the last Saxon king.

Edmund, though badly wounded had survived and once he had recovered enough to think straight, he had to decide what to do as he saw the results of William's victory materializing over the next few weeks. His Uncle Cenred was determined to stay put. Edmund had his brother to consider. Young thegns were already beginning to flee to Scotland or across the channel and he was tempted to do likewise. Perhaps he could join the Emperor's troops in Constantinople with a chance of fighting these usurping Normans on the continent. He could leave Dunstan with Cenred; but he did not want to abandon the boy. He loved him and knew that he must be responsible for him. He considered taking his brother into exile, but it would be no life for a twelve year old, particularly for the shy, gentle Dunstan. So Edmund decided to make terms. His great pride made it agony for him. There were hot tears in his eyes when he agreed to the terms proposed by the king's representatives. Surprisingly, it was not a crushing penalty. After examining the original charter issued by Athelstan, which was kept in the monastery on the hill half a mile from the northern boundary of Edmund's farm, the royal commissioners agreed to leave the freehold rights just as they had been, but to annex four hides of land from each farm.

The four hides on the northern side were granted to the monastery, the four on the village side to the royal estate.

Cenred was relieved at such leniency, thinking of all the other well-born Saxon families all over the country who would suffer much more than this, but Edmund could feel only resentment. Life went on much the same for them except that their means of sustenance was drastically straightened. The people from the four villages that made up the royal estate still looked up to the thegnly family, respectful of their birth and traditions, but it could never be the same for Edmund. He could never forget that there was a military rule imposed on him by an alien aristocracy. Hastings and the events surrounding that battle had left an indelible mark on him. A tough shell had hardened around his pride; it heightened his awareness of family traditions and it taught him to hate.

The folk on the royal estate were left in peace, if their constant state of apprehension could ever be called peace, until King William granted the entire estate to Roger De Tosny, the brother of Ralph De Tosny, one of his leading barons. De Tosny made the most of the tighter control Norman ideas of feudalism imposed on the loose Anglo-Saxon tenurial relationships. The demands on the royal estate in the days of Edward the Confessor were not heavy. De Tosny turned the screw. Even those were still officially freemen could see little hope for their grandchildren.

The Norman coveted the two farms on the edge of his manor. He considered two such freemen as anomalies in a new age. He was eager to begin large scale sub-infeudation, to set up his knights on tenancies on his estates. The farms would suit his purposes perfectly. He had tried to brush the Saxons aside, have them forcibly removed, but when he found this legally indefensible, he resorted to tempting them with offers of economic security. His reeve was so fiercely rebuffed by Edmund that he gave up the cause as lost, but Cenred was a different proposition. The old thegn was in a worse financial position than his nephews. The land annexed from his farm had been his best arable. Edmund's loss was mostly pasture. Then there had been a fire in Cenred's barn that had destroyed most of a year's barley crop. He had never really recovered from that disaster. His son was married with an eleven month old boy to care for. He had to think of them. Born down with worries, Cenred had at last succumbed to De Tosny.

As the two cousins stood looking at each other, pictures flashed through Dunstan's mind in quick succession; his father and Edmund departing with the local muster in 1066; Uncle Cenred telling Edmund that their lot could be worse; Edmund's violent reaction to the approach of De Tosny's reeve. Never once had he thought that Cenred would really sell.

'Cerdic, this is going to hurt Edmund very much.'

Cerdic was relieved that the silence was broken. He gave a terse nod. He was sure it would hurt them all.

'I know. I can just imagine that look of mortified accusation. He will never understand the element of necessity in the case. It took me long enough to understand. It will be impossible for him. But what about you Dunstan, does it hurt you? I hate to think that you failed to understand father's motives. It has been a hard struggle to reach a decision. It was not taken lightly. How do you feel about it?'

Dunstan was fidgeting with the small cross of polished wood that he wore on a piece of leather around his neck. In his concern for Edmund he had not considered his own feelings. What Edmund thought and felt was so important to him, but he knew that good terms from De Tosny could be a true benefit to his uncle. In many ways Dunstan and his brother differed, but in one aspect in particular they were worlds apart. Dunstan had none of his brother's pride. The fact that he was a thegn meant little to him. It was so vital to Edmund that Dunstan often felt the tension between his brother's aspirations and his own natural humility. He was so eager to do right and he had read so many times that pride was the greatest of the seven sins. He was not sure if this included Edmund's kind of pride. If the judgement had been left to his forgiving heart, he would have pleaded extenuating circumstances. But the authorities were so absolute on the point and they were so much wiser than he. He often prayed for guidance about it, but he was never convinced that he should wholly condemn his brother's attitude.

'I am not sure,' he answered Cerdic's question at last 'I do not think that I am hurt for myself, mostly for Edmund. I am sure that Uncle Cenred will always do what is best. I think that Edmund will come to see that too.'

Cerdic half repressed a sigh of relief. He should have known there would be no resentment from Dunstan.

'Well come on then Dunstan. We had better go back there.'

He hid the scythe under the barley to discourage thieves and they began to make their way back to the house, Cerdic hopping over the fallen barley on one leg like a sparrow and the lanky Dunstan with his long stride, crossing two rows at once.

When they began walking side by side, the contrast was comical, one cousin so small and compact, the other easily four inches over six foot with a bony frame and a shambling walk.

The straight path soon led them to the farm, a broad rectangular building about forty feet long and half that wide with a roof framed as a triangular prism and thatched with straw. The thatch was in good order with no dark, rotting patches. The framework of the house was formed by a series of vertical poles set in post holes around a flagstone base and infilled with tightly fitting horizontal wooden planks painted with a lime wash. The doors were set opposite each other in the centre of the long sides with two windows cut on each side of both doors. A porch made from woven rushes projected out over one door.

Around the house were two large barns, stables, cattle pens and a duck pond occupied by four white ducks. There was also a wooden drinking trough for the horses which doubled as a bath for Edmund and Dunstan in the warm weather. To the left of these buildings lay the vegetable plots, a patchwork of variegated greens and browns shaded by three apple trees. Beyond this was the well and behind it the ground rose to form a low embankment so that the farm sat in a hollow protected on one side.

Two dogs and a cat came out to greet Dunstan and Cerdic as they neared their destination. One dog was a sleek wolf hound of tremendous size, the other a mongrel of indeterminate ancestry. The tortoiseshell cat seemed perfectly at ease in the company of the dogs. The three of them kept pace with the cousins as they approached the house, vying for attention and circling around excitedly. There was a flurry of wings and a satin-backed jackdaw alighted on Dunstan's shoulder.

'Good morning,' said the jackdaw. Dunstan returned the salutation, so did Cerdic, bowing an acknowledgement to the bird as it watched him with one bright eye. The other eye was keeping the cat in sight. Cerdic was expecting the goats to fall in line, but they must have been up in the pasture.

Dunstan felt a sinking sensation as he ducked his head to pass through the doorway. The jackdaw flew up on to the roof and as Dunstan straightened up again, he saw his uncle Cenred sitting on a stool by the far window soberly discussing the crop yield. Edmund was standing beside him, twisting around his finger the cord of the rush blind that covered the glassless window at night. Dunstan studied his brother's face. There was no sign of frustration. Clearly he had not yet suspected what Cenred's visit portended. Edmund turned around when he heard footsteps behind him.

He seemed surprised to see his brother. 'Dunstan, what are you doing back here? Is anything wrong?'

'No.'

'Then why have you left the field? I suppose Cerdic has thought up some brilliant scheme whereby the barley cuts itself.'

Cerdic gave a wry grin.

'Well, let me tell you- 'Edmund continued, but Cenred cut him short.

'Just a moment,' he eased himself off the stool and laid a hand on his nephew's arm. 'I know you are eager to get your barley cut. Cerdic and I will give you a hand later. I asked my son to fetch Dunstan. I have something important to tell you both. The barley can wait till then.'

Edmund sighed impatiently, 'Well, why did you not say so before instead of all this secrecy? You have been here long enough. You don't often play games Uncle Cenred.'

His tone was good –humoured. He was smiling as he said it, but there was a trace of anxiety in his eyes.

'I thought you should both be here when I told you. This is no game my boy; far from it. I think you had better sit down.'

'Whatever for?'

Edmund laughed, but the look he gave Dunstan was apprehensive in the extreme. There was something ominous in the calm of his uncle's voice. Seeing that he was not going to sit down, Cenred did so himself. He crossed his legs and fixed his gaze on Edmund.

'I will come straight to the point. After a great deal of consideration, I have decided to sell my land to Roger De Tosny. I have already signed an agreement which the reeve drew up. He will be calling for it tomorrow.'

Dunstan felt wretched as he watched the colour drain out of Edmund's face.

It was worse because the more he thought about it the more he felt Cenred had done the right thing.

'God in heaven!' Edmund hissed in a fierce undertone, 'You cannot mean that. You cannot sit there in all seriousness and tell me that my father's brother is willing to be a dog-on-a lead tenant of a Norman baron. No, I refuse to believe it.'

Cerdic saw Dunstan wince and was suddenly full of anger over the intransigence that he always knew they would find in Edmund. He clicked his tongue in disgust.

'That is typical of you, immediately absolute. You will never give an inch will you? Father's visit here to reconcile you to his decision is a waste of time because you will have the knife of your thegnly pride stuck into his ribs forever more over this, without once considering why he did it. Do you think it does not hurt us as well? Do you think in your remarkable self- conceit that you are the only one who has any respect for the family traditions? Sometimes Edmund, I wish I could thump your head.'

Dunstan's grey eyes opened wide. He was astonished by his cousin's fierce attack on Edmund. 'Cerdic!'

Cerdic turned to explain himself, when Cenred said, 'That is quite enough Cerdic. That was uncalled for. Apologise to your cousin.'

Cerdic opened his mouth to speak, but Edmund interrupted him.

'I do not want to hear any apologies from him. I do not care one jot what he said. All I care about is what you have done. Just like that, without even consulting me first. You did not even tell me that De Tosny was still plaguing you. Oh, how could you do it?'

He banged his fist into the wall in frustration and Cerdic limped out into the doorway, tossing his head. This was his own inheritance they were selling not Edmund's and the arrogant way his cousin swung around on his heels irritated him. Edmund was good at the dramatic gesture; he had the looks for it. Dunstan was not sure whether he should follow Cerdic or go over to his brother. He always felt insecure in the midst of hostility, particularly between people he loved.

He was thankful for the continued calm of his uncle, who was saying, 'It is not a question of how I could do it. I had no choice. I am too old to scrape and worry any more. If we go on like this, I will not have anything to hand over to my son and what hope would little Cutha have? It is no good pointing to the good harvest. If I sold the entire wheat crop, which I cannot risk doing, I would not break even this year. I have not pledged myself to labour service; you can rest easy on that score. I have agreed to pay rent.'

'And do you think De Tosny will play fair with you? Do you imagine that he will not take the first opportunity that comes his way to push up the rent and keep pushing it up until you cannot possibly pay? He wants the land without you on it. He wants to provide for some of his knights on it. Damn it Uncle Cenred, use your head!'

Cenred refused to be ruffled by his nephew. He was sure that De Tosny would abide by the letter of the law. He had to convince himself of that or the secure future he envisaged for his family would be nothing but a chimera.

He warned Edmund that De Tosny's influence could make it difficult for him and that he too should consider some form of agreement. Edmund's reaction was predictable.

'No thank you. I would rather starve, lose the land altogether than hold it for De Tosny. As a landless adventurer I would still have my self-respect. Our ancestor, Eadberht was once a landless man.'

Cenred shook his head. 'You cannot live in the past. I do not need to tell a young man like you of that.' He turned to Dunstan. 'You have been very quiet boy. What do you feel about this?'

'You must do what you think best Uncle.'

'This is best and what is more, I know your father would have agreed with me.'

Edmund took a deep breath. The colour had come back to his face now with his passion. He had seen his father at Hastings; had heard him cry out 'God save King Harold' as a Norman broadsword had cleaved him almost in half. How dare anyone who had not seen this speak for his father?

'What do you know? He would die of shame if he were here now. He would never agree to it, never.'

'Yes he would,' Dunstan said softly.

'Oh Dunstan, are you against me too? Do you want to sell out to De Tosny?'

Dunstan reached out and touched his brother's hand.

'Of course I am not against you. We do not need to sell. All I am trying to say is that you do not understand Uncle Cenred's position. Please try. I could not bear it if you did hold bad feelings against him for it. That would be terrible.'

He glanced towards the door where Cerdic was standing. He had his back to them, but there was no doubt that he was listening.

'Please say that you will accept Uncle Cenred's decision without any more wrangling. I will not rest easy in my mind until I see you shake hands on it. Come on, take each other's hand.'

Dunstan was so concerned, so earnest. Edmund never could disappoint his brother when he spoke like that, besides his first spasm of anger was cooling and transmuting into a martyred resignation. He stared at Cenred's outstretched hand, then grasped it.

'The choice was yours uncle. I think you are wrong, but I cannot hold it against you. There is no point in making things even more difficult by bad feeling.'

Dunstan's relieved smile amused Edmund, who reached out and ruffled his hair.

'There, that pleases you does it not, peacemaker? You know if you grow much taller I will not be able to ruffle your thatch because I will not be able to reach.'

He said this with a natural affection and Cenred was surprised that he had cooled down so soon. Cerdic had turned around in the doorway. He glanced at Dunstan and then came briskly over to Edmund.

'Cousin Edmund, I have a big mouth. I am sorry that I barked at you.'

'Forget it Tich. Your spirit makes up for your lack of inches. But I truly would like to see you try to thump my head.'

Although Edmund's intransigence could irritate him, Cerdic was fond of his cousin and appreciated his sense of humour. Edmund could be full of pride at one moment and laughing at himself the next in a way that was most disarming.

'Now perhaps you two will go back to the reaping and I will join you, but I do not want to talk about this anymore. I have not reconciled myself to it enough to discuss it reasonably.'

Edmund gave both Dunstan and Cerdic a persuasive push towards the door. Then he leaned back against the wall with a sigh.

Edmund, son of Edgar was almost thirty. He was a handsome creature. He too was tall, although several inches shorter than Dunstan. His body was lithe and well proportioned, with broad shoulders, a deep chest and slim hips. He had the grace of an athlete. His strength and skill with a sword was famous locally and he rode as well as any Norman knight. His large dark eyes,

a shade of deep olive green, were striking, very intense. When they were lit with anger or scorn they could scorch. Add to this, thick, dark brown hair reaching to his shoulders, a nose that was straight, classical and a mobile mouth that was sometimes firm and strong, at others, sensuous, inviting.

It was no wonder that the village gossips were always singing his praises and folk said that the nobility of his birth showed in his face.

It was also frequently said that although Dunstan was the kindest boy one could wish to meet, he could not be compared to his brother for looks.

He was considered plain. Under that thatch of untidy flaxen hair, his face certainly fell below classical standards. His jaw was too long, his nose a shade too large. The smoky grey eyes were short-sighted and he had to strain to distinguish objects at a distance. Although his complexion was pale, his ears had a habit of tingeing pink when he was embarrassed. But it was an open, honest, compassionate face, a face it was impossible not to like and encouraged others to confide in him.

These brothers, so different in temperament and appearance were bound together with an indissoluble bond of love, which circumstance might strain, but never break.

Edmund, Dunstan and Cerdic had between them finished cutting the field of barley by midday. Edmund then left them to gather it together into stooks, while he went into the village to meet someone. 'Which lucky lady will have the pleasure this afternoon?' Cerdic asked with a grin.

His cousin did not reply, just flashed him an amused smile and began to stroll towards the village.

It was early evening before all the barley was gathered. The two families always helped each other out with their harvests, but if they had the need to catch up they would hire cottars from the village. The cottar was a man who, though he had a house of his own, did not hold a full share in the village arable. As he did not have much land to tend, he was always ready to hire himself out to work for his neighbours. All the cottars were eager to work for the thegnly families who lived on the edge of the manor. They could rely on getting paid and the prestige was valued. The Saxons still held their thegns in great respect and a villager would be proud to work for the descendants of Eadberht.

When Dunstan returned home, Edmund was already there. He had set out on the table bread, cheese, slices of pork and a jug of mead. The day's work had given Dunstan an appetite. He set about his meal with enthusiasm. Edmund however did not seem interested in his food. He said little and Dunstan was sure he had not spent the afternoon enjoying himself with a woman. His mood was too dark. He helped Dunstan clear the table and then disappeared into his own room.

There were five rooms in the house; a main hall which ran the length of the building with four smaller rooms leading off from it, divided from the hall by plaited wicker screens. The brothers had a room each, one was kept for visitors and the other Dunstan had turned into a chapel. He calculated that he had a free hour before securing the animals for the night. He tried to read, but could not settle. Edmund was too much on his mind. His brother always brought the cows down from the pasture after the evening meal, but this evening he had not left his room. Dunstan could guess what he was doing. He placed his book mark in the appropriate page and stowed the book away with care. Most material possessions meant little to him, but he had a passion for books. He had built up a small library for himself and was always eager to acquire more. Books were his one extravagance and Edmund could never grudge him something which gave him so much pleasure.

He had received an excellent education himself. He could read Latin, speak fluent French and was capable of reciting all the traditional Saxon poetry. In his youth he had composed poems and shown much interest in philosophy. But Hastings had changed him. He could find no consolation in reading or philosophising anymore.

Everything turned to bitterness. He could taste the tang of defeat and humiliation in his mouth. He rarely opened a book now. He told Dunstan that he did not have the time. He did not know how to explain to his younger brother how the old words, the descriptions of the past, gave him such pain. He still went to church, observing the outward forms of piety, but he was not sure that he could forgive God for what had happened to his nation.

Dunstan tapped gently on the screen around Edmund's room before he pulled aside the hinged flap and went in. His guess was a correct one. Edmund was brooding. He was sitting at a low table, staring at a burnished helmet that lay on the table in front of him. It was an old helmet that had seen much service. The metal was worn thin in places and was dented in others, but it had been tended with care for it shone like new.

Edmund seemed to be intent on the reflection of his own image in the surface of the metal, but Dunstan knew that he saw something beyond that. He did not acknowledge Dunstan's presence. He did not realise that he was there until he spoke.

'Edmund, I wish you would not do this.'

He looked up slowly, gazing at Dunstan as if the sound but not the words had registered with him. It was as if he was awaking from a trance.

'I said that I wish you would not sit here hurting yourself. Brooding over that helmet cannot bring father back. We cannot change what has happened. You must try to accept things as they are and put the past in its proper place'

Edmund laughed. It was a short laugh, devoid of humour.

'Have you been reading those philosophers again?'

'Do not try to pass it off like that. I know that I am no authority and I also know what Uncle Cenred's decision has meant to you, but this will not help. Father's helmet was not meant for this.'

Edmund leapt to his feet, the helmet in his hands, a strange look in his eyes.

'No, it was meant for battle, for a great conflict like Hastings. You just do not understand these things. I know you were only a lad then, but I doubt if you ever will understand. You are not made that way.'

'What is there to understand? I know what death is.'

'I am talking about what we fought for, the existence of the Saxon race, the freedom of our country. Does freedom not mean anything to you?'

'Yes very much,' Dunstan replied quietly. He was thinking of another kind of freedom, that of inner peace. He was leaning against the wall, chewing his finger nail, watching Edmund pace around the room. He longed to calm the fierce agitation of his brother's high spirit. Edmund had not missed the implication of his reply.

'You may find comfort in the peace that passes all understanding. I am sure Abbot Robert has schooled you well. But that is not what I am trying to explain to you. I did not know the real meaning of freedom until that day on the battle field.'

He thumped his fist on the table. 'I should have

died at Hastings.' He fingered the scar at the side of his neck that ran down past his shoulder blade. 'I should never have let Alfstan help me off the battlefield. I should have died beside by father and my king.'

'You were badly wounded Edmund. What would have been the point of you dying too? Everyone knows how bravely you fought at Hastings. You have nothing to be ashamed of.'

Edmund did not seem to hear him. 'Those of us who survived thought we could regroup and launch a counter attack over the following months, but it did not happen.'

He had never been able to understand how the Normans had subdued the country so swiftly. He was laid up for several weeks with his wound and the fever that resulted from it and by the time he was on his feet again all serious resistance appeared to be crushed.

His mind strayed back to that day when his whole life changed; the heaving mass of bodies, the ground slippery with blood, the screams of men and horses barely distinguishable from each other. He had slashed with his sword, parried with his shield until his arms felt so heavy, that he wondered how he managed to lift them.

He saw his father fall and tried to reach him stumbling over the dead and dying. Then he was struck from behind, a blow across his shoulder of such force that he was knocked down on to his knees.

There was no pain at first, just numbness and a strange shuddering that ran through the whole of his body. He steeled himself for the death blow, but it did not come. A Norman foot-soldier fell to the side of him, his arms stretching desperately back behind him to clutch at an axe that had cleaved through his chain mail and buried itself deep into his back. He writhed on the floor, blood frothing on his lips. Edmund was being hauled to his feet. His Uncle Alfstan, his mother's brother was barely recognisable, streaked with blood, dirt and sweat.

'Harold has fallen,' he croaked, his voice dry and cracked, 'We're finished, but I will not let you die here my lad.'

The blood was beginning to flow freely from Edmund's wound now, the numbness replaced by searing pain. The details of what happened next were hazy. Alfstan caught the reins of a loose horse, shoved him up into the saddle and swung himself up behind him. How they managed to escape the melee unscathed he would never know, but Alfstan had urged on the horse as far as he dare before he knew he must stop to attend to his nephew's wounds.

They stopped where a few wattle and daub huts were tucked beneath the sweep of the downs. The occupants were living close to subsistence level, but they gave aid willingly, washing and binding Edmund's wounds as best they could with their limited resources.

Alfstan was eager to get the boy home, but doubted he had the strength for a ride of several days. He had lost much blood and was already showing signs of fever. He tried to convince his uncle that he was fit enough to travel, but when he tried to stand, everything drifted away from him and he fell back on to the straw pallet unconscious. When he came to himself again, he was lying on his back amongst some sweet smelling hay in a farm cart that rattled along the rutted track towards Wiltshire.

Alfstan had given the peasant the gold bangle that he wore on his arm in exchange for the cart. The astonished man had never held in his hand anything worth so much. Its barter value would buy him a much finer cart and food for his family for several weeks.

Edmund could recall seeing a pure white bird, a dove perhaps, contrasted against a soft blue sky, before he slipped back into the darkness. By the time they reached home he was in high fever.

Alfstan had taken him to the mill. The wife of Alleyn the miller had acquired a reputation as a healer. She was skilled in the preparation of herbs and infusions and she tended to Edmund with great care. He lay close to death for a week, but once the fever left him he gradually regained his strength.

Musing on it now, he smiled, remembering the first face that he saw clearly when he first emerged from that strange world of shadows, distorted images and sounds. A girl, perhaps ten years old, a girl with a wealth of auburn hair tumbling over her shoulders, her pale face dotted with golden brown freckles. She was gazing at him intently. She moved closer to the bed and with a surprising lack of reserve, kissed his cheek. Ilsa, she was always bold, always independent.

He would much rather contemplate the pleasures

of Ilsa, than the thoughts that troubled him now, but he brought himself back to the present, saying, 'Sometimes I wish I had never compromised and had carried through what I stood for right to the end. If I had gone abroad- but how could I with a 12 year old brother on my hands like you were? It would have been no life for you.'

'You make it sound as if all this is my fault,' observed Dunstan, half smiling.

'Of course not, but I ask you, when you grew older, what use would you have been in the Vagaringian Guard? Faced with a horde of barbarians you would have gone off to some place like your little prayer hole and prayed about it.'

Edmund often spoke before he considered. There was no real scorn in his voice, but Dunstan was hurt. He looked down at his feet. 'I can do other things.'

Fortunately Edmund just as often thought after he had spoken. He stopped pacing and touched his brother's arm.

'Oh Dunstan, I am sorry. That was an unworthy thing to say. I did not mean to belittle you.'

Dunstan laughed as he had a mental picture of himself in the personal guard of the Emperor. He could not deny that it was funny. Edmund however would have been splendid, but he was so grateful that his brother had decided to stay on the farm with him. Their Uncle Alfstan had joined the guard and died in some distant land that Dunstan had never heard of before.

'I am not really offended, although I do know how to defend myself if necessary. I must admit that I am not much for the descendants of Eadberht to be proud of. I would not be a very welcome addition to a war band. The point is, it does not grieve me one bit.'

The tightness in Edmund's face had relaxed. 'I have never met anyone as good natured as you. You take after mother. You have her patience. I wish you could have known her. When I was your age, if anyone had made a remark like that to me I would have put my fist between his eyes with some alacrity. Come to think of it, I would not hesitate long even now.'

Dunstan did not doubt it. Edmund ran his finger over the largest dent in the helmet. It was a slow, reflective movement; then he brought his open palm down and slapped it against his thigh.

'I have cows in the pasture,' he said in a brisk voice, 'I had better see to them, but do not imagine that my work can make me forget how much I hate the Normans. Each cow that I count into the stalls will just remind me that if it had not been for his gracious majesty, William of Normandy, William the Bastard, I would have twice as many.'

Dunstan did not answer. He was thinking how impossible it was to hate a whole race.

'By the way,' Edmund added, 'If, when you have finished in the yard, you happen to be going to that prayer hole of yours, you can say a few prayers for me. I need them.'

He never referred to Dunstan's tiny chapel as anything but a prayer hole, with an affectionate irreverence. Cerdic was always Tich and Dunstan's hair never rose beyond the status of a thatch. Dunstan nodded. He knew this was his brother's way of compensating him for the careless remark he had made earlier. They rarely came away from a difference of opinion anything but the best of friends.

CHAPTER TWO

The year had been good to the villagers. The mowing was completed early. The meadow land was ready to be thrown open on the traditional date of August 1ˢᵗ for the general use of the village. The cattle found that grazing on the freshly cut meadow was more satisfying by far than on the common waste land which had fed them all the summer. The barley harvest was well in progress and by the end of this month of August, the wheat too would be ready. Wheat and barley were the major crops grown on De Tosny's manor, although around the two villages on the Bath side of the estate, a small amount of rye was planted.

The village arable was divided into two large open fields, one sown and the other fallow. The scythe and plough worked side by side, for as the crops were being harvested in one field, so the fallow field was being ploughed ready for autumn sowing. This morning the full ox- team, four pairs of beasts, were at work with the plough. The oxen trudged along patiently and the blades of the plough turned the dark brown earth inwards to make a central ridge, dipping on either side into a furrow. The shape of each glistening sillion was like an inverted, elongated letter S.

The villagers held their land in small strips, rarely consolidated into compact blocks, but dotted about the arable. The whole field was divided into blocks of these strips, which varied in size and shape and were arranged as they could best be fitted into the field. There were some unploughable patches in between and also some very odd shaped bits which refused to fit into the over-all pattern and had earned the name of gores.

Every man was obliged to put hurdles at the end of his strips. De Tosny's own land, as opposed to the land tenanted from him, consisted of whole furlongs of arable.

The village itself was small, the entire population numbering just over one hundred. It was made up of clusters of wattle and daub cottages, with mud or thatched roofs. Here and there a wooden dwelling was conspicuous. There were two features however of which the villagers were particularly proud; the small, but sturdy stone church and the water mill.

The mill was right in the centre of the village and was still referred to as the new mill, although it had been built twelve years past, under the supervision of the king's reeve. The stream which provided the power to turn the big mill wheel was the one that sprang up near the monastery on the hill to the north. In one direction it flowed down into the village, where it had been channelled to end in a circular pond, the fisheries.

In the other direction it ran through the woodland that separated the farms of Edmund and Cenred and down into the broad River Avon, crossing the flat common land where the folk of Melksham grazed their cattle. The common often flooded if the winter rains were heavy and the thegns were grateful that the boundary of their own pasture was on higher ground, so the flooding reached to their hurdle fencing only.

De Tosny's estate was famous in the West Country for its excellent eels and salmon. All four villages possessed fisheries, but only this one had a mill. It was built to serve the whole estate. The miller had long learned how to make a decent profit out of it even after he had paid the heavy dues to his lord.

Alleyn Thurkilson was of Danish origin, though his family had lived in Wiltshire for generations. He was only a cottar by status and he owned little land, but his actual wealth far outstripped most of the villeins in the village. Everyone was aware of the miller's growing wealth, but they comforted themselves by commenting that real influence in the community depended on birth and status.

The man in question, the solid, red-bearded Alleyn was not in his precious mill this morning. He was standing by the crude shelter which served as the forge of his neighbour the blacksmith, staring out with great satisfaction at the field full of reapers. What a season this would be for him. Oswin the blacksmith had no time for such leisurely speculation. He was intent on beating out a lump of hot metal into a scythe blade. This however did not impede his speech and he was full of something this morning.

'I can tell you this Alleyn, old Gilbert kept Eadwig a length of time talking and though I bent a man who claims to know everything' – a loud grunt of exertion as he swung the hammer- ' We do know that he be a man who has no trouble with his rents.'

Alleyn nodded. He was getting bored for Oswin never came to the point before he had gone miles out of his way.

'Well, there's my point see.'

As he had not yet made a point of any description, Alleyn could not follow him, but he waited, trusting one would come in time. Oswin had skilfully forged his scythe blade and now he dipped it into a clay copper. The blade reacted savagely to the cold water, spitting and hissing in protest.'

'Gilbert'

'Gilbert,' Alleyn corrected with an exaggerated French pronunciation, 'Remember- he's a Norman now.'

'Oh, I can't be bothering with that nonsense. I knowed him for years as plain Gilbert and I don't see as I should call him anything else.'

Alleyn laughed, but he was rather disappointed that what he considered an excellent joke was so obviously lost on Oswin. The blacksmith put the blade down and sat on the edge of the copper, wiping the sweat from his face. Fifteen years at the forge had determined his complexion. It was patched mauve and red. A strong inclination for mead and malmsey did nothing to improve it.

'I was meaning to say that I reckon as Gilbert had something important to tell Eadwig. As far as I can judge they were hatching up something. What do you bet there will be a meeting in the village tonight?'

Alleyn thought it was a fair guess.

'Tis more than a fair guess. Tis a running certainty. We will be hearing something tonight and if I know De Tosny, twill be to our disadvantage. I tell you, whenever I do see Gilbert with that high-flown look on his face, it do fair give I the starts. He do bring us nothing but trouble these days.'

Alleyn, always an optimistic and genial man by nature, could not bring himself to agree with his neighbour's pessimistic forecast, particularly when the sight of all that wheat and barley made his heart sing. He murmured an indistinct reply, which could have been assent or dissent and making his apologies to Oswin he began to wander back to the mill, still casting complaisant glances at those crops.

Despite his inferior status, the miller considered himself to be a grade or two above his neighbours. He felt his advantage lay in a wider experience, a greater education in the ways of the world.

His ancestors may have been seen as pagan barbarians by Saxons who had already achieved a high standard of civilization, when they could boast of a scholar like Bede and a King of Alfred's calibre, but this failed to intimidate Alleyn from his belief that he was altogether a more intelligent, better educated man than his neighbours. He had spent his early youth trading in Bath and Bristol. There he had heard and seen many things that most of his fellow villagers would not dream existed. Such boroughs, as small as they were then, twenty years ago, were cosmopolitan in comparison with the village. Many of the peasants had not strayed farther than the most westerly village on the estate and others not even as far as that. Alleyn had once been on a voyage to Bremen. This was a fact no one could forget, even if the miller had been willing to let them. He knew so much more than they. When he thought about it, he laughed at their insistent harping on his being a cottar. It was only to assure themselves.

At this point, his eyes strayed to the fields again. They were dark, shrewd eyes. There was humour in them and a hint of his vast self-confidence.

He could recognise on the edge of the field, the blacksmith's three healthy sons working side by side, stooking barley. At the busiest time of year after the harvest, when wheat and barley from all four villages on the estate were brought to the mill, Alleyn employed all three of Oswin's sons to help him with the work. Two of them loaded the sacks on to the pulley, while the third helped Alleyn heave them through the doorway of the second storey sack floor. He did not trust them to feed the hopper which sent the grain down through a shute into the hole at the centre of the runner mill stone powered by the water wheel, because they did it too fast and jammed up the shute. He undertook that task himself with the help of his wife and daughter. However Wulfhere, Centwine and Aethelberht were trusted with gathering up the flour as it was displaced from the grinding action of the mill stones. They bagged it and stored the sacks on a platform in the extended lean-to that housed the stones in their supporting frame.

In the off season when selling and transporting was Alleyn's main occupation he dispensed with the services of the three young men, relying on his own strong arms and the support of his family.

Alleyn sometimes wished that he had a son, but his yearnings were rarely profound, not when he possessed such a daughter. He fancied his daughter to be the village prodigy.

She was born in the village, but during her childhood spent some months of each year with merchant relations in Bristol. There she had obtained a fragmented education at the school of a double monastery.

Ilsa, who had been blessed with a Scandinavian name due to her father's consciousness that he had been given a Saxon one, had a lucid, inquiring mind. She was educated far above the level of the other girls in the village, but she did not feel uncomfortable in the village community.

The general opinion in the village was that it was presumptuous of a cottar to educate his daughter to such an extent, but everyone admired Ilsa. She was gifted with a healthy, vigorous body, intelligent blue eyes, and a warm smile.

Bold and independent, she was also sympathetic to the needs of others.

When Alleyn reflected, he decided that she was worth five sons. He had little land, therefore he did not need sons to work it. He was confident that he could secure a good marriage for his daughter and provide heirs enough to safeguard his beloved mill.

He studied the fisheries for a while before he strolled into the palisaded yard which led to the mill. Everything seemed good today and best of all, his wife and daughter were baking bread. He could feed on the smell alone of bread baking in the oven.

Ilsa, with her sleeves rolled up above her elbows, her arms splattered with white freckles of flour to counterpoint the golden-brown ones nature had given her, was kneading dough with expertise.

A rough awning projecting out into the yard was the kitchen of the Thurkilson family. At the back of this was the door into their living accommodation, one large room, divided off into three separate spaces with curtains to draw across for privacy. The royal reeve had struck a bargain with Alleyn when the mill was built. When the site of the mill was chosen, Alleyn's cottage stood in the way. He was offered the position of miller in exchange for permission to demolish his cottage and he agreed readily. Accommodation in the mill was limited, but he had only the one child and during the fine weather they lived mostly out in the yard.

Alleyn watched his daughter, nodding his approbation.

'You look almost as domesticated as your mother my girl,' he said suddenly. She started, for she had not heard him approach. The miller had a light tread for a heavily built man. When she saw it was her father she smiled.

'I am domesticated.'

'And what else could a girl be in this village,' chimed in her mother, a brusque, sturdy woman, who was passing into the mill with two buckets of water on a yoke across her shoulders. 'There is no room for ladies of leisure in this place.'

Ilsa laughed her agreement, but her father shook his head.

'You look better reading a book or with a pen in your hand.'

'Of course, no young woman looks very fine covered in flour and red with the heat of the oven. You should know that father.'

'And you know what I mean Mistress,' grunted the miller, slapping her affectionately across the bottom with his open palm, before he walked across to the palisade to stare down the main street. He was expecting cartloads of custom from the neighbouring villages to arrive during the day. Instead, he saw two men coming in their direction, two men he knew well.

'Here is Edgar's boy coming.'

Ilsa was at his side, wiping her hands on a piece of sacking.

'Oh, it's Dunstan.'

She tried to sound non-committal, but she could not disguise the disappointment in her voice. It did not escape Alleyn.

'For sure it's Dunstan. You don't expect to see the other young devil in the village this time of day do you? He's over at Monkton, courting the widow Aethelflaed by now.'

'Father!' she rebuked, but she was amused and defiantly resisted the urge to blush at his implication. She was not ashamed of how she felt about Edmund.

Alleyn threw back his head and laughed. It was a deep booming sound that reverberated around the palisade.

'Haven't you got some books to give back to Dunstan?' he added still laughing at his own joke.

She had. She had kept them an unforgivably long time and really must return them. She ran into the mill murmuring something about having time to wash her hands.

Dunstan and Cerdic, escorted by Ulf the mongrel dog had come into the village to collect some fencing. Tucked away behind the church was a group of slave hovels. The inhabitants of these rotting shelters were as much the property of Roger De Tosny as were his cattle. They had the right to nothing except their lives and little value was put on those. The Normans had not kept slaves in the Duchy and found such creatures an anomalous burden in their social structure. Many slaves had been emancipated to become cottars, but a few remained in most villages. De Tosny used them as sweated labour about his manor house or on his demesne land.

For years now, the two thegnly families had been taking wood to these slaves to make hurdle hedges and fencing. In this way they managed to earn some money of their own. In law, a slave owned nothing; all he had belonged to his lord, but what De Tosny did not know about he could not claim.

Dunstan was happy. Almost a week had passed since the news of Cenred's decision was broken to Edmund and nothing had changed in their relationship with their uncle. Cerdic too seemed full of high spirits. He had been entertaining his cousin on their way to the village with a description of his baby son's efforts to walk. They had just exchanged greetings with an elderly woman in a grey serge gown, the formidable Edith, village gossip par excellence, when they both saw Ilsa come out of the yard at the back of the mill and walk towards them.

Dunstan always felt his colour rise at the sight of Ilsa. It annoyed him because he was sure that Cerdic noticed it and was amused. He had known Ilsa all his life, but he still felt awkward in her presence. There was plenty he could talk to her about, more than most of the other young women in the village, but he could not rid himself of the feeling that she found him dull and ineffectual. He knew that she was in love with Edmund. It seemed natural to him that she should be. He did not feel jealousy, but he wished he could more easily understand his own emotions regarding her.

'Here comes little mistress digest it all,' Cerdic said with a grin as Ilsa drew closer, 'Having scanned the most profound literature you could find for her, she is ready to devour more. She is terrifying.'

They were level with the blacksmith's forge when they met. Ilsa had found time to wash her hands, although several stray specks of flour still lay on her dress and in her hair. Braided into waist length plaits, Ilsa's hair was an unusual shade, a deep, rich auburn; the colour of copper beech leaves in autumn. She carried under her arm two parchment books, wrapped in a white cloth. She returned Cerdic's greeting with a smile and said to Dunstan,

'I have brought your books back. I have kept them far too long. I have seen you so many times since I finished reading them, but did not think to return them. You must have thought that I intended to keep them.'

She was always so positive, so confident. Dunstan wished he could sound the same to her.

'You can keep them as long as you like. You need to read the poetry many times to many any sense of it.'

She laughed. 'Edmund once said if he read them 60 times they would be as clear to him as Turkish.'

'Well, that's nonsense because he understands them better than any of us. He used to write poetry himself, very good poetry. He does not know it, but I kept some of it. He put the scrolls out for the bonfire, but I rescued some of them and hid them under my bed. He will not admit to any joy in things of the intellect and spirit any more. I wish he would.'

Ilsa was surprised by this revelation. She was aware that Edmund's feigned indifference to culture was a defensive front, but she had no idea that he had been a poet. The thought fascinated her and she wished to know more.

'I would like to read those poems Dunstan. Could I borrow them?'

Dunstan was reluctant. 'I am not sure that he would be very pleased if he found out.'

'Well he will not find out will he, because I shall not tell him? I promise to keep them safe from flour marks and barley husks.' She held up the white cloth bag, 'Please Dunstan.'

He was not completely sure that she would not reveal the secret to his brother, but his desire to please her overrode his fears.

'Very well, I will bring them over next week.'

She clapped her hands in delight and thanked him, anticipating the pleasure of discovering a different aspect of Edmund's character. He was rarely out of her thoughts. She was longing to ask how he had reacted to Cenred's decision to sell the farm, but the presence of Cerdic held her back.

They began to discuss one of the books she had just returned, when Oswin came running out of the forge, waving his hands and trailing an air of doom with him.

'I knowed it, I knowed it. I said whenever old Gilbert do start talking with that patronising voice, we be in for something.'

He had started talking before he recognised the group outside, but when he saw Ilsa he made straight for her, stopping only to touch his forelock in respect to Dunstan and Cerdic.

'Sorry to interrupt you sirs. Ilsa my girl, where's your father?'

'In the mill of course. Oswin whatever is the matter?'

'Well might you ask; we be going to get put upon, just as we have been put upon and put upon ever since De Tosny took over this estate, may his wicked soul find damnation for it- if you will pardon the expression sirs,' he added hastily looking principally at Dunstan.

Everyone in the village was convinced that Dunstan was born for the church and would no more dream of being profane in front of him than they would the abbot of the nearby monastery.

They had far fewer scruples in the case of the unfortunate priest of their church, who spent most of his time toiling on his glebe land. They became particularly vociferous when he came to collect the tithe.

Dunstan acquiesced graciously, stealing a quick smile at Cerdic, who for some unaccountable reason had his hand over his mouth. Oswin was elaborating.

'But I can't help wishing him his deserts after what he has done to us over these past few years and as God be just, he will get them too.'

'I am sure he will,' Cerdic began, but before he could make his point, Oswin cut in. 'And for what he's done to your family too sir. Now he has got his hands on your land only the heavens above us know what he will do with it.'

'No more than we will let him Oswin, I assure you. But do not keep us in suspense, what has he done now?'

'No more have he done anything yet. Tis what he be going to do. A castle- one of they great ugly things! He is going to build a castle on the estate, right near the village. Tis all vanity, trying to keep up with that proud brother of his. I tell you, it bolds bad for us, because you know who will have to build it, dun ee?'

After that rhetorical question, Oswin set off for the mill to unburden his fears of ruination on Alleyn. Cerdic grimaced.

'And he did not even tell us the ramifications of how he found out. I wonder if it is true.'

It was Dunstan's opinion that they should treat it as a rumour only until they could uncover more details.

Oswin always put the worst construction on everything.

They walked to the mill together and before they parted, Ilsa asked Dunstan if he had a copy of the Historia Ecclesiastica that she might borrow. He had to confess that he did not, but offered to ask at the monastery. Ilsa had turned into the yard of the mill as she said goodbye, but she lingered at the gate as if she wanted to say something else.

'Dunstan.' He stopped, but Cerdic meandered on.

'Remind Edmund that I still live here. I have not seen him for a week.'

She was swinging the gate back and forth, a mixture of audacity and sweetness in her manner. Dunstan was puzzled as to how she could be both things at once. He felt that warmth rising again and tried to dismiss it.

'He has not forgotten. He has had much on his mind this past week.'

'I am told that the widow Aethelflaed might be one of the things on his mind,' she said with a mischievous smile. Dunstan looked down at his feet. He never knew what to say when Edmund's romantic exploits were mentioned. He did not expect Ilsa to joke about it. He had imagined it would hurt her.

'Oh Dunstan, do not be so embarrassed. Do you think I care about Edmund's flirtations? The widow Aethelflaed is no competition. We have a special understanding your brother and me. He always comes back to me. I would hate him to be too tame anyway.'

As he walked on to join Cenred, Dunstan was wondering if that was how she saw him, tame and boring.

His feelings about Ilsa were confused, but he was sure that he wanted Edmund to marry her. His brother had married at seventeen, the daughter of a distant kinsman. It was an arranged marriage. He met her twice before they married, but Margaret was a beautiful, delicate girl of sixteen and he had no doubts that he could be happy with her. He was not disappointed. Those first two years were more than he could have hoped for. She was the perfect wife for an aspiring young thegn, adoring, dutiful and then came that inclement spring of 1065. Margaret was always frail; she was expecting his first child. She contracted a serious fever, could find no resistance and died within a few days. The tragedy deepened, for Cenred's wife, who had nursed her, caught the fever and though she fought tenaciously, within two weeks she too was dead. Edmund had taken his bereavement with fortitude and then everything was swallowed up in the pain of 1066.

Margaret was buried next to his mother, who had died of a haemorrhage giving birth to Dunstan. Edmund tended their graves in the burial ground beside the church with care and respect. He grieved over the fact that his father could not lie beside them, instead of a makeshift pit somewhere near Battle Abbey, so many miles away.

He did not brood over Margaret, but Dunstan felt that her memory discouraged Edmund from marrying again. One day soon he would realise that he needed Ilsa and she would make a fine wife for him- that was Dunstan's firm belief.

Busy with his thoughts Dunstan did not speak to Cerdic and they skirted the church in silence, soon reaching the sprawling mess of slave hovels. Dunstan had seen this place a thousand times, but could not approach it without a tightening across his chest, shamed to think that these people should be forced to live like this, valued far less than a plough beast and little more than a stray dog. Their homes were insubstantial wind brakes, thatched awnings open to the extremities of the weather.

Two young children, as flea-ridden as the puppy that played with them, were tossing five-stones, as they sat amid the heap of refuse piled in the centre of the circle of five shelters, oblivious to the putrefying liquid at their elbows and the chicken gizzard that the puppy was gnawing. The smell of the place was so strong it had the effect of a blow.

Ulf rushed wildly at the puppy and wrested his chicken dinner away from him. The snarling of the dogs aroused an old lady, who was lying against the back of the nearest shelter with her eyes closed.

She was motionless and the faintly green tinge of her skin gave her a ghastly look, like a mummified corpse. She was emaciated and very old. At the noise of the dogs, her eyelids rolled up slowly as if they were stiff.

'Good day to you,' Dunstan called to her, 'Is Dervorgil here?'

She did not speak, but jerked her thumb in the direction of the farthest hovel, where a figure was bent over a twig fire industriously employing itself as a human bellows. Dunstan thanked her and they moved on.

The children, both around five years old, were romping round their visitors with expectant faces.

'What makes you think we have anything for you?' teased Cerdic, but the children refused to be discouraged and laughing he produced a bag of sweet biscuits and oatcakes, which he distributed to the snatching hands.

'Now share them out fairly. Don't be greedy. I stole them from my wife's kitchen this morning. So don't say a word or I shall be in trouble.'

The children promised faithfully with their mouths full of biscuit that they would preserve his secret. Dunstan bent to pick up one of the children and sit him on his shoulders, but Cerdic laid a hand on his arm.

'Not so fast. Do not get into the habit of picking him up. Your hair would be a fleas' paradise and Edmund would go crazy.'

Dunstan instinctively ran a hand through his hair as an itchy sensation passed over his scalp. Instead of giving Arthur a ride on his shoulders, he pressed a silver penny into his fist and held another out to his brother.

Dervorgil had seen them now. She left the fire and came running to them, her face wreathed in smiles. One family occupied these five shelters. They were Britons, members of a subject race, a reminder to the Saxons that they had once been conquerors of this land. Geraint the hurdle-maker, his wife, grandmother and four children called this their home. He was up at the manor with his wife and eldest son, Hugh, mucking out the pig sties and stables. Dervorgil was left in charge of the household.

'Have you come for the hurdles Master Dunstan?' she inquired, wiping her sooty hands down her equally sooty tunic, with an incongruous self-consciousness. The child was dirty all over. She was about fourteen, but her oval face was wise before its time. Knowing hazel eyes peered from under long dark lashes. The knee-length tunic she wore was patched and darned all over. Her legs were covered in bramble scratches and cuts. One was freshly done, for it was dribbling blood.

Dunstan told her that they were in sore need of those hurdles. 'That brindled cow you hear so much about from us has been on the rampage again. She has broken down an entire line of fencing on the north pasture.

We found half the cattle and all the goats having a wonderful time in the monastery meadows.'

Dervorgil made a perfect O shape with her lips. 'Twere lucky then it weren't De Tosny's meadows.'

Dunstan agreed as he began to stack the pile of wood he was carrying into one of the shelters.

'I see you have brought some more,' the girl observed, hovering around them, 'Father will be pleased with they. It means more money.'

Although the family preserved their British ancestry in their personal names and were smaller, darker than the average Saxon peasant, they all spoke with a heavy West Saxon dialect. The memory of the British tongue had melted away for them.

'What be that, that there?' she added, poking at the spotless white bag that held Dunstan's books.

The string of the bag was wound around his wrist and swung unguided as he stacked the wood. Dervorgil was curious and she never allowed her curiosity to go unsatisfied.

'The bones of St. Augustine,' Cerdic darted in before his cousin could answer.

'Jesus bless us!' cried the girl, crossing herself, her eyes opening wide, 'Where did you get them?'

'An angel passing by last night saw how innocent Dunstan looked and bestowed this great blessing on him.'

'Now stop it,' Dunstan said, amused but half reproachful, 'Do not tease the girl. There are only books in the bag Dervorgil. Do not pay any heed to what he tells you. I think that if I did have the bones of St. Augustine I would send them to Canterbury to be buried, rather than carry them around in a bag.'

Dervorgil looked at Cerdic's impish grin and then aimed her foot at his leg. He only just managed to move back in time to avoid the impact.

Her brothers had now joined them and Dunstan remarked that Arthur was growing at last. She told him that Arthur was boasting that he would be as tall as Master Dunstan one day. He looked across at Arthur, who was sharing the last oatcake with his twin brother. He was about three feet tall and slender as a withy branch. The young Saxon smiled, 'Well, he may be.'

'He will certainly have the pleasure of growing taller than me,' said Cerdic cheerily as he swung a set of hurdles over his shoulder.

'He's determined to grow big and strong because he wants to go building De Tosny's castle.'

'Castle?' repeated Dunstan and Cerdic together.

'Have you not heard about it? He is going to have a great big one, like they have in the country he comes from and none of our high and mighty villagers be going to like working on it, my father says, because they will sweat the same sweat as we then.'

'Then it isn't a rumour,' Cerdic half asked, half stated. 'Do you know this for sure or has Oswin panicked the whole village already?'

'Oswin? I don't know nothing about him. But the castle is going up for sure because Hugh were told by De Tosny's hound keeper, who got it first hand from John the cup-bearer. John was serving the wine when De Tosny talked it over with Gilbert the reeve and he went to the chief butler about it. The chief butler told the steward and he said no one was to say a word about it because the master had heard enough of his private business trumpeted about the countryside already. But John could not help telling his friend Stephen and it all slipped out then of course.'

She paused to take a quick breath. 'The trouble is he is going to take some of the village's best meadow land to build it on. That's what is worrying Father most. He reckons that if they suffer, it will come harder on us.'

Cerdic pulled an apprehensive face at Dunstan. They had been wrong to take Oswin's fears so lightly.

Chapter Three

It was late afternoon but the sun still burned with the fierceness of high summer. Dunstan glanced back over his shoulder, back into the woods as a pigeon coming to rest on a branch crashed its wings against the leaves of the beech tree causing a crackling noise like burning logs.

Dunstan was thinking about the castle. Earlier that day Eadwig, the leading villein had called the peasants together to inform them of what Gilbert the reeve had told him. Oswin's worst fears were confirmed. De Tosny had already drawn up a table of the labour services that he would require from each tenant. Building was to begin at the end of the month. Dunstan knew all this because Edmund had been to the village to fetch Ilsa and Alleyn had related it all to him.

His brother and Ilsa were now at the farm. After they had told him all they had heard about the castle, it was plain to him that he was in the way.

He decided to visit his friend Abbot Robert at the Benedictine Monastery of St Peter's on Bracken Hill with a view to borrowing a copy of the Historia Ecclesiastica for Ilsa. Father Robert allowed him unlimited access to the monastery library.

Robert Julliere had come to England from Mantes,

on the borders of the Vexin in the last years of the Confessor's reign. The Abbot of St. Peter's had met Robert at the French monastery of Bec and they had formed a strong friendship. The newly arrived Frenchman sought out his friend, was received into St. Peter's and on the Abbot's death three years later was himself elected Abbot. The Saxon opinion of Norman prelates and churchmen was often low and insulting, but Father Robert was held in respect by Saxon and Norman alike.

Dunstan first met him in 1066. When Cenred and Edmund made their peace with the king's commissioners, Cenred, wary of the soldiers who accompanied them and equally uncertain of Edmund's temper, sent Dunstan to the monastery until it was all over. He then decided with his usual wisdom that it would be best for the boy to stay there for a week or two, until Edmund's passionate grief and anger had cooled. It gave both the brothers the chance to come to terms with their father's death each in his own way.

Edmund needed the breathing space and Dunstan was spared the pain of his brother's agony.

Those weeks at St. Peter's saw the beginning of a friendship between Dunstan and Father Robert, the beginning of many journeys like this one up the gentle slopes of Bracken Hill, accompanied by Ulf the mongrel dog, to pull the weather-beaten bell cord and listen to the jangle of the bell carried back and forth on the breeze. The Abbot had taught him to read Latin over the years and found him to be a willing and able pupil. Dunstan became proficient enough to read the monastery's Bible, manuscript copies of St. Jerome's translation into Latin of the Gospels from the Greek and much of the Old Testament from the Hebrew. Dunstan felt honoured to be granted such a favour, to read the word of God directly. Such a pleasure was accessible only to monks, scholars and the more educated priests in most circumstances.

The Abbott had also talked to him about the meaning of obedience and patience; how even Jesus, the one sinless man, had learned obedience by the things he suffered. Only by his humility and by subjecting himself to God's will was he glorified. These were things that Dunstan longed for Edmund to understand and accept.

Ulf was barking. He always did when he heard the flat, discordant notes of the bell at the monastery gate. But the creak of the gate as it swung open and the be-cowelled figure, who peered out, silenced him. He sat down on his stump of a tail to watch suspiciously as Dunstan was admitted.

Brother Thomas ushered him through the forecourt and into the apartment of the Abbot. Here Ulf found the door shut in his face and resigned himself to trotting behind the monks as they went about their tasks.

Robert Julliere was sitting at a table writing a document in an elegant half-uncial script, when Dunstan was shown into the room. He rose from his chair with a smile of pleasure, extending his hand to the young Saxon. Dunstan brought it to his lips with due reverence and then the Abbot embraced him warmly.

'Dunstan my son, it has been more than a month since I last saw you and then you were so busy coaxing your ox team that you did not see me. I feared our favourite child had forgotten his second home.'

He sat down at the table once more and motioned Dunstan to sit beside him. All Father Robert's movements, gestures were elegant and none of them redundant. They all had a purpose.

Dunstan smiled. 'You must think little of my memory Father if you imagine I could forget all the happiness I have found here. I have been meaning to come and I know this is the weakest and most common of all excuses, but I have not had the time.'

Father Robert nodded. 'It is a feeble excuse, I agree. Humanity's most trusty standby. I also have intended to visit you and Edmund, but I too have found other things to do, so we are both to blame.'

He was studying his visitor's face closely.

'You look pale Dunstan. Let me offer you a glass of wine. Are you feeling unwell?'

He was at the far end of the room in a moment, pouring wine from a stone cask into a plain silver goblet. There was a cultured, urbane air about the Abbot. His manners were impeccable, his hospitality ever vigilant. It was a dignified, inbred urbanity, not an acquired veneer. He listened as Dunstan assured him that he was well, and then inquired after the farm and the village. The subjects of Cenred's bargain with De Tosny and the building of the castle soon came up. Father Robert was not at all surprised at either piece of news. Dunstan was relieved to hear that he too considered Cenred's decision to be the right one.

'Perhaps it would be better for you too,' he suggested.

'I do not know. Edmund will never think so. I have a great affection for the land. But I think it is because of the memories it holds and the beauty of it, not because it is a traditional family possession. I do not need to own it as long as I could still live there. Is it wrong Father, to be so deeply attached to something material? I find it so hard sometimes to decide if my feelings are the result of pride.'

The Abbot shook his head, smiling. 'You need not be concerned about pride my son. I know few people who have more natural humility. A little mental flagellation can be good for you, but a man is likely to faint under too much of it. Prayer is a far kinder vehicle.'

'Oh, I pray a great deal,' Dunstan assured, 'I do not find it hard. It's just that-'

'It is just that you are trying to bear up Edmund's soul as well as your own and you feel the extra weight. Things will work themselves out and Edmund must find his own way to God. You cannot carry him there.'

He began to roll up the document on which he had been writing. Dunstan watched the lines of writing, as one by one, they disappeared into the tight roll. He admired the elegant precision of the Abbot's handwriting.

'If you are looking for an interesting example of worldly pride,' Robert was saying, as he put the roll with great care into an oak chest by the wall, 'You should study our friend De Tosny. You would soon see how favourably Edmund compares. Poor Roger's conceit is fundamental to his nature. This castle is a perfect example. He does not need it for a fortification. I doubt if he intends to live in it- horribly draughty things castles and they have little aesthetic value in my opinion. For Roger it is a status symbol. To compete with his brother Ralph, he is ready to build it on other people's sweat and toil. All things must bow to his vanity and his need for status.'

Dunstan sat back in his chair, interested to hear a more impartial observer comment on De Tosny. He knew nothing of the man except by hearsay and this was warped by the natural prejudice of the Saxon peasants against their Norman overlord. De Tosny's heavy impositions on his tenants, the harsh punishments he meted out for minor misdemeanours, spoke against him, but there must be more to the man than that.

'Do you know him well Father Robert?'

'Better than he would like me to know him.'

Dunstan smiled to himself as he recalled his only direct meeting with the baron. 'He spoke to me once. It was about two months after he arrived here. He was surveying the village and when he turned his horse to look at the fisheries, he dropped a glove.

I gave it back to him when he came out. He looked most surprised as if it would be more in the Saxon character to run off with it. He did thank me though, in execrable Saxon. I could not resist the urge to answer him in French. He was even more surprised at that.

He rode off with an- I shall remember you when I see you again- expression on his face. But of course he does not. I have seen him ride by, but I have never been that close to him since.'

'He will not forget you,' the Abbot said, 'Roger De Tosny never forgets a face that he really marks.'

He glanced out of the window behind him, meticulously brushing stray flecks of dust from his habit with the tips of his fingers.

'It grows late my son. I have duties to perform. Do you wish to borrow anything from the library?'

When Dunstan asked for the Historia Ecclesiastica, he continued, 'You have borrowed it twice before. You must have a taste for Bede.'

'I value Bede very highly, but this time I wish to borrow it for a friend.'

The Abbot nodded and beckoned Dunstan to follow him into the library. He took down from the shelves, a book bound in dark leather with a gilt hasp.

Dunstan recalled the pleasure that the workmanship of that copy had given him when he first opened it. Each parchment page was decorated with illumination in vibrant colours, the work of the monks of St. Peter's fifty years past. As he followed the Abbot back through the passage ways and into the cloisters he felt the peace of the place, the cool, silent cloisters where generations of monks had walked and pondered on God's purposes.

'I could be very happy here,' he murmured, as Father Robert opened the door into the courtyard.

'I am sure you could. You never expect too much and are always ready to give yourself to others. Because of your nature, you will always find contentment.'

There was a trace of weariness in the Abbot's voice as he said this, as if beneath his calm exterior, he struggled to find a simple contentment himself.

Ulf was delighted to see his master. He had explored

the yard with great thoroughness, but found no bones, no rubbish dumps, no rabbits, not even a cat to gladden his heart and he was growing bored. They were soon at the monastery gate, staring down into the valley and the darkening woods beyond. They had said their goodbyes and Dunstan was on his way down the slope, when the Abbot called after him, 'Dunstan, the foresters have reported seeing an old wolf in the woods recently. He has had a piglet or two. It seems that he is a bad tempered fellow, so be on your guard.'

'Don't worry; Ulf will look after me.'

He sounded confident, but he instinctively felt for the knife at his belt as the monastery gate groaned shut behind him. The village was full of the tale of this wolf, until the news of the castle displaced it from the communal mind.

Peter the swineherd declared that it had red eyes that glowed like coals and his cousin Aelfric swore that it was big enough to swallow a piglet whole. Oswin was convinced that he had heard the priest say that it was no real wolf, but the soul of Rannulf Le Gros, a Norman hawk keeper, murdered in the woods some years ago, reincarnated in the form of a wolf. Dunstan recalled how Edmund could not stop laughing when he heard that story and he was laughing himself at the memory of it. When Edmund roared with laughter, he was so alive, so warm. Dunstan loved to hear his brother laugh like that.

Ulf had been probing through the bushes, when he stopped, his hackles rising and snarled in a warning undertone. Dunstan stared, trying to penetrate the growth of brambles and bracken, his heart rate quickening. He saw two luminous points of light peering from the bushes, steady green eyes fixed on him. Then Ulf leaped into the bushes, there was a scuffle and a fox, lean and bedraggled, darted away. Dunstan sighed his relief. It would make Edmund laugh even more if he admitted how scared he had been when he first saw those eyes. He restrained Ulf from chasing after the fox, but compensated him by deciding to run home. He crashed through the undergrowth, startling the wood pigeons, feeling the sting as twigs snapped back in his face. He felt exuberant as he reached the meadows, Ulf prancing by his side, excited by Dunstan's unusual behaviour.

He had almost reached the house, smiling to think how foolish he must look charging along like this, when he heard a voice. It was Edmund's voice, loud, angry.

'Now get off my land and don't ever come near it again is that clear? Norman or Saxon, I will cut the head from his shoulders if he dares come to me with intentions like yours.'

Dunstan stopped short, his excitement suspended as he tried to slow his thumping pulse. As he walked from behind the house, the first person he saw was Gilbert, De Tosny's reeve, cowering in the yard, backing away from something. He looked terrified. Then Dunstan saw the cause of his fear, for Edmund was advancing towards him brandishing a broad sword. It was plain that he was in a fury. Ilsa was standing in the doorway. Dunstan could not see from that distance that there was an amused expression on her face.

Gilbert, desperately searching for an escape route, should Edmund go for him, spotted the younger brother before the others. He darted towards him, grabbing hold of his arm.

'Dunstan, Dunstan, help me in the name of heaven. Your brother has gone mad. He wants to kill me, I swear he does. Placate him Dunstan or I'm finished.'

Gilbert's fear was real enough. His hand was hot and sweaty. Dunstan was puzzled. Gilbert had been the royal reeve before the conquest and a good friend of his father's. Edmund had never shown much respect for him after he had agreed to work for De Tosny, but he had never shown any open hostility.

'Whatever is the matter?' he asked, walking over to Edmund with Gilbert sheltering behind him.

Edmund was breathing heavily, shaking in an effort to get a grip on himself. He stared at his brother for a moment, then snarled, 'What's the matter? Need you ask? This wheedling, cozening son of a bitch has been here sizing up our land for his master, calculating what a fine knight's fee it would make.'

'That's not true,' Gilbert defended. He wanted to sound firm, but his voice would not obey. He had never seen Edmund in a temper like this and was in a state of shock. 'As I stand here Dunstan, it is not true. I came here quite openly, without one devious intention to make Edmund the same advantageous offer that Roger De Tosny gave your Uncle Cenred.'

'Advantageous offer!' Edmund spat the words out as if they offended his palate, 'That may be your opinion of it, but it is not your land that you make so free with your advice about. I do not want any of your friendly words of wisdom for my father's sake. Do not dare presume on your friendship with my father. If he could hear you now, I doubt if there would be any friendship.'

He let his sword arm drop at his side, scouring lines in the dust with the point of the weapon, but he did not look any the less fierce to Gilbert, who was grateful for the bony frame of Dunstan, interposed between him and Edmund. He began to defend his friendship with Edgar, but this only made things worse, stirring up Edmund's anger again.

Dunstan was agitated now, not sure what to do.

'Edmund I- I really think-'

'You stay out of this Dunstan. I can handle it.'

Dunstan felt a little twist of despair inside him, as he took a sidelong glance at Ilsa.

She had moved out of the shadowy doorway and was looking at him. She must be thinking how ineffectual he was. Edmund was saying, 'I have told you more than once to get off my land. So do it, now. Tell De Tosny from me, just what to do with his bargain. You can tell him to come and offer his bargains in person and I will throw him off my land too.'

'He would, I believe he would,' the reeve murmured to Dunstan, before he shouted at Edmund, 'That would be just the sort of foolish thing you would do. You thegns are all the same. You have a temper just like your father. I respected Edgar, but he was a hothead when he was your age- about as much give in him as in an iron bar when he was in a temper.'

Edmund did not reply; he just lunged at Gilbert, brandishing his sword. The reeve yelped, too panic-stricken to run. Dunstan grabbed hold of his brother's sword arm.

'Edmund, stop it. Please stop it,' he pleaded, frightened by his own temerity.

'You must not treat an old friend in such a manner. I- I cannot understand you. Gilbert is only trying to do his job. He does not mean us any ill will.'

Gilbert nodded his head vigorously but he dared not speak again, 'Please put up your sword before you do something you will regret.'

Edmund gritted his teeth. A wave of exhaustion passed over him. His anger had been so extreme he felt burned out. He threw his sword down on the ground in disgust. Dunstan turned to Gilbert.

'You must go now. You cannot do any good here. We will never sell our land to De Tosny. I am sorry that you have suffered so much abuse on De Tosny's behalf. But the principle is so important to Edmund you see.'

The reeve's brown face was full of explanations that he did not have the heart to give. He thanked Dunstan for his intercession, took a quick look at the silent Edmund and scuttled across to the barn where his horse was tied to a hitching post. As he rode away, Ulf ran barking behind the horse for some distance. Dunstan opened his mouth to say he knew not what, but Edmund turned away from him.

'I'll take you home Ilsa,' and he strode away towards

the stable, Dunstan staring wistfully after him. He was aware that Ilsa was looking at him, but was afraid to return her gaze, fearing the expression in her eyes.

'He would never hurt Gilbert,' she said, 'He was only trying to frighten him. You should have heard the flattering way the old fox was phrasing everything, trying to get round Edmund. He deserved a scare. He was like a frightened rabbit. I found it funny.'

Dunstan was disappointed by her reaction. She really was amused. 'Well I do not think it was funny,' he replied soberly, 'I am sorry that you do. I thought you would understand.'

She snorted at his assumption with a toss of her head.

'You are always so tender hearted about everything. Edmund has a right to fight for what is his. That is what a man should do.'

'I am afraid that I do not think-'

Ilsa did not let him finish. 'Oh don't be so saintly about everything Dunstan. That book you are clutching, is that for me?'

'It's the Historia Ecclesiastica. I borrowed it for you. I said I would.'

She took the book, aware that she was eager to get away from him, standing there looking like a dog that had just been kicked by his master. Edmund was waiting by the stables, with his horse saddled. She ran towards him and felt the pleasure that she always did when he swung her up into the saddle behind him.

Dunstan let out a long sigh as he listened to the

horse's hooves dying away. He decided to busy himself checking on the animals, comforting himself with the thought that he could confide in Cerdic in the morning.

Edmund was urging his horse on through the darkening woods towards the village. He was tired and frustrated. The ferocity of his reaction to Gilbert had surprised even himself. His head ached and the muscles in his jaw felt tight, unyielding. Ilsa, sitting behind him, her arms around his waist as she rested her head on his back, could feel the tension in his back and shoulders. She longed to smooth it all away with her hands.

'Edmund, you must not feel guilty about what has just happened. You had a right to be angry. You would never have harmed him. The fright was enough.'

She murmured this close to his ear as she rubbed the side of her face against his hair. He slowed the horse down to make conversation more easy.

'I do not feel guilty, but foolish because I could not control my temper. In battle it is fatal to lose control of your anger. I was trained to that. I should be able to apply it to any circumstances. But when Gilbert started using my father's name as a bargaining tool, I could hold my temper no longer. People are always trying to tell me what my father would have said or done or thought and they have no right to speak for him. I know father's mind better than they do. Even Dunstan does not understand.'

Ilsa could not help herself saying, with just a touch of scorn, 'I thought Dunstan was going to burst into tears.'

'He does not feel as strongly about our situation as I do and he wants the world to be peaceful and loving all the time. Not much chance of that I fear. Poor lad, he's convinced that I am heading for hell at a rapid rate. Mind you, he is probably right.'

Ilsa kissed the back of his neck.

'Tonight has troubled you though. Your whole body feels tense and taut. I know what you need.'

'What do I need, Ilsa the miller's daughter?'

'Me. It's not dark yet, still warm and our favourite mossy bank is just beyond these trees.'

Edmund laughed. 'You would not save me from hell. You would help to send me there.'

'Only if I could come with you.'

Her hand was now inside his tunic stroking his chest. He turned his horse off the path and dismounted, looping the reins around the trunk of a sapling. Ilsa sat in the saddle, amused, provocative. He helped her down, but instead of putting her feet to the floor, he swung her up into his arms and carried her to that mossy bank she had mentioned.

❋

Blanche curled her feet up beneath her, twisting her body like a cat trying to get comfortable in front of a fire. She possessed a feline grace, a smooth fluidity of movement. She arranged the folds of her silver-grey gown.

There was a fire in De Tosny's manor house despite the mildness of the evening. The stone building looked impressive but it was always cold and dank inside even in summer. The firelight emphasized the black sheen of Blanche's hair. She had been brushing it and it was spread about her shoulders like a mourning veil. She was watching her brother, Roger De Tosny, who was standing in the centre of the dimly lit room, pouring over a set of sketches spread out on a table. It was impossible to fathom her thoughts from the expression on her face. She sighed. It was a deliberate, loud sigh directed at De Tosny, but he failed to acknowledge it. She studied her fingers, tracing the shape of each perfect nail, contemplating whether she should paint them this evening or leave it until the morning. Her eyes darkened through several shades when she was thinking, until they were as black as her hair. The morning would do she decided and she turned her attention back to her brother.

'You are more sociable and witty than ever this evening Roger. The flow of your conversation is a perfect delight.'

De Tosny smiled, but he did not look up nor did he speak.

'Oh come! I know you do not care about my boredom, but you cannot pretend that my incessant nagging about it does not annoy you. You have never been patient and your sense of humour is limited. At least say that you wish I was back in Normandy. Be your old, discourteous self, instead of this obsessed architect that you have become. The role does not fit you dear brother.'

Her voice was deep, sinuous like her body, shot through with a vein of mockery. De Tosny turned and bowed an acknowledgement to her advice.

'And what image should I cultivate?'

'A baronial one.'

'What exactly is the essence of that?'

'Very little. Much more suitable for you. It will not subject you to strain.'

His answer was a wry grimace and he turned his attention back to the plans for his castle. Blanche had picked up her ivory backed brush and was languidly brushing her hair once more. Teasing her brother was her favourite occupation. He gave back as good as he got, although he was less subtle than his sister. She gave the impression of indolence, but her mind was sharp and active.

'When will Ralph and Eleanor get here?' she asked suddenly, 'We have been expecting them for days. I hope we do not get the old story that attendance on His Majesty is a necessity and Ralph sincerely regrets etc, etc.

If the truth were known, the real reason is that Eleanor is afraid of catching a crick in her neck because of the draughts in this barbarous house or Ralph does not want to be seen with a baron whose rent roll is so inferior to his own, even if he is his brother.'

De Tosny laughed.

'Do not laugh Roger. You know that you hate being the youngest member of the family. Every new estate Ralph acquires makes you squirm. You would not be building this castle if it did not.'

He was staring at her evenly. His eyes were dark too, but the expression in them was calm and calculating. He was considering just how much he did hate taking second place to Ralph. His brother was as thick-headed as an ox. The only thing he did well was to swing a mace and chain, but rewards, honours, estates dropped into his lap like manna from heaven. She was right; it did make him squirm. Blanche sensed what he was thinking, but she did not press the point.

'Do you think that he will come?'

'Oh yes, he will come. This rebellion by Waltheof has frightened him. You know that he was a good friend of Roger of Hereford and Ralph is terrified of being implicated. I doubt if the king has been in a very good mood these last few months. Ralph will be grateful to lose himself here with us until the rebels are completely crushed. Of course, if there is a Danish invasion, that will be a different matter. He will be out there swinging his mace for His majesty then.'

Blanche uncurled from her chair and stood in front of the fire, holding out her hands towards it.

'I'm pleased that you think they will come,' she murmured. 'I must be frank and admit that I cannot muster much sisterly affection for either of them, but I welcome any change. I will not see much of Ralph anyway because you will spirit him away to discuss your beloved project. But at least I will have another woman to talk to. It will be pleasant to have another hairstyle to criticize and a figure to be catty about. I can draw blood from poor Eleanor so easily. Do you know, I am even ready to listen to her harrowing tales of the children's spots and fevers?'

'Blanche, you are a bitch,' came the crisp reply. 'If you are so bored, why don't you get married again? Try sending a third husband to his grave.'

She applauded, pivoting around him, congratulating him on his return to what she had called his old discourteous self. Her long hair brushed his shoulder and he snatched at it, only to miss.

'That's more like my little brother. Life is brighter already. As for marrying again, no man seeks out a widow of my age unless she has considerable landed wealth and my two husbands left me nothing to bargain with. That means I would have to chase a husband and that is so undignified, do you not agree?'

De Tosny took hold of her hand, running his finger along the vein in her wrist, a blue canal in the olive skin. It was a gentle enough movement, but there was no tenderness in it. His sister was always joking about her age. She was six years older than he was, but no one would have guessed it.

At thirty six, Blanche was little different from the twenty year old girl who had married William de Beaumont or the widow of twenty seven who had followed the funeral cortege of Richard Evreux to the graveside. Her hair was just as lustrous, her skin as smooth, her figure as slender. Under her constant air of sophisticated boredom there was a hint of passion that was intriguing.

She could joke about her age because she knew she still had the beauty and the allure to attract any man she desired. She pulled her hand away from Roger and went back to her chair.

'Why don't you take a wife? I need another woman to sharpen my claws on. At least surrender your chastity and give me a mistress to get acquainted with. I love the idea of entertaining your clandestine mistress.'

'You know I hate women. You most of all.'

Followed by her mocking laughter, De Tosny returned to the plans on the table, keenly observing each small detail. Dark like his sister, with the same olive skin, he was a shade under medium height, of stocky build, giving the impression of great strength and stamina. Everything about him was exact and tidy. His hair was cut with circular precision; his clothes fitted perfectly. He moved and spoke without any wasted effort; his voice soft but brisk. De Tosny had a shrewd business brain. Beneath his calm control was an ambition driven by a domineering will that left little room for scruples. His reasonable manner hid a steely heart. He knew nothing of the depths of passion that could stir Blanche. He did not want to be loved or flattered, but he did want to be acknowledged as one of the leading barons of the realm. This castle would be a symbol of his success so far and perhaps lead to even greater things.

'Why do you not take an interest in this castle?' he suggested to his sister as she stared into the fire. 'Surely you can find something in it to engage your ingenious mind.'

'No thank you. I am not interested in your wretched castle. I realise how it will mortify poor Eleanor's pride and for that reason I am all for it, but I could never work up any enthusiasm for a cold, uninhabitable tomb. Now if you were building a new manor house, warm, spacious, elegantly furnished, I might be interested, but not a castle.

Castles always remind me of William de Beaumont's bellicose old mother. I swear she stuck a sword and shield in his hands when he was about two months old and poured a glass of Bordeaux down his throat. He never looked back either. I was never raised on milk,' she added in a deep bass voice, 'I can quite believe it. I am sure his mother never had any. Her breasts were full of blood and fire like the rest of her.'

She shuddered a little, as she ran a strand of hair through her fingers, approving the texture. She had shed no tears when William de Beaumont had been killed in a foray with the troops of the Count of Flanders.

Roger was about to answer her, when there was a rap on the door. Blanche looked at him a query in her eyes.

'I expect it is Gilbert. He has been on an errand for me.'

She was no longer interested and De Tosny walked over to the low doorway to admit Gilbert. The unfortunate reeve was still trembling from his encounter with Edmund.

De Tosny saw at once that he was frightened and the contemplation of his failure was no comfort to Gilbert. His master never raged or fumed at anyone, but his punishments could be sudden and ferocious.

'Well,' De Tosny demanded, 'What was his reaction?'

'I am afraid it was not favourable sir.'

'And that is putting it mildly?'

'Yes sir, very mildly.'

Gilbert was screwing his felt cap up in his fists,

anxiously watching De Tosny's face.

'I was doubtful of success my lord because when I put your proposition to him last year he was very angry but not to such a degree. This time he was beside himself with fury. I dare not tell you all he said sir, but most of it was very offensive. I think he would rather die than sell out to you. He nearly went mad. I knew he had a warm temper like his father, but by God's blood sir, I thought he would have killed me. Waving his sword he was, yelling at me to get off his land. I swear he would have decapitated me on the spot if Dunstan had not come along.'

Poor Gilbert began to shake at the memory of it.

'Dunstan?'

'His younger brother sir, now you could not find a more reasonable man than Dunstan. If the decision was his, you might get your land.'

'Is he that tall, lanky tow-haired fellow?'

'Yes sir, that's Dunstan.'

De Tosny nodded and fell to musing on the situation. He had heard that Edmund was obstinate, but had hoped that his uncle Cenred's example would have had an effect on the nephew. Gilbert did not know how to interpret this silence. He decided that it was a bad sign and began to excuse himself.

'I am very sorry about this sir, so very sorry. I tried as hard as I could. It was not my fault. It is impossible to shift Edmund. The devil himself could not frighten him when he's set on something.'

'Very well Gilbert,' said the Norman coolly, catching a glimpse of the amused smile on Blanche's face, 'I do not hold you responsible. I am sure you did the best you could. It is hard to be persuasive when you are threatened with a broad sword.'

'Indeed it is sir.'

Like Blanche, her brother was trying not to laugh at Gilbert's shaking legs. De Tosny looked handsome when he smiled. He had a fine set of large, even teeth.

'Sit down before you faint,' he advised the reeve, pushing him into the nearest chair. 'I would not want that to happen. So the proud thegn Edmund did not think much of my offer then?'

'I should think not! He had the audacity to suggest that you should come and make the offer yourself and then he would throw you off his land too.

'Did he?' De Tosny ran his hand over his well-kept beard in a reflective gesture.

'Just like his father sir, just like his father,' Gilbert was murmuring, grateful to be sitting down.

'I might well do that, pay him a visit myself. I would like to see if all that hot air presages a real thunder storm.'

The Norman reached out towards the table and picked up the sheet of parchment. 'Now Gilbert, what do you think of the plans for my castle?'

CHAPTER FOUR

August continued hot and dry. Alleyn the miller got his expected profit. Oswin the blacksmith was kept busy mending ploughshares and sharpening scythes. Bakers and brewers were industrious and lean cattle grew fat. The harvest was heavy enough toil in itself, but when in the second week of September, De Tosny began building his castle on some of the estate's choicest meadow land, life for the villagers became even more burdensome. He could not raise enough labour from his four villages, so he hired men from Bath, Bristol and Salisbury to speed up the work. Farmers found it hard to manage when their sons were forced to leave the crops and carry stones for De Tosny.

The villagers muttered and complained, but there was little they could do about it. Subversive words and curses became their only resistance. Peter the swineherd could feel that he had some spirit at least if he called the overseer vile names behind his back and he persuaded himself that if he had been a man of some standing, like Eadwig, the village headman, he would have spoken out openly. On the other hand, Eadwig was equally certain that if he had not been in a position of authority, did not have so much responsibility to shoulder, he would have hazarded all and refused to work on the castle. In this way both men preserved their self-esteem.

Cerdic was relieved that neither he nor his father had been forced to work on the site.

Although De Tosny had promised in the sale agreement when the land was transferred that he would request no labour services of an undignified nature from Cenred's family, Cerdic was not so sure that he would adhere to his promise. Edmund was certain of the fact.

On the day after the building had started, one of De Tosny's stewards arrived at Cenred's farm. Cerdic was just about to join his father in the fields when he arrived. He brought a polite request from their lord, asking if Cenred could spare either himself or his son to do some light work at the castle site. He was prepared to offer good wages. Cerdic had replied on behalf of his father that he considered the request to be a breach of their agreement and he was not prepared to do such duty. The steward bowed and departed. They were expecting a summary order from their lord any day, but nothing came. De Tosny had courteously accepted their refusal. When Cenred pointed to this as an indication of De Tosny's intent to keep their bargain, Edmund made a cynical comment and was unconvinced.

The conversation at the supper table dwelt long on the plight of the villagers. Cenred switched the subject without warning when he gave his son a serious look and said, 'I hope Hilde's mother will be in a better mood when we get home.'

The whole family had agreed to come to supper at the neighbouring farm, but just as they were about to cross the causeway of flat stones that afforded a crossing over the stream dividing their properties, Hilde's mother came riding up on a donkey. She could scarcely hide her irritation at the fact that they were going out. She turned down an offer to go with them declaring that she had come for a quiet talk with her daughter and to play with her grandchild, not to socialize with others. Cerdic tried to smooth over the situation, but she had never appreciated her son-in-law's sense of humour and suspected that his every remark hid some insidious insult. She was on the point of going home when a compromise was reached. The patient Hilde, who had been looking forward to the evening, agreed to stay behind with Cutha and entertain her mother, while the men fulfilled their engagement.

Cenred was secretly hoping that Aelfgifu would not be there when they returned, although he was too polite to admit it. Cerdic knew his father's secret however.

'If there is one woman who terrifies my father,' he told Dunstan, 'It is Aelfgifu of Bradford. Of course, I get along with her wonderfully well. We are always in perfect harmony.'

He winked at his cousin. Cenred grunted, but he did not defend himself.

He was content to pour out another cup of mead and reach for another hunk of bread from the platter. Cheese, rye bread, wheat cakes, sweet biscuits, apples, roast chicken still sizzling and spitting in its fat and plenty of mead filled the table. The bread that Cenred was enjoying so much had been baked by Freya at the mill for neither family possessed an oven.

Freya was the baker for most of the village with Ilsa's help, which supplemented the miller's income.

As the evening was still warm Edmund had not lit the fire, but it was made up ready in the iron basket that stood in the centre at one end of the long main room. The laden supper table stood close by it. Dunstan had roasted the chicken on the kitchen fire at the other end of the room. All the cooking was done in this area.

The cauldron for making stews and broths hung from its iron frame and all the other utensils and jars of provisions were stowed away here on or under wooden benches along the walls. In the warm weather the rush blinds would be pulled up to let the smoke from the fire and the steam from the cooking escape through the window apertures and the open doors.

The main room was divided by the passage that stood between the two doorways. Here the flag stones that provided the foundation for the house were left bare. Elsewhere the floor was covered with rushes and animal skin rugs. In the depths of winter the fires would be lit at both ends of the room, the doors firmly closed and the window blinds reinforced with thick woollen blankets to block the draught. These blankets woven in strong colours and patterns were hung along the walls to decorate and brighten the house in the warmer months.

The only disadvantage of this battening down the hatches in winter was that the smoke from the fires had nowhere to escape except to filter through the thatch above and the room could become hazy with smoke.

Edmund had welcomed his kin warmly, but then

went off to meet Ilsa, saying casually that he would be back before they went home. Cenred thought this discourteous and doubted if they would see him again that evening.

Dunstan was offering him another serving of chicken which he refused.

'Well I will then. Edmund and I did not have time to stop for a midday meal. It will take us a long time to get in the rest of the wheat without the cottars' help. Every cottar for miles has been collared by De Tosny.'

Cenred nodded, peering out of the window. 'The nights are drawing in too. It is going to be dark before Edmund gets home.'

Dunstan was carving himself two large slices of chicken.

'I expect he is walking Ilsa back home first,' he said without looking up.

'Yes and I bet they are not walking all the time either,' was Cerdic's comment.

His father frowned. 'It is about time he married that girl. He has been courting her for long enough. I am beginning to wonder if he really intends to marry her.'

Dunstan coloured. 'Of course he will uncle, very soon.'

He was quick to defend his brother. Cerdic studied his face, wondering how certain he really was. Cenred was still complaining about Edmund's lack of constancy where women were concerned. His son interrupted him.

'Oh be quiet father. It's not for us to discuss Edmund's love life. We sound like a bunch of gossipy old women. You are as bad as Hilde's mother.'

He knew that last comment was enough to silence his father.

The judgement of his relatives on his behaviour was the farthest thing from Edmund's mind at that moment. He was sitting by the stream that ran through his copse with his arm around Ilsa. With his free hand, he was tossing pebbles into the water, watching them skim along the calm surface before sinking to the bottom. It was warm; dusk was just beginning to fall. Ilsa's sweet-smelling hair was brushing against his cheek. He was comfortable and contented. Part of his contentment sprang from his recollection of his encounter with Roger De Tosny the previous morning, which he had been describing to Ilsa. He had controlled himself; so had De Tosny, but there was a suggestion of the pallor of anger in the Norman's face when he left the farm. Edmund had no doubt of his moral victory. De Tosny had made no more progress than his reeve.

The peaceful beauty of the copse, the sound of partridges in the undergrowth, the smell of eglantine nearby, all created an atmosphere akin to grace. He had no quarrel with the world that evening.

Edmund embraced the warrior ethic. He kept fit and trim, practiced with sword and battle axe several times a week. He knew that on a military campaign his stamina would not fail. He would survive the rigours of a Spartan existence without complaint, even thrive on it. He worked hard on the farm too when it was needed most. But in most circumstances of his everyday existence he was far from severe on himself or others. He was genial, tolerant, charming, a lover of music, good food, good wine and he appreciated beauty, particularly feminine beauty. As Gilbert the reeve knew to his cost, when Edmund lost his temper he was formidable and when he took to brooding he needed to be left alone, but his usual manner was good-humoured and approachable.

He did not see the sense in too much self-denial. If he fancied a piece of beef on a church fast day, he would eat it, but cheerfully confess his transgression with a disarming smile and pay his penance without a murmur. He never felt guilt when he was making love. Why God would condemn something that was so much pleasure, he could never understand.

He was naturally generous, always magnanimous in alms giving.

The financial constrictions of the past few years which forced him to watch every penny frustrated him. He hated to be thought mean but knew it was worse to be irresponsible when their livelihood depended on it.

Ilsa loved the contradictions in Edmund's nature. He was mercurial, exciting. The discovery that he had written poetry added yet another aspect to her view of him. She had read over and over again, those six poems that Dunstan had managed to save from the bonfire, marvelling at their tenderness and the sense of longing in them. She wished the rest had been saved for she was hungry to read more. She was tempted to ask Edmund about them, but kept her promise to Dunstan to say nothing.

She had loved Edmund for as long as she could remember. Even when she was a child, to see him flash through the village on a horse was enough to make her tread on air all day. She recalled with vivid clarity that day, two days after her tenth birthday, when Alfstan carried Edmund into the mill. He was wracked with fever and leaking blood from badly dressed wounds. There was an atmosphere of anxiety, even fear amongst the adults as they talked of the great battle that had been lost many miles away by the sea. Her only fear was that Edmund might die. She helped her mother to prepare lotions to heal his wounds, watched while she bathed his face and tried to sooth the delirium that gripped him. When the fever broke and he opened his eyes with recognition in them for the first time in a week, she was so relieved that she could not resist her urge to kiss his cheek. Her mother had slapped her afterwards, chiding her for her forwardness, but she did not care.

He was a thegn, but her quick intelligence and her self-confidence soon made light of any feelings of social inferiority learned in childhood. At sixteen, she had dared to smile at him when he winked at her one Sunday, as he and his brother rode to church. Her mother, who had seen the whole thing, rebuked her severely, but she never regretted it.

How could she regret it when she could feel his arm around her as it was now? She was certain that there was no place on earth so secure as in Edmund's arms. For two years now she had been the object of his caresses, the soother of his anxieties, the sharer of his highs and lows.

She knew that during that time she was not the only object of his affections, but she was certain now that she was the only one who mattered. She could listen to jokes about his sexual exploits by bucolic wits with a quiet confidence. She was convinced that he would marry her one day.

There was no hurry, as long as she could prevent her father from losing his patience and trying to find a husband for her from amongst the Bristol merchant community. Edmund loved her; that was enough for her.

'Don't watch those pebbles so closely,' Edmund said suddenly, 'You will go cross-eyed.'

'Will you still love me if I am cross-eyed?'

'Oh, I've a magnanimous nature. I should think so.'

'Then I will not mind being cross-eyed.'

He kissed the tip of her nose.

'You don't want cross eyes and freckles.'

'You like my freckles,' she insisted.

He did not confirm or deny it. Another pebble skimmed along the stream and plopped into the sandy bottom, setting up a chain of concentric circles in the water. Ilsa jerked herself out of his grasp and sprang at him. She had moved so quickly that he was taken off guard and landed on his back. She knelt on his chest, pinning his arms to the ground.

'You admit that you like my freckles or I will duck your head in that stream. I have no mercy. I will drown you if you don't yield.'

'Insolent wench,' was his retort.

He did not attempt to resist her and she applied more pressure to his chest.

'I warn you, I am not pressing with my full weight

yet.'

'Oh, very well, I love your freckles, adore them. Mercy, mercy I beg you.'

'That's more like it.'

She let go of his arms and in an instant he had pulled her down on top of him as if he intended to roll her into the stream. They struggled for a while until he realised how close to the water's edge they had rolled. He was laughing. Ilsa was a formidable opponent; he loved her boldness.

'Of course I love your freckles. You did not need to extort that from me with violence. Let me prove it. I will kiss everyone I can find.'

He fulfilled his extravagant promise in spirit if not in exactitude.

'It seems strange to hear you ask for mercy,' Ilsa reflected, only half-teasing, as she felt her skin glow with the warmth of his kisses. 'Is that not a betrayal of your thegn creed? My courageous thegn Edmund, if you roared at a lion he would flee. What chance does a Norman baron have? Edmund is a Saxon royal name. Were you named after King Edmund?'

'Yes, as a matter of fact I was and Dunstan in honour of a Saint. Rather prophetic really, seeing how different we are. I swear that boy will end up canonized.'

His tone was light, but it was not mocking.

'But how will you ever become a king?' Ilsa asked, twisting a lock of his dark brown hair around her finger.

His face clouded over and he sat up, brushing the leaves and dust from his shoulders.

'I keep praying that England will have another Saxon king in my life time.'

His voice was earnest and she knew how much this meant to him.

'Most of this shire was part of the demesne of the Saxon kings right from King Alfred's time, if not before, but they never claimed to own the whole land of England like William of Normandy. He claims that any landholder holds his land only on sufferance because he allows it in exchange for services rendered. Our estate was given to my ancestor freely by Alfred's grandson.'

'I know. You told me,' Ilsa reminded him.

'More than once no doubt,' he acknowledged with a wry smile, 'But I am proud of it. I feel no allegiance to that Norman usurper. There are times when I feel I could burst with frustration because I ought to be doing something about it and I do not know what. When rebellion flares up it is crushed before we even hear about it and the aftermath is such a catastrophe for the local population.'

Ilsa nodded. She knew her father felt that open resistance now was never worth the consequences and was preventing the King from forming a settled government. William had been conciliatory to the remaining English earls at first, confirming them in their office. It was the miller's contention that if they had used their brains and stayed loyal they would still have influence and power, continuing to do honour to their heritage, whereas now they had been swept away and replaced by Normans. He was fond of pointing out with some satisfaction that within living memory England had a

Danish King, Canute, who though repressive at first soon turned to compromise to forge an Anglo-Danish state that worked well. His memory was respected, although Alleyn would always add that his sons were useless and England was grateful when a scion of the Saxon royal dynasty was restored to the throne in the shape of good King Edward. Logically Ilsa knew her father's argument was valid, but she was always stirred by Edmund's flashes of thegnly indignation; it was the light in his eyes.

'When the Northumbrians rebelled six years ago terrible vengeance was wrought on the countryside,' Edmund was saying, 'It is common practice for the victor to destroy the land and property of those who rebel, but this was beyond all proportion. William's army burned and destroyed everything that was capable of sustaining life-crops, livestock, gardens, houses, filled in all the wells. A whole swathe of the countryside was left desolate, a barren desert. I have heard tell it is still like that to this day. Those people who escaped slaughter died of starvation, thousands of them. He says it was purely a military tactic to make sure there was nothing to feed the Danish army if it invaded, but it was more than that. It was done in anger, in the spirit of revenge with no respect for the lives of English men, women or children.'

Edmund had no taste for slaughtering the defenceless. To be ready to fight, kill and perhaps die in battle was the essence of the thegn's creed, but not to murder women and children.

'William does not care for this country. He spends half his time in Normandy skirmishing with neighbouring states. A true king should live in his kingdom.

If I see an heir of Edgar the Atheling on the throne, then I will feel like a king too. Until then I cannot even be a real thegn. What does true nobility mean to a race of half-civilized ox brains?'

He sighed, wondering why he had allowed his bitterness to disturb the contentment he was feeling earlier and he did not wish to inflict his frustrations on Ilsa. He brushed his lips across her fingers. 'Enough of this yearning for a true king. If I can charm your intelligent, searching mind into believing that I am made of kingly stuff that will do for me.'

He stared into the stream trying to pick out the pebbles on its bed. In the last few moments it had grown appreciably darker and he found his task difficult. He jumped to his feet, holding out his hand to help Ilsa up. She sat there looking at him, willing him to sit down again. She did not want to go home yet.

'It's no good reclining there looking seductive. You know what an iron will I have,' he said, amused at his own sarcasm, particularly when she twisted her mouth in an incredulous grimace. 'Seriously though, it will be dark soon and I promised your father I would bring you home before dark. He has still got that wretched supernatural wolf on his mind. The ghost of Rannulf le Gros indeed! From what I can remember of Rannulf Le Gros, I'd say that his very essence had been scorched up in fire and brimstone long ago'

She laughed, pulling herself up with his hand and they set off towards the village.

Edmund enjoyed Ilsa's company so much. Her bright face, intelligent conversation, the smell of her hair, the way she responded to his embrace. He could laugh and feel free when he was with her.

On a hot day when he was toiling in the fields or worrying how to stretch their income to meet their needs, he would hear her clear laughter in his head and contemplate the pleasure her body gave him. Then he would long for the evening when they would be together.

He spent more time with her than any other woman who took his fancy, but did not admit to himself that he was in love with her. Ilsa was mistaken to assume that he intended to marry her. It had never entered his head. He underestimated her commitment to him, the depth of her love. It was convenient to persuade himself that her understanding of their relationship was as casual as he wished his own to be. As far as he was concerned it could continue on the same footing for as long as she wanted it.

They had stepped out of the copse just where the end of Edmund's south pasture, fenced with hurdles, abutted on to the meadows of the manor. He could see the torchlight in the village ahead of them and when he looked back over his shoulder he could also see a faint gleam in the direction of the farm house. He smiled.

'I see that the torches are alight in the yard back home. I did not realise that it was so late. We had better get a move on young lady. Cenred and Cerdic came over for supper tonight and I told them I would be back before they went home. Uncle Cenred was a bit grumpy because I left them. Besides, once those three set about the roast chicken, there will not be much left for my supper. I expect Cenred has just refilled his cup for the umpteenth time and is saying in that grave voice of his- well I cannot see that Edmund is in any hurry to share our company.'

His impersonation of his uncle was very accurate.

Cenred was indeed filling his cup for the umpteenth time, but he was not discussing his elder nephew. He was listening with great pleasure, nodding his head from time to time, as Dunstan read aloud from a small brown volume, stories of King Alfred's wars against the Danes. Cenred greatly admired King Alfred and delighted in these tales. His sight was deteriorating and he found reading difficult.

Cerdic had lit the fire and was sitting beside it, running his hands along his twisted leg, feeling the benefit of the heat as it coaxed away the ache that often troubled him.

Dunstan stopped reading.

'Listen, did you hear anything?'

'What sort of anything?' Cerdic asked.

'A banging noise. I think it is down by the barn.'

His cousin smiled. 'You have ears like a donkey Dunstan. I cannot hear anything.'

Cenred stood up and listened by the window, his face wrinkled up with concentration.

'Something is disturbing the chickens. I can hear them squawking.'

Dunstan was on his feet in an instant, taking from the corner a gigantic stave of knotted wood.

'It may be that wolf. The dogs were barking earlier.

He may be on the prowl. I had better take a look.'

He stepped out into the yard, the others close behind him, Cerdic feeling for the dagger at his belt. It was dark now, silent except for those noisy chickens.

The first thing that caught Dunstan's attention was the torch down by the barn. It had gone out. He was puzzled. There was no wind and recently lit, it could not have burned out already. The other torches still burned. Cerdic had noticed it too and pointed it out to his cousin. Dunstan was afraid and was not sure why. He felt a prickly sensation under his skin and sensed his heart beat accelerate. He stood still, just listening, trying to decide if the noise he heard again came from the barn or was just his own heartbeat. Cenred and Cerdic were walking down towards the chicken coop. He chided himself for his fear and was about to follow them when he saw something move down by the barns, a figure darting through the gloom from one barn to the next.

'Wait,' he called softly to the others, 'There is someone down there.'

'Where?' his uncle demanded.

'By the barns.'

He was already hurrying in that direction. Cerdic grabbed a torch from its bracket, holding it out in front of him in an effort to pierce the darkness.

There were no sounds now, just an obtrusive silence.

'Who's there?' Dunstan called. 'Is that you Edmund?'

There was no answer.

'We know someone is there. Who are you?'

Suddenly things began to happen. There was a

scuffle. Someone shouted. A horseman galloped away from the barn. There was confusion as more horsemen appeared. Uncle Cenred was shouting 'Thieves,' and grappling with a man who rushed out of the cow stalls. Another horseman rode into Dunstan, who grabbed at the rider in an instinctive attempt to protect himself.

The man was unseated and fell on top of him, the horse galloping on. Dunstan, his mouth full of dust, scrambled to his feet coughing and snatched hold of his stave. The intruder was up already. A sword gleamed in the darkness. He was lightly armed; dressed in a short surcoat of chain mail. He swore at Dunstan in French and lunged at him with his sword. Dunstan managed to step aside and catch the fellow a blow on the side of the head that felled him and he pitched forward on his face.

The Saxon knelt beside him trying to distinguish his face. There was a sudden rush of light. Cerdic was rekindling the torches that had gone out.

The man on the floor was a stranger, but his armour was Norman. Dunstan had no time to speculate on this, for looking around him he could see neither his uncle nor his cousin. Then he saw Cenred. The old thegn seemed to be entangled in the stirrups or the girths of an escaping horseman. He was dragged along as the horse gathered speed, the rider striking at him with his fist, as eager to shake him off as Cenred was to free himself. Cerdic, still carrying his torch, was trying to run after his father, when another group four riders charged out into the yard. He was right in their path.

'Cerdic!' Dunstan yelled frantically.

His cousin half-turned to see the riders bearing down on him. He tried to throw himself out of their path, but his weight was on the wrong leg. His twisted limb gave way. He was still falling when the first horse drove into him. There was a flailing of hooves, the next horse and the next; they all rode over him as if he were not there. The thunder of hooves died away, the uproar was gone. It had all happened so quickly. Dunstan was paralysed. He wanted to run to his cousin, but he could not move for a moment. He had to force himself to put one foot in front of the other. There were no coherent thoughts in his head.

Cerdic was curled into a ball, his arms thrown around his head for protection. Dunstan had seen him do this a hundred times when he was playing with the village children. He would curl up like a hedgehog, taking all their punches on his arms and yelling in counterfeited agony. Dunstan wanted to tell him to get up and stop fooling, but he knew that this time Cerdic was not fooling. He dropped down on his knees and gently brised his cousin's arms away from his face. His head was in a pool of blood. One side of his head was crushed, blood and brain matter smeared across his face, garish in the torchlight. Dunstan lifted the body up in his arms and burying his face in it he began to weep. He wanted to pray. Cerdic was dead. He must pray, but all he could do was cry.

The knight he had felled in the yard had come to his senses. He raised himself on his elbows, shaking his head. Once he had gathered enough of his wits to think straight, he scrambled to his feet and disappeared into the darkness.

Dunstan did not see him go. All he was aware of

was the body in his arms. He did not know how long he sat there, holding Cerdic close to him, rocking backwards and forwards in his grief.

'God in heaven Dunstan, what's happened?'

The voice floated around in his head, the words not registering. He glanced up to see Edmund standing over him looking pale and wild.

When Edmund approached the farm he found dead chickens scattered around the coops, their necks wrung; two goats and a young calf outside the stalls with their throats cut and the stable door off its hinges, the horses nowhere to be seen. Hurdles were strewn in disorder all over the yard.

His mind was clear enough to conclude that this was Roger De Tosny's doing. He had resorted to a different form of persuasion. Nothing else could explain this wanton destruction. He was as inarticulate with anger as Dunstan was with grief. All he could do was curse De Tosny. Dunstan stared at him.

'Edmund, Cerdic's dead.'

Edmund stopped cursing. In the poor light and taken up with his own anger, he had failed to realise what was in his brother's arms. He crossed himself, kneeling down beside them.

'Tich, poor little Tich, what have the bastards done to you?' He ran his hand across Cerdic's close-cropped hair in an affectionate gesture. 'Oh Dunstan I am so sorry.'

He sat in silence for a while, his arm around his brother's shoulder, then he asked, 'How did this happen?'

'They were getting away- horsemen and Cerdic was

in their way. He was not quick enough. It was his leg; he fell and they rode over him, four of them.'

Even the battle-fledged Edmund shuddered and then he thought of his uncle.

'Where is Uncle Cenred?'

Dunstan had forgotten him completely. He looked around him helplessly, trying to order his thoughts.

'I- they were dragging him away. I- I can't think,' he stammered.

'You must think,' Edmund insisted, taking him by the shoulders, 'Which way did they take him? Which way Dunstan? Pull yourself together. Stop weeping boy!'

'I can't'

All Dunstan's efforts to control himself broke down under this barrage. Edmund saw it was useless to question him further. Instead he embraced his brother and jumped to his feet.

'We will take Cerdic into the house and then I will go to look for Uncle Cenred. Come on, there's a good lad. I will take him.'

Dunstan did not want to let go, but Edmund coaxed the body away from him. As he took Cerdic in his arms he was struck by how light he was; no heavier than a child. He kissed his cousin's bloody forehead and Dunstan was so grateful to see that love in Edmund for Cerdic. He knew there was so much kindness, even gentleness in Edmund's nature and grieved to think that it was so often overcome by anger and hatred.

They wrapped Cerdic's body in a sheet and laid it before the altar in Dunstan's chapel. Then Edmund set off on his search for Cenred. Dunstan went into the chapel and knelt beside Cerdic's body.

His cousin had died without a blessing, but he was sure that there was no sin in Cerdic bad enough to keep him from God's mercy. He prayed for his soul, for his uncle Cenred, for Hilde and Cutha and for Edmund. He was worried that his grief was too selfish. Cerdic was now taken into the light of eternal glory and all he could feel was his own loss, instead of rejoicing for him. He asked for forgiveness.

It was almost two hours before Edmund returned. He had found no sign of his uncle and had given up the search until daylight. He had gone through the harrowing experience of telling Hilde the news and was thankful that her mother was still with her. She was a firm support in her daughter's distress and agreed to stay the night and take her and Cutha home with her in the morning. Edmund was grateful for this. He was worried about Cenred, who could be lying somewhere, bleeding to death and the difficulty of their plight was also on his mind. Every pig was dead in the sty; so were half of the chickens. Five cows had been maimed and all the farm tools broken up. No doubt more damage would come to light in the morning. At least they did not have the time to fire the barns.

As he threw himself into a chair, he recalled his uncle's words, that his intransigence towards De Tosny might be the undoing of him. He had no doubt this was De Tosny's work. No wonder the Norman was so cool during their encounter the previous day; he had an ace up his sleeve. How he hated that man who had murdered his kindred, devastated his farm; he and all his ilk, the conquerors who had subjected a proud people, killed his father, despised his rank. He must take revenge; he was a thegn. It was his duty to avenge his kin.

He was brooding for some time. Then the thought that Dunstan was still in the chapel irritated him. He called for him with impatience in his voice.

Dunstan had not heard his brother return. He came into the room, his face drained of all colour. Edmund was pouring himself a glass of mead.

His tone was brusque when he said, 'It is about time you came out of there. You cannot sit in there praying forever. What good does it do? It will not find Uncle Cenred.'

He was immediately sorry that he had sounded so sharp and tried to explain his search for his uncle and the visit to Hilde in a factual, passionless way, but he could not keep it up. His anger spilled out and he jumped up from his chair.

'Damn it, what is the matter with me? I should not be talking; I should be doing my duty.'

'Duty?' Dunstan repeated hollowly.

'Yes, we are thegns. Our kinsmen have been murdered. We must avenge our blood. That Norman devil must answer for what he has done today.'

'But you cannot be sure it was De Tosny.'

Edmund snorted. 'You said yourself that fellow you brought down was dressed in De Tosny's livery, one of his knights. What more proof do you want?'

'I said I thought it was. It was shadowy Edmund, I could

not see properly. I cannot swear it was his livery. We must not accuse a man of such a terrible crime without proof.'

'Proof, hell and damnation Dunstan, do not be so naive.'

Edmund was pacing up and down the room. Dunstan wished he would not argue. His head was aching and he felt sick.

'Of course it was De Tosny. Who else would do this to us? I should have known he would retaliate after yesterday. Well, he will suffer for this. I may not be able to rid the country of the Normans, but I can manage De Tosny.'

'What will you do?' Dunstan was frightened by the look in his brother's eyes.

'Blood asks for blood. You know the thegn's creed. I will kill him.'

'No Edmund, you cannot do that.'

Edmund assured him he could look after himself.

'No, I do not mean that. It is wrong. The days of the blood feud are past. Centuries of kings with a conscience have tried to stamp it out. It's pagan and we are Christians. God does not want blood. De Tosny's blood will not help Cerdic's soul and Edmund it will not help yours.'

Edmund pointed a frustrated forefinger at his brother.

'Don't you start weeping again. You cannot accuse me of not feeling for Cerdic and Uncle Cenred. They have both been good friends to me. I loved them. It hurts me too you know.'

'I –I know-I did not say' he stopped in despair for

Edmund was not listening.

'A thegn must show his love for his kin by avenging them as they would expect. Tears are no use. Cerdic meant so much to you. You should burn to avenge him.'

'You do not understand. I love him too much to avenge him.'

'You are right, I do not understand. I do not understand you at all. You are willing to be trodden on. God does not want us to be trodden on.

The God who led Deborah and Barak to victory over Sisera's host, who went before the Israelites in all their battles, resting in the ark, is the kind of God who demands action, vindication.'

'Christ told us to love our enemies, do good to those who hate us,' Dunstan countered.

He was afraid that Edmund was ready to walk out of the house and try to kill De Tosny right then. 'Father forgive them for they know not what they do our Lord said when he was betrayed. I do not know why this happened. We must trust. That is all we can do.'

Edmund was standing with his hand hovering over the sword at his waist

'Blood asks for blood,' he murmured through gritted teeth.

Dunstan put his hand to his forehead.

'I cannot stand any more of this.'

He felt faint. Sounds were beginning to drift away from him. He caught hold of the table to steady himself.

'Dunstan, what's wrong?' Edmund was beside him, his voice softened with concern. 'I thought you were going to faint then.'

'So did I.'

'Look, you are badly shaken. We both are. Besides you must have cried yourself sick. You better go to bed. I will never make a thegn out of you and you will never be able to teach me obedience and humility. We will not discuss this anymore tonight.'

'Edmund, promise me that you will not do anything reckless tonight, please.'

'That's a promise. Now go to bed. I will clear up what I can here and will start looking for Uncle Cenred again as soon as it's light.'

Dunstan had one more request.

'Do not let hate override everything else. I am afraid that it will consume you.'

Edmund had begun to clear away the supper things. He did not answer and continued to stack the plates.

'I think I will pray a little more before I go to bed.'

'Suit yourself. I will see you in the morning.'

Edmund did not turn around and Dunstan looked disconsolate as he left the room. Edmund stopped his work, listening for the swish of the chapel screen closing, then he banged down the brass platter that he held in his hand with such force that he dented it.

'Oh God, I swear that Roger De Tosny shall be paid for this. Requite me if I do not fulfil my vow. Roger De Tosny, you will pay.'

A shaft of light struck through the narrow window slit, soft autumn sunlight, buoying up moats of dust and playing on the silver cross that stood on the altar. The beam fell on a bundle, wrapped in a white cloth, lying at the foot of the altar. The whiteness of the cloth was accentuated by the patches of dark red that had soaked through it like ink on blotting paper. The light came to rest on the face of a young man asleep, sprawled on the rush-strewn floor. The eyelashes flickered and Dunstan stared into the light. He lay motionless for a while, wondering where he was, puzzling over the haze of brightness. Then the painful memories came flooding back.

He had prayed for a long while after he had left Edmund the previous night. He had exhausted mind, spirit and body and fell asleep while he was still on his knees. He stretched out his leg, feeling stiff. The floor was a hard bed. He listened. There was a bee buzzing somewhere, an hypnotic drone in the stillness. Now a dog barked, the hostile bark provoked by the approach of strangers, but it was not a bark he recognised, not Ulf's or the wolfhound's.

Minutes passed. Still he lay on his back, listening harder. Someone was talking in the yard. The voices drifted down the shaft of light with the dust.

'It is good of you to come so soon Father Robert.'

It was Edmund's voice. The Abbot had heard of the tragedy from Brother Raymond who was in the village when Edmund escorted Hilde, her mother and Cutha through the village on their way home. Robert asked after

Dunstan. Edmund expressed concern for his brother's state of mind. What of Cenred?

'I found him at the top of the north pasture Father, almost on the boundary with the monastery land. He had been killed with a sword. I took him down to his own house and locked it up. It would only grieve Dunstan more if I brought the body back here. The poor lad looked truly ill last night.

I saw the priest in the village. He will be over this afternoon. I am at a loss to know what to do next.'

Edmund sounded subdued, bewildered. Dunstan's heart went out to him. He was so relieved to find that he was not so taken up with his own sorrow as he had been; that his first thought was for Edmund and not himself.

He got to his feet. There was no one he would rather see than Father Robert. The Abbot was never glib or trite when he gave words of comfort. He hoped that Robert could help Edmund in some way too, although it was not his brother's way to turn to the church in times of stress.

Edmund was indeed dispirited. The damage was as bad as he had imagined. Even the dogs were dead; the first to be silenced. The barking that Dunstan had heard was Mankel, Cenred's dog. Edmund had brought the dog back with him when he locked up his uncle's farm house. There was one small comfort. He had found the horses grazing in the meadowland. He was sure about his resolution to repay De Tosny, but what he was going to do about their situation he had no idea.

The three of them sat together far into the morning in earnest discussion. It was almost midday, when

Mankel, who was sitting in the doorway, rushed out into the yard, growling. Edmund heard horses' hooves and thought it was the priest arriving early with the village coffin. Father Robert went to the window. His reaction was an apprehensive one.

'I am afraid not my son. It is Roger De Tosny and his sister.'

Edmund turned pale. He gripped the arms of his chair, but he did not stand up. Dunstan joined the Abbot at the window. Sure enough De Tosny was reining in his horse in the middle of the yard, twisting around in the saddle, looking for any signs of life. Blanche, dressed in a jade green riding habit, the very latest fashion from the continent, was trying to sooth Mankel as he snapped around the hooves of her mount. De Tosny called out, asking if anyone was at home.

'I must credit him with courage,' Edmund said in a fierce undertone, 'Daring to come here without a bodyguard after what has happened. He is quick off the mark, coming to crow over us as soon as this.'

'You do not know why he is here yet,' corrected the Abbot, 'He is aware that he is unpopular and that most of the village will immediately jump to the conclusion that he was responsible for this raid. He may have come to clear himself.' Edmund gave him a sardonic smile. 'Besides, your uncle was his tenant. I think he may be here to offer his condolences in his capacity as their lord. Roger is always scrupulously correct.'

'Of course, you are a Norman. You would know all about that.'

Julliere smiled. 'I am an abbot Edmund. My race has nothing to do with it and I see Roger as a man, not a Norman.'

He looked out of the window again. Blanche was growing impatient, but De Tosny seemed disposed to wait. Father Robert suggested Edmund should go and speak to him.

'I cannot. I would not be responsible for my actions. I would kill him as soon as look at him.'

Dunstan, fearing the truth of his brother's remark, volunteered to do the talking, but he looked nervous as he went outside. Father Robert patted Edmund on the shoulder and followed Dunstan.

De Tosny made some comment to Blanche that he knew someone would come out, when he saw Dunstan walking towards them. He was surprised to see the Abbot and bowed him an acknowledgement. He had come to respect him as a man of good sense and business acumen, as well as a spiritual advisor. The polished manners and informed conversation of the Abbot pleased him.

'Why do you wish to see us Sir?' Dunstan asked.

De Tosny glanced over at his sister, his eyebrows raised. The last thing he had expected was any show of courtesy, particularly in French.

'I do speak your language.'

'I think I speak French well enough for you to understand.'

'Indeed you do. Very well, we will stick to French. You must be Dunstan. You were not here when I called on your brother the other day, but we have met before. You retrieved a dropped glove for me in the village.'

Father Robert smiled to himself. He knew that De Tosny would not forget it. The baron pulled in his rein to stop his horse from fidgeting, but the bay was so disturbed by Mankel prowling around him, De Tosny decided to dismount.

'Your French is good,' he complimented, as he swung out of the saddle, handing his reins to Blanche, whose docile grey mare was indifferent to the behaviour of the dog.

'I had a good teacher,' was Dunstan's reply. 'My brother speaks it far more fluently than I. But perhaps you can imagine that it would choke him to converse in French now. He has not come out to speak to you because he fears he will not be able to control his temper.'

'Ah yes. My reeve can vouch for the fire of your brother's temper, although when we spoke together the other day he was calmness itself. I did not come here to exchange pleasantries. My errand is a serious one. I was truly shocked this morning when my steward told me of your great loss. I come to tender my deepest sympathies.'

He had in truth heard about the raid the previous evening, when his knights came scurrying back in the darkness. His amazement in front of his steward was a charade, but he did have regrets. He had meant the raid to be devastating, but he had intended no loss of life. It could prove awkward, particularly if they had been recognised and he was furious with them. He had no feeling for the murdered Saxons, but he had not meant it to happen.

'I feel even more oppressed,' he added, 'To think that

men in my own employ, men for whom I am responsible, have done this thing to you.'

Dunstan was astonished at such forthrightness. He had not expected the baron to admit they were his men. He hoped this was the honesty of an innocent man. He did not want the further burden of apportioning blame.

The Norman put out his hand and touched Dunstan's arm in a kindly way.

'I hardly know how to apologise, to you and your brother. I understand how Edmund must feel and why he might blame me. They are my knights after all. But let me assure you both that I had nothing to do with this. The kind of man, who is most useful as a knight, is not the easiest creature to control. Many of them have done nothing but fight since boyhood. Murder and plunder are second nature to such men and they grow restless in peace-time. Besides, they are not over fond of Saxons. I am sure you can understand that emotion. But I cannot relinquish my responsibility for them and they will be severely punished.'

It was so convincing. Dunstan wondered if he was being too credulous, but he wanted to believe him. He glanced at the Abbot, eager for confirmation of his hope, but Father Robert's face was impassive. He would have to decide for himself and he chose to believe. The relief was immense.

'I can only hope,' De Tosny continued, 'That you have not suffered too much.'

'I think Roger there is little point in such a hope. His suffering is written plainly enough on his face.'

It was Blanche who spoke. Dunstan had hardly noticed her. Now he looked at her. She was studying him closely. He had not expected such kindness; it touched him. He would have been disappointed if he knew what Blanche was really thinking. She had been intrigued by the thought of someone who could so terrify Gilbert the reeve. It was the fiery Edmund she had come to see and was wishing he would make an appearance. One of her serving women had repeated to her mistress some of the gossip about the handsome thegn that she had heard in the kitchens. It seemed he had quite a reputation as a lover as well as a firebrand.

De Tosny was pleased with the progress he had made with Dunstan, although he knew he had little chance of convincing Edmund. He was not even sure that he had convinced the Abbot, who still had not spoken and was watching him with a shrewd interest.

'Well,' he slapped his gauntlets against his thigh, 'I am also here as the landlord of your unfortunate uncle. I suppose you realise that as the land belongs to me, so all the stock and revenues from it reverts to me, as the grandson is a minor. As their lord, it is my duty to take the child and his mother under my protection. I will see that they are treated well.'

'Roger,' Father Robert spoke at last, 'Has it not occurred to you that Hilde may prefer the protection of her own kin.'

'That is a Saxon custom. I am the lord of the manor and now the Norman custom prevails. I consider the fulfilment of my duty more important than a woman's preference. I think women are given too many rights in

Saxon law. Always a dangerous thing to give women choice.'

Blanche laughed her mocking laugh and De Tosny turned to Dunstan.

'I have no idea of the scale of your loss, but if your brother would care to make out an inventory, I shall willingly reimburse him. And then there is the question of wergild or whatever you call it. I am ready to pay full compensation for the lives of your cousin and uncle.'

He knew full well that Edmund would never accept any money from him, so he could offer freely. His tone had become that of a business man, brisk and practical. All signs of sympathy were gone and Dunstan was bothered by his sister's mocking laugh. He was startled by this sudden transition. Perhaps he had committed himself too readily. He resolved to be more guarded.

'The matter of compensation will be settled by the shire court,' Dunstan said.

'My dear young man, this will not go as far as the shire court. It is entirely a personal matter. Men in my employ committed a crime, killing my tenants. The manorial court will deal with this. '

'Yes, but the crime was committed on our land, not yours. The king endorsed our charter. We have full rights, soke, sake, toll, team and infangentheof, independent rights of justice and we can choose to go to the shire court.'

The Norman nodded his head. 'Well, you are a lawyer too are you? It seems that we both have our rights, but I advise you not to trade legal quibbles with me. I am an old hand at the game. The manorial court is legally constituted. Your countrymen have a large enough say in it. I assure you, the offenders will get just what they deserve.'

He meant that. He had no intention of forgiving the knights for their blunder.

'I believe you did have something to do with this after all,' Dunstan accused, disappointment sweeping over him, 'All that sympathy was a lie.'

'You can believe what you wish.'

'I wanted to believe you, but Edmund was right; you are guilty. You talk about wergilds and compensation as if Cerdic and my uncle were just chattels on your estate, to be disposed of at your will. You do not care about them at all. I was praying last night that if you were indeed guilty, God would help you to feel remorse. I still hope that will be so.'

De Tosny looked surprised, then amused. That attractive smile spread across his face, as he stroked his horse's mane.

'I do believe that you are expressing concern for my soul young man,' he said genially, 'And are offering me forgiveness in the bargain. What impudence! If I did not believe that you were a complete innocent, I would take that as a studied insult. As it is, I marvel at your temper. Not at all Saxon. I do not think you hate me one little bit.'

'Do not mock the boy,' Father Robert reproved, frowning, 'You need his forgiveness very much. Do not encourage him to hate you.'

'I do not, indeed I do not. But give me leave to be astonished. I had heard from Gilbert that Dunstan was a good-natured young man, but I imaged that he was a Saxon nevertheless. He looks so Saxon.'

He stared thoughtfully at Dunstan, then without warning, he slapped him across the mouth with his gloves. The leather gauntlets were backed with a light chain mail. Dunstan turned his head with the blow, a thin stream of blood beginning to trickle from the corner of his mouth. He could not understand why De Tosny had done that. The Abbot stepped forward protesting, but the baron interrupted him.

'No, no father, there was no malice behind my action. You must forgive me, but I was eager to see how he would react. Now I am satisfied that he is genuine. If that had been his brother I would have been half throttled by now.'

He should never have said that; it was prophetic. A lithe figure hurtled across the yard from the direction of the house and before anyone had time to think, had thrown himself upon De Tosny. Edmund had been watching from the window, debating whether he should join them or not. He was worried that Dunstan would be taken in by smooth words. He too was marvelling at his brother's patience and to see it rewarded in such a way was too much for his self-control. He had his hands around De Tosny's throat. All his grief and anger were in those hands.

The Norman was fighting for breath. It was as much as Julliere and Dunstan could do to pull Edmund off him. He struggled as they held him back.

'Have you not done enough to us? Aren't you

satisfied with killing my uncle and Cerdic that you have to take it out on Dunstan too? If you had seen how this boy has suffered because of what you have done, you would not dare speak to him. Go away for God's sake and leave us alone.'

De Tosny had scrambled to his feet and was brushing the dust off his clothes. He tried to appear unruffled, although he was red in the face and was no longer smiling. After smoothing down his hair and straightening his garments, he put his foot into his horse's stirrup.

He paused to say, in a voice that was more constricted than usual, 'I came to offer my apologies, but there is little point in repeating them to you. No doubt your brother will explain. I am sorry he has suffered. I am sure that you both have. It is a pity that you cannot bear it with his patience. The manorial court will sit next Monday. I will send my coroner to look at the bodies as soon as possible.'

He lifted himself into the saddle and coaxed his horse away.

Blanche had been silent through all this. She had gained her wish to see Edmund and it had been a spectacular introduction. She was impressed with his looks and convinced of his passion. On the whole her morning's trip had proved diverting. She lingered after her brother had moved away, moving her horse towards Dunstan, angling her position to give Edmund a good view of her. Then with calculated grace she reached out an elegant hand and wiped the blood from Dunstan's mouth with her fingers.

'My poor child, you did not deserve that one pain

more. Please forgive my brother. His manners are not refined. Most young men kiss my hand when I leave them.'

She was balancing her hand delicately in front of him. Dunstan was confused, but on an impulse he raised it to his lips. She smiled at him, nodded to the Abbot and turned her horse. As she turned she glanced at Edmund. It was a quick, enigmatic glance, but she was certain that it had the desired effect. He was looking at her with intense dark eyes and she sensed those eyes following her as she rode away. Roger De Tosny may not have been fully satisfied with the outcome of his visit, but as she spurred on her horse to catch up with her brother, Blanche was very satisfied indeed.

CHAPTER FIVE

Edmund had done it. He could hardly believe that it was so, but it was done. The fact slowly sunk in as he rode out of the manor yard. He did not even notice the flaxen-haired dairy maid, lingering in the doorway of the dairy, swinging her milk pails backwards and forwards. He had noticed her right enough when he rode in, for he had winked at her and she was waiting for him to come back that way, but she was disappointed for Edmund had other things on his mind. As he headed for the village, he began to feel proud. It had stung him acutely at first, but not now. Edmund, son of Edgar the thegn had taken a job as supervisor of the castle construction.

After all the business of the funerals was over, he had to decide what to do about their losses. He would not accept De Tosny's money as compensation. Father Robert had advised him not to fight a lawsuit with the Norman concerning investigations into the incident at the shire court, for De Tosny's influence in the shire was considerable and it could make their position worse. Edmund saw the sense in this. However he refused to abandon Hilde and Cutha, to give them up to De Tosny's protection without a fight. This case he did take to the shire court. He argued cogently that as Cutha's closest male relative and a freeman, he had the right to a say in what happened to the boy and he supported Hilde's wish to put him under the protection of her brothers. He offered De Tosny a deal. The family would surrender to the Norman all rights to return to the tenancy, if he relinquished his claim of wardship. Edmund knew that Cutha would not lose out in such a deal, because his maternal uncles were partners in a lucrative wool business and one of them had agreed to bring Cutha up as his son and train him in the business in due course. His future was assured. De Tosny found that Edmund was well regarded in the shire and opinion at the court tended to favour his suggestion. Roger decided that he would make little profit out of the wardship anyway and he could rent the land out to another tenant, without any restrictions, so he accepted the deal. It was a relief to Edmund to know that Cutha's upbringing would be a Saxon one, but he still had the problem of how to rescue his own economic position.

He heard that the lord of the manor was in need of a supervisor for the building site. The Gascon he had appointed had not come up to his standards. He was asking for a man of intelligence, responsible and authoritative. Edmund searched his pride long and hard about how it would look to others, but he decided in favour of it.

He explained to Dunstan that if he was willing to manage the farm on his own, with some support from a cottar for a few months, he might be able to earn enough money from the supervisor's job to put things right. He professed in convincing terms, his willingness to work for De Tosny for a short while. He would not see much of him personally and although he could not forgive and forget he would let things lie.

He was worried about Dunstan, who was so pale and listless in the days after the funeral, when Cenred and Cerdic were laid side by side in that part of the burial ground reserved for the descendants of Eadberht the thegn, who had contributed generously to the building of the church. Even Edmund's success at the shire court did not seem to raise his spirits. He had no appetite and his dejected look haunted Edmund. He realised that his brother was anxious about his determination to avenge his kin. The uncertainty of what Edmund might do was playing on his mind.

When he told him about the supervisor's job and expressed his willingness to accept the situation, Dunstan brightened up rapidly. His appetite returned and with it his energy. But Edmund was not being completely honest; he was lying to his brother, lying to him because he loved him. He had always told Dunstan the truth, because the boy was so open himself and he was sorry that he had to deceive him now. They did need the money that this job would bring, but the main factor that had inspired Edmund to apply for it was his hatred of De Tosny. It would provide him with an opportunity to kill the Norman. His nature was not suited to guile, his temper was too quick, yet the more he thought about it now, the more he liked the idea. It would be revenge indeed if he could lull De Tosny into the belief that he had worn down the Saxon's spirit and then mock him for his misjudgement with his death.

He turned the morning's conversation over in his

mind as he entered the village. He had acquitted himself admirably; controlled but terse, withdrawn but courteous. He had given a fine performance of a man who had swallowed his pride but was suffering from indigestion as a consequence. He was sure that he had given De Tosny no room for suspicion. In fact the Norman's arrogant smile had almost broken his control. He was too new a hand at this game of guile not to feel the tension with his natural temperament. He wanted to place a fist against those strong white teeth, but resisted the urge and now he could feel the pleasure of having fooled him.

Roger had no doubts that he would make a good supervisor. He had been impressed by his showing at the shire court and felt that the Saxon workers would be more inclined to obey him than a Norman overseer.

Oswin called out a greeting to the thegn from the forge and Wilfred the tanner trotted along beside his horse for some way, complaining to him about the price of ewes. An old dame asked him if he wished to buy her flowers. He answered them all, but he hardly knew what he answered, preoccupied as he was with his own thoughts. He did not think to follow his usual custom and look over into the compound around the mill, in case he saw Ilsa there, brushing the dust out of the house, or up to her elbows in flour. This was a rare omission on his part. There was a woman in his thoughts, but it was not Ilsa, it was Blanche.

She had been present during the interview that morning. She said nothing, but intimated much. Curled up in her favourite chair, she had watched his every movement. She was too mature to be coy, but she was not forward. He decided that seduction for her was a fine art. Beneath the air of boredom was a sensuous creature sending him signals that were unmistakable. It might complicate matters, getting involved with Blanche, but he was excited by the prospect.

So Edmund the thegn presided over the building of the castle. By the end of November the outline was clearly definable. The villagers were startled at first to hear that Edmund had taken such a job, as he had never made any secret of his hatred for anything Norman. There was some talking behind his back, allusions to principles bowing to the need for money and the occasional 'Oh he's doing alright for himself he is.' But there was no real resentment. They were far too practical to brand a man for taking a way out of his troubles. Besides, he was not one of them. He was a thegn, free to do what he wished and they had always accepted his authority. Many of them were very sorry that such a noble young man as Master Edmund should be reduced to taking wages from his social inferior, as they considered De Tosny and hoped he would soon mend his fortunes.

Another thing that predisposed them towards him was his attitude as supervisor. He treated them leniently, good-humouredly, quite ready to fool the wages clerk, a neurotic little man from Aquitaine, into paying them a few shillings extra or to turn a blind eye if a tenant failed to make an appearance on the site. The work was done all the same, for they were willing to make an effort for him. He was like an angel compared to the boorish Gascon who had been their first supervisor.

Edmund often came into contact with De Tosny, discussing the progress of the project. Roger considered him an asset and was pleased with the work rate. They had been hunting together in a small party when De Tosny's brother came for a short visit.

When Roger had invited Edmund to join this hunting party he explained that although his brother Ralph was a member of the king's intimate circle of friends, he was avoiding William for a while.

Ralph was a close friend of Roger of Hereford, who the previous year had joined Ralph, Earl of East Anglia and Waltheof, Earl of Northumbria in a rebellion against the king. Earl Waltheof was one of the few men of Saxon ancestry still holding high office.

'My brother knew nothing about the plot of course,' De Tosny had assured Edmund, 'But he considers it wiser to lay low for a month or two. Why the three of them did it is beyond me. They all stood high in the king's favour and had nothing to gain by it. The rebellion was poorly organised – no coordination- soon put down. Ralph managed to escape by fleeing to Brittany. His father was a Breton by birth, so he has estates there. His wife proved to be the better soldier. She held out in his castle at Norwich for some weeks. Now the king is back in England he has generously allowed her to join her husband in exile. Roger of Hereford has been thrown into prison.

He will not see the light of day for many a long year. Waltheof of course was executed, beheaded at Winchester some weeks ago. He could expect no mercy.'

'No indeed, he was an Englishman,' Edmund had replied in a flat voice, refusing to be drawn into an argument if that was De Tosny's intention. He had heard that Waltheof had repented his actions before Archbishop Lanfranc and travelled to Normandy to beg the king's pardon. But on his return he was arrested and condemned to death, the only outcome in law for an Englishman found guilty of treason. He was the last of the earls with a Saxon ancestry.

Ralph De Tosny was a short man with a barrel chest and bull neck. His square face wore a constant expression of pugnacious suspicion. He did not resemble his brother in manner or in looks. He found it hard to understand why Roger should invite the overseer of the castle construction to ride with them particularly as he was a Saxon. He was even more puzzled at the courteous way his brother treated the fellow. He decided to ignore him, act as if he was not there, which suited Edmund fine. He would have struggled to hold a civil conversation with him.

Riding just behind the De Tosny brothers he caught snatches of their conversation and it was clear that Ralph was uneasy about the effect of the recent rebellion on his relationship with the king.

He heard Roger comment with a touch of sarcasm in his voice, 'I am sure William will never forget you were one of the first to rush outside to protect him from that angry mob at the coronation.'

Edmund found it hard to restrain an urge to laugh aloud. He had heard the true version of what had turned a solemn ceremony into an undignified and bloody fracas outside Westminster Abbey. After Hastings William had waited a few weeks to make sure his conquest was fairly secure before he accepted the crown. Once his wife Matilda had joined him he fixed on Christmas Day for the date of his coronation. Archbishop Stigand was out of favour with the Pope, so William judged it politic to ask Eldred Archbishop of York to conduct the ceremony with the help of the Bishop of Coutances.

Although he believed the crown was his by right, he knew that in the eyes of many he was king by conquest only. He did his best to stress the continuity of rule and that he was the legitimate successor to King Edward. It was Harold Godwinson who was the usurper. His grandfather's sister Emma was Edward's mother which meant he was of royal blood, William argued. Besides Edward had named him as his successor and the magnates of England had elected him. Never mind the fact that Edward just before his death, had changed his mind and endorsed Harold and that the magnates of England had little choice but to elect William, Edmund thought.

The coronation was important because the ceremony was an ancient one which underlined the continuity that William wished to stress and legitimized his rule with the sacred rights of the Church, investing him with God's approval. While a strong contingent of soldiers guarded the doors, Westminster Abbey was packed with Normans, most of whom spoke only French. This meant the ceremony had to be conducted in two languages, extending the length of it. When the congregation was asked to acclaim their new King shouts of Yea and Oui blended in a sound so loud and raucous that the soldiers outside, unused to the proceedings of a coronation and edgy because some of the crowd looked sullen, were convinced that a revolt had broken out inside the abbey. Their reaction was to attack the crowd with ferocity and set fire to some buildings nearby. The Normans inside, hearing the commotion and thinking there was a riot taking place, all rushed out to join in the slaughter.

So the new king was crowned and anointed in an empty abbey and while he was promising to rule as a just king in the manner of his predecessors, innocent Londoners were being murdered and robbed by his knights. This was the truth behind what made Ralph De Tosny so proud of himself.

Blanche had confirmed this version of the events to Edmund. She had told him, 'Ralph can barely concentrate for long enough to sit through a Sunday church service. The coronation ceremony must have been a great trial for him. He could not wait to escape outside and lay into innocent bystanders with his sword. Believe me there was no angry mob threatening the king.'

The hunting party rode through the growing settlement of Melksham into the royal forests beyond, which stretched to Chippenham and the banks of the River Marden at Calne. As their horses followed the paths winding between thick hawthorn bushes, beneath a canopy of oak, birch and hazel Edmund felt the power of the forest, how it spoke of the past.

His mind dwelt on stories Edgar, his father had told

him of hunting in these forests with Earl Godwin and his sons Harold and Leofwine in the days of King Edward. Calne had been a special place for the Saxon kings, part of their demesne land. A royal hunting lodge stood in the town where the king stayed when he was hunting. Edgar had known the royal steward Wulfwine, who took care of the building and dined with him on several occasions.

Wulfwine's father Aelfric had attended the meeting of the Witan in Calne when Archbishop Dunstan was miraculously saved from falling through to the ground below, when the floor of the second storey room in which they were meeting collapsed, hurling everyone except the Archbishop down in a heap. Two unfortunates were killed and Aelfric fractured his elbow and wrist. It was talked about as a great wonder at the time. Edmund was dubious regarding the belief that the Archbishop was saved by a miracle. He was inclined to the view that St. Dunstan, canonised only 40 years after his death, was lucky to be standing by a wooden support beam and reacted swiftly enough to grab hold of it.

These memories filled Edmund with a stinging sensation of loss. As he watched De Tosny, immaculate in his tailor-made hunting gear, giving orders to his companions to fan out wider to disturb the deer they were seeking, Edmund thought, 'What does he or his king care about Calne?' The royal lodge had been demolished some years past and no doubt William would soon be distributing the rights of the manor to his knights.

He hated De Tosny so much at that moment he contemplated killing him right then, him and his arrogant, sneering brother. Then he could die himself, fighting valiantly against the Norman's knights.

He was aware that he had let several opportunities to kill him slip by. His hate was still alive, his sense of purpose undiminished, yet he had not done the deed. He questioned his own hesitation. He did not recoil from the act of killing. In Roger's case it would be retribution, justice.

Perhaps it was Blanche. He spent part of most evenings with Blanche, often in a hunting lodge, a mile or so from the manor. There was something about her, a fascination that he had never encountered before. She could be teasing and casual one minute and then seductive, passionate the next, pleasuring him in so many subtle ways.

She was daring in her love making, inventive, sometimes submissive, at others dominant. He enjoyed this constant change of roles, this variety. He convinced himself that he could break off the relationship with ease, but he did not want to make the effort, not yet. He was still hungry for her. Desire for Blanche checked him from taking impulsive action in the forest that day. He was disposed to drift along until she grew tired of him. He would still be ready to fulfil his vow. He risked the danger that he might leave it too long.

He had promised to give Dunstan a hand with the farm in the evenings, but in practice he often came home so late, that most of the work was done. The younger brother was coping with the aid of a few hours' help from a cottar, moonlighting from the castle with Edmund's blessing.

It was not the farm that worried him; it was Ilsa. Edmund had gradually dropped his intimacy with the miller's daughter. He still called to her when he rode through the village, told her his news, gave her an affectionate kiss or two, but he was sorry, he could not see her that evening. He was too busy.

The servants at the manor house loved to blazon abroad the affairs of the manor and it was soon all over the village that Blanche and Master Edmund were more than casually acquainted. He must have been aware that Ilsa knew it. Dunstan could not understand how his brother could behave that way. He found himself wanting to avoid Ilsa because he could sense her hurt and felt ashamed on Edmund's behalf.

It was now four weeks before Christmas. The good weather had lingered through October and the first two weeks of November, but during the previous week the temperatures had dropped and icy rain began to fall. This early morning was dry however, crisp with frost. The gaunt prickles of the hawthorn bushes were tipped with silver. Dunstan looked up at the sky. The sun was just penetrating the pastel grey. There was little warmth in the rays, but they highlighted the intricate, frosty cobwebs spreading across the grass. A thrush, full of bravado, flung its song into the cold air.

Dunstan was fulfilling a promise. At the edge of their copse was a fine holly tree and he had promised Steven the priest that he would bring some to the church for the traditional Christmas foliage decorations. He was carrying branches covered in glistening berries in a basket.

As he trudged on he was grateful for his leather boots and thick worsted cloak. He was beginning to feel apprehensive as he neared the mill for he could see the sturdy frame of Alleyn inside the palisade, but his attention was diverted by the sounds of a scuffle.

A ragged figure dodged between the houses and out into the road. It was Dervorgil. She was pursued by a young man who was shouting imprecations after her and waving his fists. When she saw Dunstan, relief lit her face and she made a dash in his direction, but the man was long-legged and fleet of foot and had caught her before she reached Dunstan. He took hold of her wrist, wrenching back her arm and she yelped with pain and fear.

'Now you little thief, you're not going to nip off so easy,' said Thurstan, eldest son of Eadwig, the village headman. 'Where's that cross you stole?'

'I never stole nothing,' Dervorgil threw back at him, trying to wriggle out of his grasp.
His response was to twist her arm even harder.

'Stop that!' Dunstan called, running over to them. 'You are hurting the child Thurstan.'

Thurstan touched his forelock. 'Begging your pardon sir, but she do deserve it. She's one of them damn dirty slaves. Tis a pity she was never taught to keep her hands off other people's property. Little thief that's what she is.'

'What has she stolen?'

'My mother's cross sir- been in her family for years. Fine gold with a jewel in it and on a gold chain too. Marched in the house and took it as bold as you please.'

'I never Master Dunstan. I never, I never!' she defended, 'I never touched his cross. I only looked inside his doorway. I don't suppose I be good enough to come near his precious threshold let alone go right inside.' She had been acting brave and defiant, but now she changed her tactics. Hoping that a few tears might help her cause with Dunstan, she began to wail loudly.

'Push us slaves about like cattle they do, as if we be an insult to decent folk. How can I tell anybody anything when he's pulling my arm out of its socket?'

The last word was one long drawn out howl. Dunstan demanded that he let her go. He did so reluctantly and she poked her tongue out at him, moving closer to Dunstan.

'Now Dervorgil, did you steal it?'

'No Master,' she sniffed. 'I stepped to his door to look at the little cat that was playing by the table. A pretty little white thing it was'

Dunstan turned to her accuser with a smile.

'I think perhaps you were mistaken. I do not think she has taken anything.'

'Don't let her fool you sir,' Thurstan muttered, thoroughly disgusted with the girl's lies. 'She is only trying it on. Them slaves is all the same. You wicked girl, telling lies to a man who is trying to help you. She took it alright.

I saw her take it off the table with my own eyes. This is the only way to treat them.'

So saying, he took her by the shoulders and began to shake her, lifting her frail body off the ground.

'Don't do that Thurstan. It will not help if you

frighten her.'

Thurstan let go and stepped back, a resentful expression on his face.

'I hope you were not lying to me,' Dunstan said, 'If you have taken the cross you must give it back now. You know as well as I do that it is wrong to steal.'

Dervorgil hung her head. She was an accomplished thief. Sometimes it was the only way she could provide food for her young brothers. But she felt a pang of conscience, lying to Dunstan who had always been so good to her and her family. Slipping her hand down inside her tunic, she pulled out a handsome cross and chain. She held it out to Dunstan, not daring to look at his face.

'Oh Dervorgil!'

She squirmed, hating the note of reproach in his voice. Thurstan let out a whoop of triumph, seizing the cross out of Dunstan's hand and holding it aloft.

'There, I said she had it.'

Dervorgil reverted back to defiance in an effort to justify herself.

'Well, them that has nothing must be given it by them that has. So seeing that nobody around here thinks us slaves worth spitting on, let alone giving us anything, we got to take it.'

Dunstan was shaking his head. 'I am sure your father has a sounder sense of values than that. Thurstan, you have your cross back, can you be satisfied with that? There is no point in getting her into trouble.'

The villein was dubious. He studied the cross, turning it over in the palm of his hand, watching the light reflecting on the amethyst at its centre.

'Please, as a favour to me,' Dunstan asked.

'Very well sir, if you ask it, but tis more than the wench deserves. If I catch her round our house again, I'll have her ears off. If I had my way, all them slaves would be druve out of this village. Nothing but a menace they be.'

He started to walk away after bidding Dunstan good morning, only looking over his shoulder to call out in a disgruntled tone,

'You want a damn good hiding my girl, that's what you want.'

After he had gone there was a momentary silence. Dunstan stood there trying to look severe, but he did not feel it. Dervorgil was so miserable that he felt sorry for her. Suddenly she burst out with more explanations.

'Master Dunstan, I never meant to steal it, honest I never. I have stole before, when we needed food and the boys was going hungry, cos nobody misses a bit of food do they? I did go to the doorway to see his cat, but there was this cross shining up on the table. It was so beautiful and they never should put such temptation in poor folks' way. I had to take it. Don't be angry with me. We haven't got a friend in the world save you, specially now poor Master Cerdic has gone to heaven,' she added, crossing herself.

Every time he heard Cerdic's name, Dunstan felt a stab of loss and hoped that in time it would soften to a gentler regret. He smiled at the girl.

'No, I am not angry with you, although I should be. You must not do it again.'

'No, no Master Dunstan. I won't honest.'

At that precise moment, she meant it. He began to walk towards the church and she hurried along beside him, taking three steps to his one. She was wearing the same short tunic she had worn throughout the summer, although the patches and darns were now working loose. Her bare feet were mauve with cold, her hands too. Dunstan wondered how anyone so inadequately dressed could survive the winter.

'What would you have done with the cross if you had managed to get away with it?' he asked as they turned into the church yard.

The sun was beginning to melt the frost that lay on the graves and thin streams of water like tears were running down the wooden and stone crosses. 'You could not have worn it because someone would have recognised it.'

'I should have put it away in a box, under the straw where I sleep. At nights sometimes, I would have worn it, when there was no one to see. I have always wanted a cross on a chain. I don't covet other things. I know some folk have got to be poor and others rich. But that is one thing I have always craved.'

Her voice was full of longing, her eyes wistful, as she conjured up a picture in her mind of drawing out that box from the straw and fastening the cross around her neck. Dunstan instinctively felt for the cross he wore. His tastes were simple. It was only a plain cross of polished wood on a leather thong. He was tempted to give it to her. His hand went up to untie the leather, but he stopped. Cerdic had given it to him for his fifteenth birthday. He could not part with that. Instead he said, 'If you wish hard enough, you may have one someday, but please do not try to steal one or you may end up on the gallows.'

She knew that he was going into the church and she must run home to keep an eye on her brothers. She resisted the urge to stay.

'I must be going now. The boys will be wondering where I be got to.' And she was gone, scampering through the churchyard to disappear behind the low stone wall at the far end, as Dunstan wandered into the church.

The villagers valued their church, small and plain as it was. They were proud of the pair of stone angels above the porch and the four carved saints on the pillars either side of the nave. It was the only church on the estate and folk from the other villages attended it. Fenestration was limited and the main body of the church alone was well served with light, from the window high above the altar. The walls were dank and there was always a musty smell even in the summer.

On a Sunday when a sweaty, restless congregation were jostling each other on the hard benches and Steven the priest incanted Latin sentences which he had learned by rote, but barely understood, Dunstan would find the atmosphere oppressive rather than spiritually uplifting. He found more inspiration in his own little chapel or in the peace of the monastery.

He stepped into the aisle and glanced around the shadowy church. He could see Steven in a far corner, bent over double, peering underneath the pews. He was uttering rebukes in an irritated voice. The pews, the altar steps and the aisles were strewn with a variety of greenery. Steven and his church warden had already been at work, entwining the pillars with trails of intermingled leaves. A girl moved across from the pillar she was decorating to bend over beside the priest. In doing so she passed into the light and out of it again. For a moment the bright auburn of her hair was caught in the sunlight. Dunstan felt the urge to put down his basket of holly on the nearest pew and leave the church in a hurry. The unexpected sight of Ilsa threw him into confusion. He had put the basket down and turned to go, but turned back again when Steven, straightening up with an exasperated wave of his hands at whatever was causing the aggravation, spotted him.

It was too late to flee now. Dunstan picked up the basket and walked towards the priest. He greeted Steven and Ilsa hoping that he did not look as apprehensive as he felt.

'Master Dunstan, you remembered the holly. How kind of you to bring it yourself. As you see, we are a bit short of holly this year. Ivy in plenty, but holly is scarce.'

Steven the priest was from the same social background as his congregation, a villein, tenuously literate and possessor of all the prejudices, superstitions and frustrations of his class.

His income was negligible and he was forced to rely on the cultivation of his glebe land and a small share in the village arable. The toil of agriculture took up much of his time, but he was aware of his responsibilities as a priest, striving to visit his congregation in all four villages, as often as he could. He always responded when called to administer any rites and lived what he considered a respectable life. He had no scruples about what the bishop thought of his having a wife, for the reverend gentleman had three mistresses to his knowledge and he was far less honest about them than Steven was about his Elizabeth.

He launched into a discussion about the reasons for the dearth of holly and Dunstan was spared the awkwardness of talking to Ilsa. Then Steven broke up the one-sided conversation, darting back to the pew that had so interested him earlier.

'Tis still there look. I think tis stuck. Oh come out you silly creature.'

He knelt down and began to poke about under the pew. Dunstan looked at Ilsa with a puzzled smile. 'What is it?'

'It's a kitten. When Steven tried to catch it, it jammed itself between the pew and the wall and will not come out. We have been trying to coax it out.'

'Mischievous creature,' Steven scolded as he lay on his side groping under the pew. 'I don't want it shut in here. If the villagers catch sight of an animal in here, they will all start bringing their beasts. I have a job now to keep them from bringing their favourite animals on a Sunday. On market day I don't mind, but not on a Sunday. Tis not right. I cannot help but remember that our Lord did drive out them that did buy and sell in the temple.'

Ilsa and Dunstan exchanged smiles. Steven's conscientiousness was endearing.

'I had to drive Wulfhere's pigs out one Michaelmas,'

the priest added as an indignant after-thought. 'Come here you little varmint. Got you!'

He sprang up from the floor holding in triumph, a tiny black kitten with green eyes that was spitting at him with startling ferocity for one so young.

'I know who owns it. I will take it there before it gets loose and jams itself somewhere else.'

He left the church, holding the wriggling kitten out in front of him, wary of the angry claws. Dunstan did not want to be left alone with Ilsa and was ashamed of his cowardice. She returned to decorating the pillar and he decided to help her, handing up the greenery when required.

As she stood on the pew, winding ivy around the stone, he had ample opportunity to study her face as she concentrated on her task.

Her skin was as healthy and bright as ever. She still held her head up in that spirited way. There were no obvious signs of any distress.

When she had completed her task, he helped her down off the pew and they both stood back to view her work.

'That looks very fine,' he complimented. 'Very natural.'

'Thank you. I value your opinion.' She pushed her hair back over her shoulder. 'I have not seen you for some time Dunstan. How are you? You look much better than you did a couple of months ago'

'Well, I have come to terms with what happened now. I have been too busy to dwell on it.'

'Yes, it must be hard doing most of the farm work on your own. But it is a good thing Edmund had the chance of that job. I have not seen him to talk to for a week now. Is everything going well?'

She wanted to ask Dunstan if Edmund spoke about her, hear any hint that he still loved her. She did not want to reproach him; she just wanted to see him, to feel his arms around her again. Dunstan was assuring her that they were very satisfied with everything and the farm was restocked already. He was well aware of what she really wished to say and she sensed his sympathy. It was enough to persuade her to let down her defences and swallow her pride.

'Could you tell him that I am still eager to see him in spite of – Blanche? I mean, he may think that I have no desire to see him anymore. Dunstan, would it be any use to tell him that I love him? I was proud and angry at first. I called her all kinds of unholy names. What was he doing fooling around with this dried up old widow, I stormed. I intended to ignore him, but it is no use. I think about him all the time. He does not love her does he Dunstan? He cannot love a woman like that surely.'

Dunstan searched for the right words. He had to admit that he had wondered if he was in love with Ilsa himself, but now he knew he could not be, not in the way she loved Edmund. If he had been, he would have taken her in his arms, kissed her, assured her of his love and support, instead of standing there shuffling his feet, lost for words.

'Don't worry,' Ilsa assured him, aware of his

embarrassment, 'I will not weep all over you. I have more pride than that.'

'He does not love Blanche. You know as well as I do that Edmund has always been self-indulgent when it comes to the pleasures of women. She is beautiful and she is different. She knows the ways of the wider world and that intrigues him. She has woven a web around him, but it is not one that he cannot break. He knows that he is only a diversion to relieve her boredom. It is not a true relationship, not like the one he has with you.

Do you remember saying to me when he was flirting with Aethelflaed of Monkton that it did not worry you because he always came back to you? Blanche is no different. I think part of his interest in her is linked to how he feels about the Normans. He enjoys impressing her with his Saxon virility.'

'Oh he will have no trouble doing that.'

Ilsa was amused by Dunstan's effort to avoid phrases that were too explicit, the way he drew back from contemplating anything sensual too closely.

'I know he loves you, but he may not be fully aware of it himself. I will talk to him; make him understand how much he means to you. He would not wilfully hurt you.'

'Thank you. I am sorry to burden you with this, but I know you are always ready to listen to the troubles of the world. I need an advocate and Edmund heeds your opinions more than anyone else's. If anyone can make him see it, you can.'

Dunstan nodded. He was determined to make his brother understand. He looked around to see Steven the priest come back into the church, followed by Wilfred the tanner, his chief churchwarden. The kitten had been safely restored to its owner and all was well. After discussing the prospects for the coming Christmas season, Dunstan made his excuses and left Steven and Wilfred to continue their decorating. He walked with Ilsa as far as the mill gate. Neither of them spoke until they were about to part.

'You should take these back,' Ilsa said.

She pushed her cloak aside and took from a pocket inside her dress, just above her breast, two small scrolls. They were tubular no longer, as they had been flattened by lying in that pocket for some time. Dunstan recognised Edmund's poems. When he took them in his hand the parchment was warm from the heat of her body. Her smile was self-conscious.

'You may think me foolish, carrying them around with me like some love-struck twelve year old. But when I read them they give me comfort, convince me that there is a part of Edmund that is out of Blanche's reach.'

Dunstan suggested that she keep them.

'No, I have read them so often, I know them all by heart anyway and I have copied out my two favourite ones. You must keep them.'

All the way home Dunstan was rehearsing in his head what he would say to his brother. He was pleased to think that he had the whole of the afternoon to ponder over it, but when he entered the house, he found to his surprise that Edmund was already home. He was sitting in a chair with his feet on the table, drinking wine from a leather bottle.

He looked pleased with himself and was humming a lively tune. He looked up when Dunstan came in and flashed him a broad smile.

'Hello young un,' he greeted him in an exaggerated Wiltshire burr, 'Where have ee bin then?'

Dunstan winced and did not reply. Edmund pulled a face at his brother's failure to respond to his high spirits and offered him the leather bottle.

'Do you want a drink? You look cold.'

'No, thank you.'

'Go on. It will warm you up.'

Dunstan shook his head. He was about to ask why his brother was home so early, when Edmund said, 'Suit yourself. I will finish it myself then. It is none of our good old Saxon mead. It's best burgundy, straight from De Tosny's cellar. I may have an aversion to Normans, but I have no aversion to emptying their cellarage.'

He was full of good humour and Dunstan began to fear that his resolution to tackle him about Ilsa would fail him. He would despise himself if it did. He hung his cloak on the peg behind the door. Edmund was watching him thoughtfully, then an amused smile spread across his face.

'You know, you are a vision of rustic simplicity in that outfit. Sometimes I wish you would dress a bit more respectably. That old tunic of yours should have been pensioned off long ago. Anyone would think we were penniless to look at you.'

Dunstan looked down at his calf length tunic. It had been a russet colour but was very faded. The edges of the long sleeves were frayed. Sometimes he wore a leather belt around it, but just as often he tied a piece of rope round his waist. It was belted with rope now. He never thought much about clothes.

'Never mind, they only have to look at you to know that we are not penniless. Besides, there is little point in looking fashionable when you are cleaning out pig sties.'

'True, but you have just been down to the village, not cleaning out pig sties. I think you would feel as uncomfortable as a man in hell in a well cut suit of clothes.'

Blanche had asked him that very day why he let his brother go around dressed like a villein. He ran his hand over the hem of his own tunic. It was a pale blue worsted garment, finely tailored. Over it he wore a surcoat of brown leather, lined with rabbit fur. His cloak, hanging over the back of his chair, was a dark wine colour with a silver clasp at the neck. He had always taken pleasure in fine clothes, a trait he had inherited from his father.

The reason he was absent from the castle site became apparent when he asked Dunstan if he could cope, if he went away for a few days. De Tosny's sister wished to visit her brother and his wife, whose estate was just the other side of Malmesbury, to deliver Christmas gifts. She had requested that Edmund escort her and Roger agreed.

'We will be off later this afternoon. It will be good to ride a fair distance again.' He stood up, slapping his scabbard against his boot. 'I have not been to Malmesbury for years. I would like to pay respect to King Athelstan. He is buried in the abbey. Father took me there once when I was about ten.' Dunstan was staring at the ground. He did not look impressed.

'You do not mind do you?' Edmund asked. 'The castle work is slackening off for Christmas. You will be able to hire an extra cottar. I will not be gone long. Four days at the most.'

He patted his brother's shoulder, but Dunstan did not respond. He did not worry about the work. He knew why Blanche had asked for Edmund as an escort.

'What is wrong Dunstan? Why the sour face? You look as if you have been sucking an unripe sloe berry.'

'Is Blanche taking a big retinue with her to Malmesbury?'

Edmund smiled with a wry curve to his mouth.

'Well, there is the coach driver and then there is- me.'

'I thought so. This is just an excuse for you to spend time together undisturbed.'

'My dear boy,' Edmund teased,' I did not realise you knew about such things.'

Dunstan sighed. It was almost as impossible to make his brother see sense when he was in one of these irrepressible moods as when he was angry, but he forced himself to say, 'I met Ilsa down at the church just now. She asked after you.'

'Oh-' Edmund stood up with a casual gesture of his hand. He did not want to talk about Ilsa. He was not as indifferent to his own behaviour towards her as he wanted to be and did not wish to be reminded of it. His gaze fell on the parchment scrolls in his brother's hand. Dunstan had forgotten that he was still clutching Edmund's poems.

'What have you got there? Another indigestible, scholarly treatise to take to bed with you?'

He had taken them out of Dunstan's hand before he had time to pull them back out of his reach. Edmund was astonished when he discovered what was written on the scrolls, in his own bold handwriting.

'Christ Dunstan,' he exclaimed, 'Where did you get hold of these?'

'I rescued these two, when you put them all out to burn. I will never understand why you destroyed them.'

'I burned them because they were a part of my life that did not exist anymore. They came from a time when I saw hope and romance in the world. When my eyes were opened, I saw how irrelevant they were- better consigned to the flames. Why are you carrying them around with you?'

'Ilsa asked if she could read them, so I loaned them to her. She returned them to me this morning when I met her in the church putting up the decorations.' 'And did she laugh at the expression of my youthful innocence?'

'No, why should she laugh? They are good poems, thought-provoking, profound. She was impressed by them. We met by accident, she was not expecting to see me there. She was carrying these with her, tucked into her dress, next to her heart.'

Edmund had thrown himself carelessly back down into his chair, but he sat forward when Dunstan said this, his eyebrows raised quizzically. Now Dunstan had begun, it all tumbled out.

'You are breaking her heart Edmund. She loves you so much and you do not seem to care. She does not deserve to be hurt like this. I cannot believe that this thing with Blanche is serious. I know that you do not mean to give Ilsa up, so why do you not assure her?'

'Slow down, slow down! When did you become such an authority on Ilsa's heart? I doubt if she is pining away over me. I am very fond of Ilsa; we have had good times together, but she has never given me the impression that she regarded our relationship as binding and I certainly did not give that impression to her.'

Dunstan was shaken by his brother's statement. 'Not binding, but you were going to marry her!'

'Marry her!' Edmund repeated, staring at Dunstan in disbelief, 'Did she say that?'

'No, but we all assumed it. I am sure she did too. Alleyn is hoping so. That is why he has not found her a husband yet. I mean, she's twenty. Most girls are married by that age and she would make a good match for anyone.'

'Alleyn Thurkilson is too much of a realist to expect to marry his daughter into the family of a thegn. Father would have disapproved of the idea I can guarantee you that. I can just see the look on his face. He would have forbidden it in no uncertain terms.'

'Not if he got to know Ilsa, saw her worth,' Dunstan protested. He had not imagined for one moment that status played any part in this.

'It's not about her worth. Ilsa is the equal of anybody. Look, you did not know father very well. You cannot expect to understand him as I do' Dunstan flushed with indignation. He was twelve when his father died, not a small child and reminded Edmund of the fact.

'Yes, but you never got close to father because you were frightened of him. Do not try to deny it. You know you were. You thought that because you had no interest in weapons, stories of battle, anything military, that he was ashamed of you. Any approaches you made to him were always filtered through me. He was not ashamed of you- a bit puzzled perhaps- but not ashamed. He was proud of your eagerness for knowledge, your skill with animals, your capacity for hard work without complaint and your sympathy for others. He could seem forbidding at times, but it troubled him that you could not confide in him.'

Dunstan had to admit that it was true. He loved his father, but had never felt at ease in his company. He was a stickler for tradition and Edmund was right to suggest he would have disapproved of his marrying Ilsa. But his father was dead and Edmund was his own man. Why was he talking like this?

He was saying, 'I do not intend to get married again. I see no reason to do so. I have no wish for any children. What future would they have under the Normans? When Cutha is old enough he can take a share in this farm if he wishes. I admit that I should see Ilsa more often, but the castle keeps me occupied – very well- Blanche too. When I have more time, I will spend more of it with Ilsa. I may not be around much longer. Ilsa needs to look to her own future and not think about me.'

In his eagerness to defend Ilsa, Dunstan had missed the significance of that last remark.

'But you cannot cast people off like old clothes and

take them up again when it suits you. You treat Ilsa like a whore.'

Edmund laughed aloud. 'Ha! I would like to see anyone attempt to treat Ilsa like a whore. He would scarce escape with his life. Anyway, what do you know of whores? Have you ever been with a woman Dunstan? No, you haven't have you, nor would you outside marriage, my pious little brother. You would not so offend the teachings of mother church. But have you never felt the desire, that ache that nothing can quench- wait a minute- have you felt it for Ilsa? Is that what all this is about, why you are such a brave champion on her behalf?'

Dunstan knew the cause was lost. Edmund's vitality was too strong for him today, but he made one last effort.

'No. It is not like that at all. Ilsa is my friend and her pain hurts me too. I do not want to see you do something so dishonourable as to abandon her. I want you to do what is right, right for you as well as her and right in the eyes of God.'

Edmund snorted scornfully. 'Well, when I stand before the judgement seat, I shall be called to account for my pride and the sins of the flesh, but I trust I will take my punishment without complaint. I won't be doing much grovelling. As noble as your concern for my honour and my morals may be, I've had enough of it. I did intend to have a meal with you before I left, but now I think I will just pack and go up to the manor house. This odour of sanctity is too much for a sinner like me to bear.'

Half an hour later Edmund was ready to leave. He embraced his brother, but Dunstan felt that the hug lacked

Edmund's usual warmth. There was a stiffness in it. He watched him ride out of the yard on Midnight, his black stallion and turned away with a heavy heart. Edmund too was dissatisfied; the high spirits he had felt earlier that morning had evaporated.

He was irritated with Dunstan for ruining it all by making him think more deeply about Ilsa. Surely she had not expected him to marry her. He did not want to believe it.

He was also annoyed with himself for leaving his brother in such a cool, offhand manner. He almost turned back, but thought of Blanche waiting for him and changed his mind.

Chapter Six

The ox stopped in its tracks, looking back over its shoulder to see why the pressure on the plough had relaxed. Dunstan was leaning over the handles, coughing. He was angry with his cough this morning, for it was interfering with his work and he was far enough behind with that already. He was eager to finish off the winter ploughing before the snows came. In a normal year it would have been finished long ago, but this was not a normal year. There were no relatives on the neighbouring farm to help out, Edmund's contribution had been limited because of his work at the castle and now Jacob the cottar who had been helping, had been poached by Gilbert, De Tosny's reeve, to drive a cartload of goods to Bristol. He would be gone for days.

Dunstan considered looking for someone else as Edmund had suggested, but that would take up valuable time. His brother had been away two days; in another two he would be back. There did not seem much point in searching around for help. He could manage for another two days, but when he had made that decision, he did not know he was going to make the promise he had done earlier that morning. Now he stopped to think about it, he wished he had made an effort to find extra labour.

The ploughing was completed on the arable that

once belonged to his Uncle Cenred. He had taken a look a few days before. De Tosny had not yet put new tenants in the farm house but he sent workers from the manor estate to maintain the fields. The animals had been added to the livestock at the manor and Gilbert the reeve checked the house regularly to make sure it was in good order. Dunstan wished Cerdic was beside him now, sharing the toil and lightening his mood. He missed his cousin's humour and support more than he could ever put into words.

It was bitterly cold, the wind cutting like a two edged sword through everything that tried to resist it. It blew in Dunstan's face as he drove the plough up the twisting furrow, penetrating his cloak and his leather jerkin. He pulled the hood of his cloak up over his head and urged the ox on. The beast stumbled on the hard ground. The frost had compacted the soil so that some of the clods were like stone. Sometimes the curved blades of the plough stuck fast, jolting the ox to a halt and it was as much as Dunstan could do to free it. This was the penalty for leaving the ploughing so late.

He tried not to think of the rashness of his promise. Ilsa came into his mind. He had promised her something too and had not been able to accomplish it. He had gone to church on the Sunday after his confrontation with Edmund knowing that he would meet Ilsa and with no idea how to tell her.

He had prayed all through the service to be shown the right way to do it. When he left the church, Ilsa was standing beside his horse by the gate. Her mother was already hurrying home and Alleyn was in conversation with Peter the swineherd, haggling over a consignment of corn that had gone through the mill. Dunstan went straight to Ilsa, hoping he had been granted the strength to say it in the right way. She was fondling the ear of his bay mare. He did not ride often, preferring to walk, but he always rode to church on a Sunday. It was a family custom.

He was about to speak to her, but she shook her head. The whole village knew that Edmund had gone to Malmesbury with Blanche. The leakage from the servants' quarters at the manor was swift and sure. Ilsa already knew the answer and Dunstan's manner confirmed it.

'There is no need to say anything Dunstan. I know he does not love me. I am sure you tried your best, but no one can dictate to Edmund. Thank you for your concern.'

And that was it. She had gone to join her father before he could reply. It was all over, the thing that had kept him awake for two nights.

He blessed her for making it so easy for him, as he skilfully guided the ox through a turn at the end of the field to begin another S shaped sillion. The wind was at his back now and he was more comfortable.

He wondered if he would be able to cope with what he had undertaken to do for Dervorgil's family. She had come jumping over the furrows towards him early that morning, her face full of worry. She had no one else to turn to she declared and poured out her story. Geraint, her father had been working on the castle carrying a hod of stones up a ladder and his foot had slipped. He fell some distance, injuring his back and bruising himself all over. He would not be fit for work for some days. William the temporary supervisor insisted that another member of the family take his place. Here lay the problem. Hugh, Dervorgil's older brother, had run away with two other young slaves from Bradford. They were heading for Bristol, hoping to find work in a busy town where no questions were asked. They might even be taken on as crew on a merchant ship. Hugh knew that unless he was legally manumitted, he would never have any status and De Tosny could still claim him as his slave, but he gambled that the Norman would not consider him worth bothering about.

'Twould be no trouble if Master Edmund were here,' Dervorgil had said. 'He would turn a blind eye. All the workmen like Master Edmund, but this William from Salisbury is a swine. When he reads the roll and finds there is no worker from our family, he will check at the manor and find that Hugh is not there either. Then they will catch him before he gets to Bristol and De Tosny will throw us all out. He talks quiet, but he's a hard man Master Dunstan.'

This would happen when Edmund was away. It aroused again in Dunstan the disappointment he had experienced when Edmund told him he was going to Malmesbury with Blanche. The journey was not necessary. Edmund was concerned with his own pleasure and in the meanwhile Dervorgil's family might be facing starvation. He knew that none of the villagers would lift a finger to help the slaves. The only solution he could see was for him to work at the castle to represent Geraint's family. William the supervisor did not know him and the villagers would not give him away.

Now as he clicked his tongue to encourage the patient ox and looked at the amount of ploughing he had to get through, he thought he was mad to offer. But Edmund would be back in two days he reminded himself. Then there would be no need to cover for Geraint if he was still unfit to work. Surely he could cope for two days.

Geraint the hurdle maker could not refuse Dunstan's offer of help. He sent his daughter with his thanks and a promise to get back on the site as soon as he was able. Dervorgil would go up to the farm as often as she could be spared, to check on the animals while Dunstan was at the castle.

Work on the site began at six and as he imagined, the local workmen were astonished to see Dunstan. It was a struggle for them to understand why he should do such a thing. They might have done it for kin or a good friend, but for a thegn to worry his head about a family of slaves was something they could not fathom. They did not tell on him though. When the roll call came he was accepted by William as the representative of Geraint, though Peter the swineherd had to smirk at the thought. Dunstan's greatest problem was to stop them calling him sir or master within earshot of the supervisor.

The work was harder than he had imagined. He was not a stranger to toil, but hauling great stones, climbing ladders, digging ditches, rigging up scaffolding and splitting rocks all day at a steady pace was draining. His back, arms and legs were soon aching. William was from Wilton in Southern Wiltshire and was fond of impressing on others that in early times it was the chief town of Wessex, the administrative centre for the royal court. He had come from Salisbury with some hired labourers.

Proud of his temporary promotion he made the most of it. He was everywhere at once, chivvying and swearing, rooting out malingerers.

That afternoon when Dunstan sat down on a pile of stones for a moment or two, to recover from a bout of coughing, William was behind him in an instant, demanding to know why a young fellow of his size should need to take rests at that time of day. Peter the swineherd swore under his breath and nursed his fist belligerently.

The castle was taking shape, a great shell of walls, the outer one eight feet thick, thrusting up into the leaden winter sky. A gang of workers had started on the keep. These were men hired from the towns who had worked on construction jobs before. Dunstan's group divided their time between hauling stones into the keep and digging the ditch that was to serve as a moat. He was thankful when the day was over.

Trudging home with the villagers, he hoped they were right when they assured him he would get used to it.

By the time he had attended to the needs of the animals it was past midnight when he finally fell into bed. Despite his exhaustion, he was so stiff that he found it hard to sleep.

It snowed over night; three inches of snow, turning slushy by mid-morning, lay over everything. It was a nightmare on the site. Every stone was slippery, the ground treacherous, footholds difficult to find. There were numerous accidents, one fatal, but somehow the work went on.

Sigeberht, a caustic, old Cornishman who had worked on buildings most of his life, assured them that these conditions were easy compared with what he had seen. He could remember working on a manor house in Surrey that was being thrown up in a hurry to honour a visit by Edward the Confessor, when there was a mighty hurricane raging. He had seen a man torn off a scaffold by the wind and hurled more than a hundred yards away. His story was little comfort to his companions.

Each day seemed like a week to Dunstan. He understood now why there was such consternation in the village when the news of the castle first reached them. The snow did not stay long. It was washed away by icy rain that fell continuously for the next two days. All the men could talk about was their two days holiday at Christmas. He marvelled at their endurance.

He had expected Edmund back on Thursday, but Saturday found the young thegn desperately weary and still his brother had not returned. His cough was now very bad, his breathing constricted. His chest felt as if it was raw inside. It was difficult hauling stones when his head and limbs felt so heavy and he could hardly breathe.

He encouraged himself with the thought that tomorrow was Sunday. Anyway, Edmund must come home today and then there would be no need for him to go to the castle on Monday, even if Geraint was still unfit.

He was grateful for the meal break at midday. The last thing he wanted was food and he gave his dinner to

Peter, who had become his constant companion on the site. The man wolfed it down. His appetite was a joke amongst the villagers. He was a stringy man, about five feet four inches tall and could not have weighed more than seven stone, but he had the appetite of a horse. He was perched on the edge of a wooden beam, eyeing the hunk of bread and cheese in Sigeberht's hand and chattering to Dunstan, who had stretched out on the floor, his head resting against the beam. He was trying hard to listen to Peter's polemic on the Norman landed gentry, but he could not stay awake.

He had jerked back from the brink of sleep several times, but now his companion's voice was nothing more than a drone. He was vaguely aware of how heavy his eyelids felt and then the voice and everything else faded away altogether. He had been asleep for some time before Peter realised that he was talking to himself. He was still sleeping soundly when the break was over.

Sigeberht who considered himself the unofficial foreman of the gang, let out his belt a notch to make room for his dinner, picked up his spade, then jerked his thumb at Dunstan.

'You better wake up your young friend Peter. If old sour-faced Bill catches him asleep there will be all hell to pay.'

Peter swung himself up onto a section of scaffolding as agilely as a monkey and surveyed the site. William was nowhere to be seen.

'Oh let him sleep a bit. If anybody sees William, they can give a shout and I'll raise him quick. He needs some rest.'

'Don't we all,' commented the Cornishman. He had rolled up his sleeves, oblivious to the cold and was driving his spade into the earth. 'You caint afford to be delicate on this job.'

Peter felt the need to explain.

'He's no villein like us. He's a freeman. Comes from a long family of thegns. His brother, Master Edmund is our regular supervisor. He's gone off to Malmesbury with the Lady Blanche. Giving her an early Christmas present no doubt- showing her what we Saxons can do. He's a great one for the ladies is Master Edmund. Fair supervisor too. He's on our side see. Be damn glad when he gets back. But Master Dunstan has been doing all the work on the farm on his own and working on the castle.'

'Well, that's his hard luck,' Sigeberht grunted, unimpressed. 'That still don't give him the right to sleep while we are working.'

Peter's indignation at this lack of sympathy was cut short by a sharp whistle. Someone farther down the trench had spotted William. He was jumping up and down waving his spade. Peter gave him the thumbs up and hurried off to wake Dunstan. He shook him hard. Dunstan sighed, rolling over on to his side, but he did not open his eyes.

'Come on lad,' Peter urged. 'Sour faced Bill is coming.'

'He's come!' snapped a voice from behind him.

Peter spun around to see the supervisor swinging off his horse with a face like a storm cloud. He was not accustomed to being called sour faced Bill, although had he but known it, it was one of the least offensive names he had collected on the site.

'What do you people think this is then?' he demanded. 'A winter palace? What does he think he's doing?'

'The lad's exhausted,' Peter defended glaring at William.

'Well he's lucky it's Sunday tomorrow. His dear mother can let him stay tucked up in bed, but today he's supposed to be building a castle.'

'He's got a bad cough.'

'Yes and I've got the bone ache, but you don't see me slacking.'

'We don't see you doing anything,' was Sigeberht's inaudible aside.

'There's a sure way of waking him up.' The supervisor was reaching for his saddle. He pulled a short whip from the pommel and with a neat flick, raked it across Dunstan's side. The young Saxon, already disturbed by Peter shaking him, was half awake when he was startled by that sudden stinging sensation. He moved forward into a sitting position, wondering whatever it could be. The first thing he saw was the thick-set supervisor standing over him, curling his whip around his hand.

'Tickle a bit did it? I thought I had better wake you up gentle. Now, if it wouldn't be too much for you, would you mind getting up off your arse and doing some work?'

Dunstan scrambled to his feet, apologising. 'I am sorry. I did not mean to fall asleep.'

'I am so glad.' William returned with a sarcastic

bow. 'It would cut me to the quick, if I thought that you did not care, but just so you will not do it again --'

With another expert flick of the wrist, he brought the lash across Dunstan's face, causing a red wheel to appear on his cheek. Peter the swineherd, who had seen enough of William's bullying in the past week to write a book on it, if he had been able to write, decided that this was the final straw.

He dived at the supervisor's feet, knocking him over backwards and began banging his head against a wooden bucket.

The men in the trench, seeing the prospect of a scrap, threw down their spades and raced over to the spot, shouting encouragement to Peter. Dunstan was calling for him to stop, but he could not make himself heard. Then suddenly the shouting stopped, the men melted away like shadows before the sun and returned to their digging. Dunstan turned around to see what had dispersed them. Standing a few feet away from them, slapping his gloves into the palm of his left hand, was Roger De Tosny. Peter, realising that everything had gone silent, stopped struggling with William and looked up.

'Get up!' the Norman ordered briskly. 'I do not employ a supervisor so that you Saxons can punch holes in him.'

Peter obeyed and raised his knees from William's stomach. The supervisor was then free to stagger to his feet.

'I'll have you sacked,' he threatened.

'No you will not William.'

'But he attacked me my Lord.'

'I am quite aware of that. I have been watching for some time. I do not recall giving you the authority to use a whip on the workmen.'

The man coloured. 'He's only a slave my Lord, from Geraint the hurdle maker's household.' De Tosny glanced sideways at Dunstan, half smiling. 'Gives himself the airs of a freeman. He thinks he can sleep on the job.'

'While I cannot condone sleeping on the site, you had no right to use that whip and I do not want to hear of it again. When Edmund returns, you can take yourself back to Salisbury. I shall not want you on the site any more. Is that clear?'

'Yes my Lord,' murmured William, cowed.

'Good, now get back to your job.'

The unfortunate supervisor could not remount swiftly enough. At his first attempt, his foot slipped out of the stirrup and his face banged into the saddle. His sheepish exit delighted Peter, who was grinning all over his face.

'And you,' De Tosny was pointing at him. The grin disappeared. 'Do not let me catch you manhandling my officers again. Clear off!'

Peter galloped off down the bed of the trench, eager to put some distance between himself and the Norman.

'Well, you must be the cleanest member of Geraint's family by far.'

Roger did not need to ask what Dunstan was doing there. He already knew.

'You know you could be in dire trouble, aiding a

slave to escape,' he said evenly, studying Dunstan. 'Oh yes, I know all about Hugh. There is very little that happens on this estate that I do not know about. I have an efficient intelligence network. We Normans are known for our efficiency. I will not take it out on Geraint as long as my work is done. If the work falls behind schedule- well then I may turn nasty.'

Dunstan had no desire rise to his mockery; in fact he had no wish to speak to him at all. He wiped the blood from his cheek, picked up his spade and began digging.

'Of course,' the Norman added, 'When your brother comes back, I am sure he will sort it out for you. I expected him back several days ago, but no doubt my sister is finding something to occupy his time. If you see him before I do, give him my regards.'

He had begun to stroll away, but stopped with his back to Dunstan, waiting for a reply, when nothing was forthcoming, he flicked a stray speck of dirt from his shoulder with his gloves and disappeared amidst the bustle of the site.

Edmund did not come home that day. Dunstan meant to get up early on Sunday, but the crowing cockerel and the sound of Mankel barking failed to wake him that morning. It was past midday when he finally woke. He was astonished to see the sun so high.

His devotions would have to be done in his own chapel this Sunday. He realised that he was too ill to do any heavy work. He managed to milk the cows and stack some wood in the barn but that was his limit. He sat by the fire and tried to read, but he was too weary to concentrate. When Dervorgil arrived in the early evening he was dozing in the chair. He was pleased to see her, but her news was not as welcome as her person. Her father was still unable to work, but hoped he could be on the site by Wednesday. He was not sure that he could last until Wednesday. He did not argue when Dervorgil offered to attend to the animals and he was sorry to see her leave. In the morning he felt a little better, but he took the precaution of riding to the site. He managed to get through the day and still Edmund had not come.

What was Edmund doing when his brother dragged himself to bed on Monday night? To give him his due, he was on his way home; meandering back from Malmesbury in easy stages, at a pace dictated by Blanche. As he pushed a gold coin into the hand of the ostler of the White Swan inn, he calculated they would be home by Tuesday afternoon. He was amused by the obsequiousness of the man when he saw the colour of the coin in his palm.

Since Edmund had been supervisor of the site, he had been able to indulge his natural generosity more freely. This journey had been a breath of fresh air. In the past few years he had not travelled far from the farm. Since his father's death he had knuckled down to his work, become the most responsible of brothers. It was a relief to throw off the responsibility for a while. He liked this life of a sauntering gentleman, particularly with a companion like Blanche.

They had reached the handsome manor house of Ralph De Tosny, built on an elevated piece of ground halfway between Malmesbury and Tetbury, to find the family not at home. They had gone up to Warwickshire to spend Christmas with Eleanor's parents. Edmund suspected that Blanche hoped this would be the case. She showed little surprise and less regret.

She declared her intention to stay overnight because she wished to visit a silversmith in Tetbury who had been recommended to her.

That night they made good use of the luxurious bed in the guest room and Edmund had no objections when Blanche wished to spend a second night at her brother's mansion.

When they travelled back through Malmesbury, Blanche decided to stay there for two days. On the first morning there, Edmund rose early, leaving Blanche still sleeping and went in search of his father's old friend, Alfred. He did not know if the man was still alive, but his family had lived in Malmesbury for generations and he hoped to hear something of them.

Edmund had last seen Alfred on the eve of the battle of Hastings, striding about the camp, distributing ale to his retinue and casting vulgar aspersions on the ancestry of William of Normandy. He had fought on the far side of the line from Edgar and Edmund and no word of his fate had ever reached him.

The family house looked much as he remembered it ten years before. There was a large courtyard with a central beech tree and he could see several people coming in and out of the yard from the house. When he enquired after Alfred he was referred to the owner of the house, a pompous pot-bellied grocer who was very offhand with his visitor. Alfred had indeed survived Hastings, but reprisals had ruined him and he was forced to sell the family home. As far as the grocer knew, he was still about the town somewhere, but he had little respect for redundant nobility. He had hitched his wagon firmly to the Norman cause.

Edmund did not like his tone, but he let it pass. He made inquiries around the town and eventually tracked Alfred down. He was lodging in the house of a shoemaker, in one dingy room.

If a housewife leaned out of a window from a house on one side of the street, she could touch the wall of the house on the opposite side, the roadway was so narrow.

It was hard to recognise the wan, ageing man, his red hair streaked with grey, who now earned his living teaching the sons of aspiring merchants to read, as Alfred the Wild, the warrior who had always acted as if he had stepped straight out of the Beowulf story.

Edmund took him to the nearest inn and bought him a meal and plenty of ale. Talking about old times revived Alfred's spirit for a while and a sweeping gesture, a grand pronouncement here and there, hinted at what he was formerly. But the spark of life was only brief and his eyes soon took on that expression of dull hopelessness that troubled Edmund. When they parted he clung on to the son of his old friend Edgar, who looked so prosperous and full of the spirit he had lost, in a long embrace. Edmund untied the cloth purse from his belt and pressed it into Alfred's hand.

'I have no wish to insult you, but I can see you are in

need. Take it for my father's sake. You were a trusty friend to him often enough.'

Tears welled up in Alfred's eyes and Edmund walked away briskly to save the man further embarrassment.

He strolled around the town for some time, trying to clear from his mind that look in Alfred's eyes. He found himself in front of Malmesbury Abbey. He stopped to gaze up at the roof and tower. It was an ancient foundation, established hundreds of years before and watched over the town with a quiet dignity.

He wondered what part of the building had served as a platform for the flying monk. He remembered his Uncle Alfstan telling him the story when he was about ten years old. It happened in the last years of the reign of King Ethelred, the ruler they nicknamed evil counsel because of his inability to listen to wise advice. A young monk called Eilmer had been pondering on the mechanics of flight and tying wings to his hands and feet, jumped from the tower of the abbey. He broke both his legs and was lame for the rest of his life, but he defiantly claimed that he would have succeeded if he had added a tail for balance. How long had he remained in the air? What were his thoughts as he plummeted to earth? Edmund had a vivid picture of this man bold enough to test out his theories, flying through the air, the skirts of his monk's habit spreading wide on the breeze. He smiled at the thought of such daring.

The main attraction of the abbey for Edmund however was the fact that King Athelstan was buried there, the king who had valued the thegn's ancestor Eadberht highly enough to grant him part of the royal estate, the land Roger De Tosny so coveted now. He had always admired Athelstan, the courageous warrior who had pushed the boundaries of his kingdom to its farthest point.

He was the first King of Wessex to be acknowledged ruler of the whole of England, when he conquered the Danish dynasty based in York. He also subdued the Scots and Welsh. It was said he had never lost a battle. But like his grandfather, the illustrious King Alfred, he loved and encouraged scholarship and learning. He was a collector of works of art, manuscripts and religious relics. He had a particular fondness for Malmesbury Abbey and stated in his will that he wished to be buried there instead of Winchester with his distinguished forbears.

Edmund thought of Eadberht fighting beside Athelstan at the victorious battle of Brunanburh, driving the invading Scottish king back over the border with his tail between his legs.

His own experience of a great battle was very different. He had tasted victory at Stamford Bridge, but it was small comfort to him after Hastings.

He was so taken up with imagining the old, glorious days that he was startled by a gentle touch on his arm. A lay brother from the abbey was standing next to him.

'You may enter the abbey church my son, if you seek some solitude in which to pray,' he said in an encouraging tone of voice.

Edmund thanked him and the man walked on. He did not do much praying, perhaps he should do more, but he reckoned on balance that Dunstan did enough praying for the both of them.

He told himself that Dunstan would love this place with its ancient traditions. He would be thinking how all those years of prayer and devotion to God had given an atmosphere of peace and spirituality to the abbey and here was Edmund inspired to dwell on the battle of Brunanburh. He shook his head and said aloud with wry amusement,

'Oh Dunstan, your brother is a lost soul indeed,' because he had decided against going into the abbey and would soon be in the arms of Blanche.

The lamentable state of his father's friend Alfred stayed with him for the rest of the day and his meditations on the past had stirred up his hatred of the Norman yoke. He was restless and irritable that evening and at first he was aloof with Blanche, keenly aware that she was Norman and his mission in life was to kill her brother on behalf of all those dispossessed Saxons like Alfred and to avenge his kin.

He would have killed De Tosny that very night had Roger been there, but Blanche gradually coaxed him out of his mood, stimulating his desire in a dozen subtle ways. By the morning he was again willing to drift on until this relationship dissolved.

They had lunched with Blanche's friends and visited a nearby shrine. Blanche declared that there was nothing that fascinated her more than to see rows of pilgrims queuing to kiss the tombs of saints, hoping to be cured of blisters, which would never have plagued them if they had stayed at home. She enjoyed shocking others with her irreverence.

Now they were almost home. Edmund, as he lay on the hard bed in what the landlord had called the best room in his establishment, brushing his lips desultorily over Blanche's smooth breast, was discontented at the thought of returning to routine. He did not mind farming; a picture of his own land, of his untidy, flaxen-haired brother ploughing, was welcome to him. But the mundane activity of shepherding the villagers on the building site was not. He had worked for De Tosny long enough and must bring this game to a conclusion.

He ran his hand over Blanche's thigh, the olive skin shining darkly in the light of the candles. She was listening to the raindrops beating a delicate rhythm on the eaves. Edmund murmured, 'It would be good to have another fall of snow so deep we could not travel on for another day or two.' He stopped to listen to the rain with her. 'Or it might even flood.'

She smiled, rubbing her head against his chest with feline grace.

'Do you not wish to get back to your respected job and all that admiration your peasants give to their thegn? Surely you cannot be content to wander about the countryside from one bed to another.'

'As long as you were in them.'

'Liar! As long as some girl was in them.'

He laughed, making a pretence of biting her ear, but she twisted her head away from him.

'Are you not worried about your little brother? You protect him so fiercely. I am sure he followed you around all the time when he was a child, wanting to be like brave brother Edmund.'

'Oh yes, he followed me around, but I doubt if he ever wanted to be like me. You remind me of how the time passes. I was thirty last month. I shall be feeling old soon enough.'

'You will never feel old Edmund.'

'Do you mean that I will not live long enough?'

'Interpret it how you wish. Do you know how old I am? Take a guess.'

Edmund grimaced. 'I prefer not to commit myself in case I walk into one of those traps you women set. Does she want me to tell the truth? Will she be offended if I hit the mark? If I gauge her to be younger than she is will she accuse me of flattery? Oh no, I'm not falling for that one. You have been married twice, so you must have some years behind you, but you are the timeless Blanche. It does not matter one jot how old you are. You will always beguile and conquer.'

'A perfect answer.'

She leaned across and kissed him. Again the pattering of the rain infiltrated into the room. In the dim light the shadows of the furniture built strange cities on the walls. Blanche's voice seemed suspended on the raindrops.

'What does Dunstan think of this trip?'

Edmund was very sure of Dunstan's opinion of it, but he chose not to share it with Blanche.

'He knows what it is all about. He was twenty two in August.'

'Yes, but he is such an innocent; a rare commodity.

He is much safer in this world than you are.'

'A paradox my lady.'

'A paradox indeed, but I think you understand me.'

'I would never attempt to enter the subtle labyrinth of your mind Blanche. I would be lost for ever. I am only a simple Saxon remember.'

Laughing, she wound her long hair around his neck like a noose.

'You are wise. It would be a mistake to think that you know me.'

She increased the pressure on his neck, knotting the hair as if she was about to garrotte him and he ran his hand over the rope of black silk.

'Many a thief would savour hanging if your hair was the last thing that touched his throat. I believe I would rather be strangled with it than never to have touched it.'

'How courtly, positively central France! You never learned that from the Normans.'

Then she dropped her voice to a low, purring register, tugging at the noose of hair again and putting her face close to his.

'Shall I strangle you Edmund? Because after tonight, you will never touch my hair again.' He gave her a keen look, but did not reply. 'When we get back to the manor, you will be simply Roger De Tosny's supervisor, just another Saxon; a handsome, spirited one, always worth looking at, but not in my social orbit. Are you prepared for that?'

She had moved away from him and was sitting with the bed cover pulled up around her, studying his reaction.

'Just like that Blanche? Is your body so obedient to your whimsy? Not even the slightest doubt?'

She shook her head.

'Then it is all so easy.'

'Quite, quite easy.'

Blanche was not so confident that it would be easy. She was accustomed to dropping lovers when the moment suited her and had never intended this affair to go on beyond the winter months. She had wanted something to relieve her boredom until the spring social season began. Now she was terminating it before she had planned and not through whimsy. At the age of thirty six, after two husbands and several lovers, she had at last found what she had been seeking, the deepest sexual satisfaction she had ever known. It was such an irony – a Saxon thegn. She could not let him become essential to her. The situation would be impossible. There had been times when they were together when she surrendered all her control to him with a willingness that surprised her. This had never happened to her before. It was too dangerous. She must always be the one in control. She must put a stop to it now.

She unwound her hair from his neck and lay there, curling his chest hair around her finger and stroking his diaphragm. He was asking himself why he was antagonised by something that he had known was inevitable. He had never been brushed off with such economy of emotion before. Could she really dispense with him so easily, with no regrets at all? He decided that she could and it galled him.

His pride was hurt but he was determined not to show it. It would not hurt long. Soon everything would be eclipsed in the accomplishment of his vow.

'There are certain things you will miss,' he told her, rolling over on top of her and holding her fiercely tight, 'And I have a few hours left to remind you.'

'Yes Edmund,' she thought, 'I will miss this more than you will ever know.'

She let herself relax in his arms, ready to deny all regrets but he smothered her answer with his kisses. He could do what he wished with her that night; her resolution was not due to begin until the morning.

CHAPTER SEVEN

Edmund left his fair travelling companion at the front door of the manor house and rode straight back to the farm. On the journey back from the Swan Inn, he had made good use of the knowledge that his relationship with Blanche was finished. He had smothered any nagging discontent and stirred up the flames of hatred. The hour of his revenge was close at hand. He would send De Tosny to eternal damnation for what he and his race had done to England. He would not allow himself to dwell on the consequences. There would be no more waiting for opportunities. He would create one.

When he reached home, he was greeted by Mankel, who had taken to following Edmund everywhere and had missed him. The thegn made a fuss of the dog, patting his head and rubbing his back with affection. He was surprised to find that Dunstan was not at home and looked for him around the yard to no avail.

When Dunstan came back from the castle site, wet and shivering, he found his brother sitting at the table, cleaning his sword. He was so relieved to see him. He tried to speak but his throat constricted and he was seized by a violent bout of coughing. Edmund looked around to see Dunstan leaning against the wall for support, desperate to control his cough. He dropped his sword and strode over to him.

'Dunstan, what has happened to you? Where have you been? You are soaking wet.'

Dunstan was swaying unsteadily and Edmund put an arm around his shoulders to support him. The younger brother had meant to say nothing about working on the site, but he felt too weak to lie.

'I was working up at the castle.'

'Why in Christ's name were you doing that?'

'Don't be angry Edmund. Geraint was injured badly and could not work and Hugh had run away. I filled in so no one would get into trouble.'

Edmund was bewildered. 'Who in the devil are Hugh and Geraint?'

'Geraint the hurdle maker. He makes all our fencing.'

'The Briton, the slave? You have been filling in at the castle for a slave and doing all the farm work as well. I told you to hire extra cottars.'

'I know but I did not think you would be away as long as this and I thought I could manage. Oh Edmund, I am so pleased that you are back. You were gone so long.'

Edmund embraced his brother and held him tightly.

'I am truly sorry. I did not intend to be that long, selfish fuck-wit that I am!'

It was then that he noticed the lash mark across Dunstan's cheek.

'This welt across your face, is this a present from the castle? Oh, I know who did that. You do not need to tell me- William of bloody Salisbury. He will regret that.'

Dunstan was wracked by another bout of coughing. 'We must get these wet clothes off you.'

Edmund supported him towards the fire basket and cursed because the fire was not lit. He stripped off Dunstan's clothes and rubbed him vigorously with a blanket muttering, 'Why must you give solace to every waif and stray in creation? I know the prestige of having a saint in the family is great, but I would rather have a less noble brother who was still living.'

He wrapped his brother in two dry blankets, sitting him down by the fire and set about lighting it, venting his frustration with a string of oaths because the wood took so long to catch up and burn.

Dunstan submitted to his ministrations without protest, grateful for Edmund's decisive energy. It reminded him of his childhood. He had never known his mother and Edmund, almost eight years his senior, often found himself fulfilling that role, insisting that he take a bath, scrubbing his neck, rubbing his hair dry, tending to any cuts and bruises sustained in the rough and tumble of growing up.

Any disapproval concerning Edmund's behaviour that had been building up inside him, criticism that he could not always banish from his mind about his treatment of Ilsa and his absence from the farm, all melted away then. Love and warmth for his elder brother suffused all over him with the comforting feel of the blankets. He smiled as he heard him rooting around in Dunstan's room in an effort to find him some dry clothes, still swearing. The profanity of Edmund's language often troubled Dunstan, but not today. He knew it was his brother's way of releasing his anger at himself for allowing this to happen.

He was soon wearing fresh clothes, but still swathed in blankets, drowsing before the fire. Edmund had made him a bowl of vegetable broth, but he had little appetite. His cough made swallowing difficult. Half asleep, he saw that Edmund was putting on his cloak.

'Where are you going?'

'You need something to blunt that cough. I am going over to the mill to ask Freya to make up one of her potions.'

'Do not go. Do not leave me.'

He knew it was foolish, but he feared to be parted from his brother now that they were so close, as if something might happen to force them apart again.

The appeal brought a lump to Edmund's throat and his voice was husky as he replied, 'There is no need to worry. I shall not be gone long. I will not abandon you again. You sleep; you need some sleep.'

He stroked Dunstan's damp hair before he ran from the house. As he urged his horse on at break-neck speed, he was aware of nothing around him. Two villagers returning from driving their pigs to the pannage, greeted him respectfully, but he did not see them. His head was crowded with confusing thoughts. When he had returned earlier that day he was so clear where his duty lay and determined to force the issue. Now he began for the first time to consider the consequences. If he failed, he would die. If he succeeded and escaped, he would be outlawed and unless he could disappear into the forests and mountains of Wales or get over the border into Scotland, he would be hunted down for certain and hung. Whatever happened, Dunstan would be left alone and he had present evidence of the dangers of that. The farm would be confiscated too. He had sworn an oath to avenge his kin. It was his sacred duty to fulfil that oath. But when his mother lay dying, he had held her hand and promised that he would always take care of his new-born baby brother. He was not quite eight years old; the baby was not even named, but it was a promise he had kept. He did not see how he could do his duty as a thegn without hurting Dunstan.

When he walked into the mill without knocking, Alleyn and his wife were seated at a table eating a meal of rabbit stew. Taking wild rabbits from the estate was considered poaching, but the miller bred his own rabbits at the back of the mill. Alleyn jumped to his feet, surprised by Edmund's unceremonious entry.

'Master Edmund, is anything wrong?'

The thegn's cloak was streaked with dust and he looked agitated.

'I apologise for bursting in on your meal like this, but Dunstan is unwell. He has an evil cough and I fear he may have caught a chill. I have seen too many people die of a chill. I have come to ask Freya for a potion to relieve the cough and reduce fever.'

Freya looked at her husband. Alleyn was so solid, standing there encased in his buckram apron, barley husks entangled in his beard. His arms were folded and he was frowning. A few months back, he had allowed himself to believe that his daughter was good enough for a thegn. He entertained the hope that Edmund would marry her. The cooling of the relationship on Edmund's part was a slight to him as well as Ilsa. Freya knew how he felt. She was waiting for his permission before acceding to the visitor's request.

He gave her a terse nod and she hurried out into the awning that served as their kitchen, where all her herbs were stored.

'Too much hard work,' Alleyn said, staring keenly at Edmund, 'He had more need of you than milady Blanche. She must have a bewitching power when you choose her not only over my daughter, but your own brother as well. Why did you not go to her for aid? Has she tired of you?'

For a moment Edmund was offended that the miller dare speak to him in that tone. He almost rebuked him, but held back. It was true after all. He had chosen the pleasures of Blanche and left his brother to cope alone. He had no defence. He did not try to justify himself or stress the foolishness of Dunstan's decision to work on the castle. He said quietly.

'I deserved that, but it would be best for both of us if you did not touch on the subject again.'

Alleyn was about to reply, when the door that led into the mill proper opened and Ilsa stood there. She was wearing a plain green gown, simply cut without adornment, but it emphasised the contours of her figure and the colour set off her auburn hair to perfection. She caught her breath when she saw Edmund. It was as if her heart had moved its position and could not find its way back to its original place. All the previous week she had been regretting her appeal to Dunstan to be her intermediary, embarrassed by her lack of pride.

The whole village knew that Edmund had gone to Malmesbury with that haughty Norman bitch and nobody imagined that it was to honour any saints. She stared down the women gossiping in the road, dropping their voices at her approach. When she thought of him in that woman's bed, she was angry, could feed her pride, tell herself that the next time she saw him she would make a barbed remark to demonstrate clearly just how little she cared about his indifference. Now he was standing in front of her, she could only think how much she loved him. If he had seemed arrogant; if he had expected to resume their old relationship as if nothing had happened; if he had smiled at her in his old confident way, then she would have been angry still. But the expression in his eyes as he gazed at her was unsure, vulnerable.

Her father was uneasy. He stepped between them, explaining briefly why Edmund had come and told her to help her mother prepare the medicines. She hurried into the kitchen. Edmund watched her go. She felt his eyes follow her out into the awning; could still see those intense, dark eyes although her back was turned to him. Even in his agitation, Edmund was struck by how fresh and vital she looked in that simple dress.

'She has grieved over you,' Alleyn growled, 'If that means anything to you at all.'

Edmund did not reply. He did not want it to mean anything. He had enough to worry about; but he was wondering now about the depth of her attachment to him, heard in his head Dunstan saying, 'You cannot cast people off like clothes.' Alleyn's surly attitude irked him and he was relieved when Freya and her daughter came back into the room carrying two clay jars full of strange smelling liquid. One potion was a mysterious green, the other pink. Freya explained which was for the cough and which to prohibit fever and how often they should be administered. He listened, but all the while he could not take his eyes off Ilsa and saw that she looked at him in the same way.

His hand went to his waist where he often wore a coin bag at his belt and realised that he did not have it with him. He spread his hands helplessly.

'I fear I cannot pay you at present. But I shall tomorrow.'

Freya was aware that Alleyn was about to bluster. She was all too familiar with that aggressive set of his jaw. Before he could say anything, she pressed the jars into Edmund's hands and said with sincerity,

'We do not ask any payment. We are only too pleased to help Master Dunstan regain his health. We value the friendship of your family.'

He was grateful for her kindness. As he turned to go, Ilsa put her hand on his arm.

'I will go with you. The stoppers on these jars are loose. They need to be held upright. It will be hard to do that and control a horse, even for the best horseman in Wiltshire.'

There was a touch of archness in that last phrase. He almost smiled.

She added, 'Besides, a woman's care may be useful

to Dunstan.'

'I would welcome your help Ilsa.'

It seemed an age since she had heard him speak her name. Her father had moved across the doorway and adopted a truculent pose. She feared that he would refuse to let her go. Edmund looked him straight in the eye.

'I appreciate your daughter's generosity and understand full well that it is not easy for her. Now stand aside Alleyn. I can waste no more time.'

There was authority in his voice and reluctantly the miller stepped aside to let them pass. His wife moved next to him and patted his arm.

'Tis a pity he saw fit to waste so much time this past week,' Alleyn muttered through his beard. 'The girl still loves him; that's plain to see. She will be humiliated all over again. I must make a greater effort to find her a husband. Perhaps if I sent her to Bristol.'

Freya shook her head. 'There is no hurry husband. Don't give up on Master Edmund yet. You underestimate Ilsa. No one else will do for her and did you not see the way he looked at her?'

'Aye, lust is one thing -'

His wife tutted. 'Twas more than lust. There was something in that young man's face tonight that gives me hope.'

Alleyn snorted and made a comment about the failure of women to be realistic as he returned to his meal.

Ilsa was back in her familiar place, sitting behind Edmund in the saddle, her arms around his waist. The two jars were squashed tightly between her body and his back.

She could feel the liquid sloshing around in the containers as they rode. He was silent, lost in his own thoughts. She knew that she must not assume that because she was with him now, everything would return to the way it was before Blanche, before he took that job as building overseer at the castle. His action had surprised her and she had tried to coax him into talking about it, but he would only say that it was the easiest way to restock the farm. Then he stopped calling for her. She could not count the number of times when she heard the sound of a horse in the yard, that she expected to hear her father's familiar call of 'Master Edmund's here for you' and swallowed down her disappointment when it was not so. Recalling this now, prompted her to throw her dart.

'Did you enjoy your jaunt to Malmesbury? It took a very long time for such a short distance. Did she pleasure you all the way there in her carriage? Does she have the power of witchcraft to enthral you so? She must have some secret knowledge of lovemaking of which I know nothing, to excite you and make you follow behind her like an obedient dog.'

The moment that it came out of her mouth, she regretted it. The words sounded far more bitter than she had intended.

'I wondered when you would shoot your dart Ilsa. Well, your arrow has found its mark. You can fill my back with arrows, but I will not talk to you about Blanche. There is no point.'

She had no desire to let loose any more arrows nor for any conversation concerning Blanche. The rest of the journey was completed in silence.

The weather was gentler than it had been the past week. The light was clear and soft. There was freshness in the late afternoon air that betokened a frost. Dunstan was sleeping fitfully in the chair when they reached the farm. It was a shame to wake him, but Freya had given instructions to dose him with both medicines as soon as possible. Still half asleep, he coughed and spluttered as Edmund spooned it into his mouth, ordering him to swallow it.

The taste was strong, but not unpleasant and after the coughing had died down, he began to feel a warm sensation in his throat and chest. Before long, he fell into a deep, comfortable sleep. Edmund dragged the bed from Dunstan's room. It was a simple construction of wooden slats, nailed across a box-like frame, softened by a mattress of straw and goose feathers. He arranged it in a position near enough the fire to feel the advantage, but not near enough for sparks or falling ashes to reach it. Ilsa admired the ease with which he lifted his brother out of the chair and onto the bed, as if he had been no great weight at all, instead of a large boned man, bigger than the lifter. Then she was touched by the tender way he covered Dunstan with blankets and smoothed his hair back from his forehead as he tested for the signs of fever.

It was not until all this was done that Edmund could find the time to explain to her why Dunstan was in such a state, or at least as much of it as he had managed to gather. He knew Geraint the hurdle maker and his family existed, although he had never paid much attention to their names.

He was the one who paid out for the fencing they made, but it was always Dunstan and Cerdic who had collected the hurdles and handed over the money. Edmund had no idea that his brother had formed a friendship with the family, a bond strong enough for him to cover up a slave absconding from the estate. He did not wonder at it. On reflection, it was just what he would expect Dunstan to do. He ran his hand through his hair. It was a weary gesture.

'You need some sleep yourself,' Ilsa said. 'You look worn out with anxiety. I will stay the night if you wish it.'

He shook his head. 'No, I do not think your father would be too pleased. He is angry enough with me already. Angry enough to insult me to my face and I will not take that from him again. I best take you home.'

'If it worries you to leave Dunstan, I can walk home.'

'Take one of the horses. I know you ride well- best horsewoman in Wiltshire.'

She smiled at his reversal of her earlier comment.

'Not my stallion though. Midnight is high tempered and headstrong, does not care to be ridden by anyone but me. You can take Dunstan's mare. She is gentler, kinder. Like master, like horse,' he added with a wry smile.

The bay mare looked up in expectation as the barn door swung open.

Edmund stroked her ears and the arch of her neck before turning to Ilsa and saying, 'Ilsa, I must tell you something. When I took that job at the castle, I had a plan in my mind, a purpose far higher than the earning of wages.

Blanche was not part of that plan. She just happened. She diverted me from my purpose, winding me up in her web. I admit I did not put up any resistance. Her web was a wondrous place to be for a while. But that is finished now. No more Blanche. No more diversions. My purpose is still firm and I will bring my plan to fruition very soon.'

She felt a thrill of exultation to hear him say no more Blanche in that way. She was sure that he meant it, but the exultation was mixed with fear.

'What are you talking about? What are you going to do Edmund?'

'I cannot share the details with anyone. The burden is mine alone, so do not ask me again. But should my plan succeed or fail, Dunstan will have sore need of good friends. I have no fears for his spiritual welfare. His faith is unshakeable and he has Father Robert for support. It is his bodily well-being that worries me. Promise me that you and your family will always look after him.'

He knew he need not ask; could take it for granted. She nodded. He was not expecting what she said next.

'I love you Edmund son of Edgar. I have loved you since I was six years old. I will always love you. And if my father manages to marry me off to some pot-bellied merchant, I will take no pleasure in his bed. You have my heart for ever.'

She was aware that her eyes were filling with tears and tried to hold them back, but they clung to her lashes and trickled down her cheeks.

'Do not weep for me Ilsa. Save your tears for a more

worthy cause.'

He took her hair plait in his hands and raised the auburn braid to his lips. Then suddenly she was in his arms and he was kissing her eyelids, her throat, her breast and she responded eagerly. They fell into the hay and soon he was deep inside her and for a short, sweet while everything else was forgotten.

❈

Dunstan was astonished by Edmund's energy and application over the next two weeks. During the first few days he would not let Dunstan move away from the fire, let alone step out of the house, except to use the privy. He had managed to hire another cottar, who was only too pleased to be released from duties at the castle.

Edmund would rise before dawn, attend to the animals, prepare Dunstan's breakfast, make sure his brother took Freya's medicine and when the cottar arrived, would ride off to the castle to supervise the construction. Back by early evening, he would prepare another meal, finish off any work that needed doing and still have the energy to read to Dunstan before they went to bed. He was on fire with purpose.

The rest and Freya's concoctions worked well. By the second week Dunstan's cough was less frequent and the soreness had gone from his chest and throat. The third week saw him ready to start work again. His recovery was aided by the knowledge that Edmund no longer spent time with Blanche. He did not speak to Dunstan about it, but it was clearly so. Ilsa came to the farm several times a week to help out where she could, but also just to be with Edmund. Dunstan sensed there was something different about their relationship now. It was calmer, more tender, but it was more than that. He could not quite figure out what it meant. Sometimes he would catch them looking at each other in a wistful way that he could not interpret, but what really mattered to him was the simple fact that they were together and he was happy.

Edmund had the burden of knowing that his brother's happiness would soon be shattered. The date for his attempt on Roger De Tosny's life was now fixed. The Norman had sent out invitations to a New Year gathering at the manor. All the important people of the shire were expected to come.

He was eager to show off the progress that had been made on his castle and he told Edmund that he needed to be present to answer any questions about work schedules that might arise. This would be the perfect opportunity. Roger would spend the evening flaunting his wealth and his influence. When all the guests had gone, Edmund would find a reason to stay on and show him just how much his influence counted with a sword at his throat.

His only worry was that Dunstan might not be well enough by the beginning of January and he would see the opportunity slip by. But his brother's recovery was rapid enough for Edmund to believe that with the support of Ilsa's family and of Father Robert, Dunstan would be able to bear the consequences of his action.

On Christmas Eve, Edmund had distributed alms to the poorest members of the village community, a duty that his family, as the local thegns, had carried out for generations. Steven the priest lined them up in the churchyard to receive the charity. Part of the tithe was set aside to support the poor, but it was customary for the thegn to add money of his own.

Edmund was thankful that he now had resources enough to be generous and the recipients went away well pleased with their Christmas gift.

He and Dunstan attended the Christmas services together, sitting in a packed church, brightened with foliage and holly berries. De Tosny and his sister did not patronize the church on the estate. They travelled a few miles to a small market town nearby. The church there was grander. The Bishop of Bath sometimes preached there and it was a fashionable place to be seen.

The villagers groused about their church not being good enough for the likes of De Tosny, but in their hearts they were relieved not to be under the eye of their earthly lord as well as their heavenly one when they were at worship.

A wooden crib was placed before the altar to symbolise the nativity. Edmund, as he joined in the responses and tried to concentrate on Steven's sing-song recitation of the service, could not help feeling hypocritical. Dunstan loved the message of Christmas- 'God so loved the world that he sent his only begotten son ----' The key words of this season were peace and love, whereas Edmund's heart was longing for revenge. The incarnation was a profound mystery. He tried to link what he intended to do with the notion of sacrifice. God sacrificed his son to save the world. He would sacrifice himself for his Saxon heritage. But he could not make it fit. He would save nothing but his own honour and his sacrifice involved killing someone else.

Dunstan left the church that day radiant and refreshed; Edmund perplexed and uneasy, eager for the appointed day to arrive so that it would be too late for anxiety.

It arrived soon enough, a crisp January day blest with pale sunlight. Edmund decided that it would be fitting to use his grandfather's sword to fulfil his vow. It was a family treasure, kept in a box lined with velvet in Edmund's room. Dunstan went into the village that morning on an errand about which he was coy divulging details and Edmund took the opportunity to burnish the sword. It was a superb piece of craftsmanship. The blade measured thirty inches long and three inches broad, double edged, with a groove down the centre to channel away blood. Curling designs were incised on either side of the groove. The triangular iron pommel and cross guard were decorated with silver and the horn grip wrapped in soft leather. The weight and balance of it in his hand was perfect.

This sword had not been used for more than fifty years and Edmund was sure Dunstan would ask questions if he wore it to De Tosny's New Year gathering. So when he had burnished it until it gleamed and tested the sharpness of the edges, he wrapped it in a blanket and stowed it behind his saddle in the stable.

Most men of standing carried swords for self-protection and many Normans, even after ten years in this country were wary of ambush. All De Tosny's male guests would arrive with weapons, which they would lay aside during the social activities and take up again when they left. Dunstan would not question his brother wearing a sword, but he would this particular one.

Dunstan returned from the village mid- morning.

He had ridden there and back; Edmund insisting that he conserve his energy, despite his protests that he was well now. They worked side by side doing the routine tasks on the farm and then shared a simple meal. Edmund was eager to spend what time he could with his brother that day because he might never see him again. It was a thought hard to bear, even for a man so determined on his mission.

The darkness came down early in January. By five o'clock Dunstan had lit the torches around the yard. Every time he did so, he thought of that terrible night of the raid and tried not to picture Cerdic curled up on the ground. When he came into the house, Edmund was standing in front of the fire, warming his back.

'Is it not time that you got dressed up for your visit?' Dunstan asked.

His brother nodded. 'But first, those poems of mine that you loaned to Ilsa, do you still have them squirrelled away somewhere?'

'Of course.'

'Can I read them? Just to refresh my memory of how

bad they were.'

Dunstan was surprised at this request, but happy to comply. Edmund read through the six poems, his lips pursed.

'Well, perhaps they are not as bad as I thought.'

'They are fine poems. I wish I had saved them all.'

'No, I am not sorry that I burned the others, but on the other hand, I am pleased that you kept these- not for their quality, but because they will always remind you that your brother had some interesting ideas in his head once.'

Dunstan laughed. 'You still do. I do not need the poems to remind me of that. I have you, always full of good ideas.'

Edmund handed the scrolls back and went into his room to change. He emerged ten minutes later wearing his finest clothes.

Dunstan stood back to admire him. 'You will cut a splendid dash tonight.'

'Well, I cannot let all De Tosny's Norman friends think that we Saxons do not know how to dress. And I promise I will hold my temper, be courteous and know my place, so there is no need to worry.'

That was the truth at least. It was essential to his plan that he seem respectful to the guests. 'Do you like my extra little detail?'

He held up his hand to reveal that he was wearing on his wrist another family treasure, a leather armband studded with gold rivets. Dunstan approved. He had no interest in fine clothes himself, but he always enjoyed the sight of his brother when he was well-dressed. He had never felt a shred of jealousy about his brother's looks. He was pleased that Edmund was handsome.

'What are you going to do this evening?' Edmund asked, as he put on his cloak and pinned it with a silver pin.

Dunstan pointed to the manuscript spread out on the table.

'I shall be working through this, the history of St. Peter's monastery since its foundation. Father Robert gave me permission to bring it away from the library, which is a great honour. What time do you think you will be home?'

'I have no idea. Depends if De Tosny wants me to stay on and discuss any work plans after the guests have left. I may be very late, so you go to bed when you feel like it. I better be off.'

Dunstan was already engrossed in the manuscript, but he said, 'Do not drink too much of that Norman wine. I do not want you falling off Midnight on the way home.'

'Oh, there's not much chance of that.'
Edmund lingered in the doorway. He wanted to embrace his brother, tell him how much he loved him, how he regretted having to betray him like this, but that was impossible. It was a fitting image to keep in his mind, Dunstan, his face bright with interest as he studied the manuscript; his little brother, always so eager for knowledge.

He walked across the yard with determined stride. Uncovering his grandfather's sword, he slid it into the scabbard at his belt. He had just saddled Midnight when Mankel began to bark. Looking out into the shadowy yard, Edmund saw a small figure walking towards the house. It was someone Mankel knew, for he had stopped barking. A closer view revealed to him a skinny girl, inadequately dressed for such a cold night in a tatty tunic and a cloth jacket in no better state. She jumped back, startled when Edmund came out of the stable.

'And who might you be?' he asked in a genial voice.

'Dervorgil sir, Geraint's daughter.'

'Ah, one of Dunstan's waifs and strays.'

'I bent straying sir. My father knows where I be.'

He laughed. 'I am pleased to hear it.'

'I come to tell Master Dunstan news about my brother Hugh.'

'The one who ran away?'

'Yes, as Master Dunstan was so kind as to work at the castle in father's place to give Hugh more chance to get away, I thought he might like to know that we got word today that he be taken on as a sailor.'

'Good for him. I hope he prospers. I would hate to think that Dunstan endangered his health for nothing.'

She hung her head. 'I be very sorry that Master Dunstan got sick on account of it sir. If father had hurt himself when you were on the site it wouldn't have mattered, because you would have let him stay home.'

'So it was my fault was it?'

'Oh no Master Edmund, I didn't mean---'

He stopped her protests with a smile. 'I was only teasing you.'

She looked up at him and said with great satisfaction, 'You hit him didn't you sir, that William of Salisbury, cos he was cruel to Master Dunstan. Peter the swineherd said that you knocked him down and he slunk off back to Salisbury with a black eye and a fat lip. All the workers cheered and so would I if I had been there.'

Edmund did not confirm her statement, but he was amused by the relish with which she contemplated William's humiliation. She was standing there full of spirit in her tattered outfit, shivering in the sharp wind that had arisen. Her legs were blue with cold.

'Are those the warmest clothes you have child?' he demanded.

She nodded.

'Well, we must find you something more stylish in which to visit Dunstan.'

He went into the stable and came back with the woollen blanket in which he had disguised his grandfather's sword. He put it around her shoulders like a cloak.

'There, that's better. It may smell a bit of horse, because it has been in the stable all day.'

'Oh, I loves horses Master Edmund. I don't mind that. It feels so warm.'

'We need something to fix it with.'

He took the silver pin from the shoulder of his cloak and pinned the blanket firmly.

'Just the thing. Now you are ready to visit your guardian angel. Off you go!'

He pushed her gently in the direction of the house. 'Dunstan will be glad of company tonight. He has his head buried in a manuscript. No doubt he will read some of it to you.'

Dervorgil had been rendered speechless by his actions. She did not even thank him, but walked on towards the lights of the farm house.

As he led Midnight out into the yard, Mankel trotted up ready for action. The dog loved to run alongside Edmund's horse when he rode to the castle or the village. He bent down and stroked the animal's ragged ears.

'Not tonight old lad. You cannot come with me tonight. You go back and look after Dunstan for me.'

When he rode off, Mankel ran beside him at first, but when Edmund ordered him to go back in a commanding voice, the dog turned back with a disconsolate droop of his head.

The thegn tried to clear his head of all the images of the day, all those things that might cause him to hesitate. He must concentrate on his task alone. He tied his horse to the hitching rail near the main gate of the manor, expecting to see a whole row of horses there, but only two turned to look at the newcomers. He must be early. He was shown into the main hall by a servant, who indicated where he could leave his weapon, on an oak coffer by the door. He unbuckled his sword and lay it down with care, throwing his cloak beside it.

'You do look splendid,' said a voice close to him.

He turned to see Blanche standing there. She was dazzling in a gown of gold coloured satin, bound at the waist by a green sash shot through with gold thread. She wore a matching headband and at her throat an emerald pendant. She pulled his sword part way out of the scabbard and ran her fingers over the silver chasings on the blade.

'A handsome weapon too.'

'It was my grandfather's,' he replied in a flat voice. 'I only wear it on special occasions.'

'You consider this a special occasion?' She raised her eyebrows quizzically.

'Oh yes, a very special occasion.'

'You surprise me. Roger was doubtful that you would come. He will be pleased though. I believe he has some boring details to discuss with you about alterations to the plans.'

Edmund nodded an acknowledgement. That would serve his purpose well.

She could not resist asking him if he missed her.

'Not in the least milady.'

She had her hand on his arm and could feel no reaction from him. She sensed that his indifference was genuine. There was something about him, something different, calm on the surface but tense and focused beneath it.

'Well, you will fill the wives of Roger's boring guests with lust tonight-give them something to talk about. Roger has no idea how much I loathe playing host to his friends.'

'And yet you are happy enough to live off his wealth,' Edmund said. 'Do you love your brother Blanche?'

'What a strange question! We are used to each other. That is enough for me.'

'And if you were set adrift from Roger's bounty

how would you survive? Would you go to Ralph and ask him to keep you or would you ensnare some unsuspecting baron and get married again?'

'You are in too strange a mood for me this evening.'

She moved away from him to greet newly arrived guests, but his whole demeanour troubled her shrewd mind. She watched him during the evening. Wine was flowing freely, but she noticed that Edmund did not keep refilling his cup like the others, as if he wanted to keep a clear head. He spoke to Roger's Norman friends in a quiet, courteous manner, answering questions about the castle construction, seemingly untouched by the haughty attitude some of them showed towards him. But now and then she glimpsed him looking at Roger and the look in his eyes confirmed her suspicions. The antique sword, the abstinence, the questions he had asked her, that look – they all convinced Blanche that Edmund intended to do something desperate. She made up her mind to prevent it if she could, for whose sake she was not yet sure.

When some of the guests began to leave, she sent word to her coachman to get her personal coach ready and pulling the hood of her cape up over her head, she slipped out of the hall by the side door.

※║※

Dunstan was delighted to see Dervorgil standing in the doorway, swathed in her woollen cloak. He beckoned her to come to the fire. Then he recognised the silver pin that held the blanket around her shoulders.

'That is Edmund's pin. He was wearing it in his cloak just now.'

'He gave it to me,' she announced with pride. 'He put this blanket round me, took the pin from his own cloak and fastened this together. I was so surprised I never even thanked him. He did not want me to be cold. That was kind of him.'

'Edmund is kind,' Dunstan told her. 'He likes to act tough sometimes and pretend that he does not care about things and he has a quick temper, but it soon blows over. He has a very kind heart. I could not ask for a better brother.'

'He called you my guardian angel.'

'Did he indeed?'

'But he's right Master Dunstan; you have been a guardian angel to my family.'

Dervorgil settled down by the fire, snuggling up inside the blanket. It was such a luxury to feel warm.

She told him the news about Hugh and what a relief it was for the family to know that he was safely out of De Tosny's reach.

'How did he get a message to you?' Dunstan asked, puzzled.

''Twas the evangelist,' she replied.

The evangelist was a rogue pedlar, so called because of his ability to preach fine sermons at market crosses. The genuineness of his religious convictions was dubious. His main intention was to attract folk to buy his wares. He walked the West Country from Bristol to Salisbury and was well known around the area. He had passed through the village the day after Christmas Day. He called on Geraint the hurdle maker, pushing a scrap of parchment into his hand and departing mysteriously without a word. On the scrap was a message from Hugh, incoherent and hardly legible, for the boy's grasp of writing was rudimentary. It had been scrawled in a hurry, but it told his father all he needed to know. Hugh had found a ship. A master mariner had taken him on as a cabin boy, paying him two pence a day. He was to sail all the way to the Rhine the very day the note was written. It was such a blessing that he should recognise the evangelist peddling his wares on the quayside.

Dervorgil's face was radiant as she told the story. The idea of her Hugh sailing in a ship to some faraway place, meeting strange people and earning two pence a day was wondrous to her. She had no idea how hard and dangerous life at sea could be. She gazed at the manuscript spread out on the table.

'I would have been so happy if I could have read Hugh's note myself. Seemed strange to think that he had writ it and yet when I looked at it twere just squiggles. Like all that on the table- just squiggles to me.'

'Would you like to learn to read?'

'Very much, but mother says there is no point, me being a slave.'

'I believe that everybody should have the chance to learn to read and write. It makes such a difference to your life. I could teach you to read.'

She shook her head. 'No, I be too stupid.'

'You are far from stupid. You are a very bright girl. Come over here and look at these letters.'

Dervorgil edged up to the table and he spent some time encouraging her to trace her fingers over the large, illuminated letters at the head of each page and repeat after him what they were.

'This one is a D – a d sound like at the beginning of your name, Dervorgil and mine, Dunstan.'

She was fascinated at first, but after a while she began to tire of the effort needed to concentrate on so many different sounds.

Dunstan realised that she was flagging and there was something else that he wished to show her. He told her to reach up to the shelf behind her and take down something wrapped in a cloth. She did as she was asked and laid it on the table.

'I was going to bring this over for you tomorrow. It is a gift.'

'A gift for me?'

'It was good of you to come to the farm and help with the animals when I was working at the castle, walking all the way here in the freezing weather. I wanted to thank you.'

She stared at the roll of cloth.

'Go on, open it.'

She unrolled the cloth slowly, enjoying the suspense of it, but when she saw what was inside, she let out a shriek of delight that woke the cat dozing by the fire. It was a silver cross, plain except for a cabochon garnet at the centre. It hung on a silver chain with a sturdy clasp.

'Master Dunstan, this is what I wanted most in the world. You remembered that.'

She was turning it over in her hand to catch the reflection of the fire light on it. 'It must have cost a terrible amount.'

'No. Oswin made it. He only finished it yesterday. He is very skilful. He could make a living as a silversmith. The chain we had in the house already.'

She was fastening it around her neck, declaring that it was the most beautiful cross in the whole world. Then her face grew solemn.

'When I go home wearing this and the blanket with Master Edmund's pin in it, my mother will say I have stole it.'

'I will write you a note to tell your parents that we have given you these things and they are yours to keep. I know your father can read.'

'I won't let mother sell them either, no matter how poor we get.'

The fear had suddenly entered her mind that her precious gifts would be taken away from her and bartered for food.

Outside Mankel was barking. The sound of horse's hooves rang in the yard, the clatter of wheels. Dunstan looked at Dervorgil. Surely Edmund was not back already. Someone was knocking on the door and Mankel continued to bark. As he went to the door, Dunstan was tempted to pick up the cudgel. The raid that so changed their lives, had made him nervous of unexpected visitors at night.

He opened the door slowly and was astonished to see Blanche, Roger De Tosny's sister standing there. She was hugging her fur cape around her, but the wind had blown her hood back from her face.

She had lost some of the pins from her hair and part of the tightly wound, black knot was beginning to uncoil. He invited her in, but she shook her head.

'There is no time for ceremony. You must come with me to the manor. We may be in time to save Edmund's life.'

A sick, icy feeling rose up in the pit of his stomach.

'What do you mean, save Edmund's life?'

'I believe that he intends to try to kill Roger this evening.'

'He told you this?'

'No, not in words, but I know Edmund better than you may imagine. I read the signs. He has your grandfather's sword. Does that mean anything to you?'

She could see from his face that it did.

'I think you may be the only person who can dissuade him. We must hurry. My coach is outside.'

He followed her towards the coach, calling back over his shoulder to Dervorgil, would stood in the doorway, her eyes round with bewilderment,

'Go home Dervorgil and say nothing about this.'

The coach was a small, closed in vehicle designed for a lady and her maid servant to travel in. There was a padded seat on one side, facing the driver, to accommodate two passengers. It was never intended for someone Dunstan's height. There was insufficient room for his legs and he was obliged to draw his knees up to his chest to fit himself in. As he sat hugging his knees, trying not to bang into Blanche with his elbows, things began to make sense. Edmund had been so affectionate with him all day and then the poems- what had he said? - they will always remind you that your brother had some interesting ideas in his head once. He was saying goodbye! That look between his brother and Ilsa that he could not fathom; he understood the significance of it now. She knew and they had shielded him from the truth. How could he have been lulled so easily into such a false feeling of security about Edmund's state of mind? He was appalled at his lack of insight.

'Why did you not just warn your brother?' he asked Blanche.

'If I had told Edmund that I was going to warn Roger, he would have made the attempt anyway. Had I warned Roger, he would have allowed Edmund to declare his intentions and incriminate himself. Besides, Roger can look after himself. Your Edmund has a noble streak. He is no murderer. He will offer Roger the chance to defend himself. My brother is not in the least noble.

He must always win, at all costs and he will use any dirty trick to do so. Even if Edmund is victorious, he will not escape capture for long. I have no desire to see him at the end of a rope and your life ruined.

I know the peasants on the estate call me the Norman bitch and no doubt far worse, perhaps with some justification, but I have a few finer feelings. That handsome brother of yours awakened some of them. Let us hope that we are not too late.'

She banged her fist on the wall of the coach, nearest the driver, calling out loudly, 'Faster Gaston, faster.'

❈

It was a great relief to Edmund when Roger's guests began to leave. As the evening wore on, he found it increasingly hard to appear courteous and submissive. He had no idea what De Tosny had told them about him, but it was obvious that some of them found this example of a humbled Saxon amusing. They were patronizing, expressing surprise at his command of French and the breadth of his knowledge. If only they knew he thought with grim amusement, how much I despise their ignorance, their total lack of understanding concerning the achievement of Saxon civilization, the kings, the scholars, the craftsmen, the churchmen. These shallow friends of Roger's, most of them landowners, lords of other manors, saw the Saxons only in terms of a defeated warrior race.

That evening he attempted to show them otherwise, but it was a strain to remain good-humoured while warding off their half-veiled taunts.

There was one fellow in particular, boorish, loud-mouthed, a distant relation of De Tosny's, who insisted on pouring scorn on the Saxon tactics at Hastings. Wine had loosened his tongue and red in the face, his close-cropped hair standing up bristly like a hog, he harangued Edmund about Saxon indiscipline in battle. It hurt all the more because it was partly true. Failures of discipline may indeed have lost them the victory at Hastings.

King Harold had given clear instructions that on no account should the militia break ranks without orders to do so; but they did. On three occasions when sections of the Norman army retreated, some of the inexperienced militia ran down the hill in pursuit, leaving them exposed and easy prey for the Norman knights, seriously depleting the Saxon ranks. This meant that when Duke William made his final push, there were no Saxons in reserve to fill the gaps made in the defensive phalanx of house carls at the top of the hill.

The thegns had the responsibility of marshalling the militia and Edmund had a vivid memory of adding his shouts to his father's and screaming at the jubilant militia to hold the line, but to no avail for their voices were lost amongst the triumphant war cries, as whole lines of men chased after the Normans.

His Uncle Alfstan had seen King Harold fall around sunset, the battle having raged all day, with several lulls in the action. He saw him stagger and clutch at an arrow that had struck him in the face. Then he was overwhelmed by a group of knights hacking him down with their swords. At this point Alfstan came to search for his brother-in-law and nephew. It was too late for Edgar, but he was determined to save Edmund.

Harold's house carls fought on devotedly around the bodies of their king and his brothers. They died to a man under the banner of the golden dragon of Wessex. The noise, the smell, the chaos of it filled his mind now and he felt again the guilt of having survived; but this night he would atone for it.

The Norman was calling Harold a string of vile, depreciating names and Edmund had to bite his lip to hold back a bitter verbal retaliation in defence of the man he admired so much. Harold was a great leader and a fine general. It was true that the blood of the royal Saxon dynasty did not flow through his veins, but when the Confessor died, the legitimate heir, Edmund Ironside's grandson Edgar, was a young child and with two separate invasions threatening, a boy king would have been a disaster. The Witan, swiftly and unanimously voted Earl Harold Godwinson to be their king.

Edmund's family supported the decision wholeheartedly and were ready to fight beside him. Few leaders could have inspired their men to march 180 miles in four days and defeat Hardrada's formidable army of Norwegians and Scots at Stamford Bridge. It was Edmund's first taste of battle, facing that fearsome weapon, the Viking battle axe. He had acquitted himself well. King Harold had complimented him in person, slapping him on the back and assuring his father that he had a son well worthy of his family's traditions. It was the proudest moment of Edmund's life. He could not have dreamed that it would all turn to ashes so soon.

Harold was never vindictive. Magnanimous in victory, he had allowed Hardrada's young son Olaf and the youthful earls of Orkney to leave without paying ransom. He also gave his treacherous brother Tostig a decent burial in York. Hardrada's body however was never recovered from the battlefield. Harold had promised him seven foot of English soil or thereabouts and that was all the Norwegian warrior ever got.

Some said, with the benefit of hindsight, that Harold went to meet William too rapidly. He should have stayed longer in London and let the Normans move farther in land, away from their supply bases. They said that his brother Gyrth had strongly advised him to wait. But the Normans were devastating the coastal area, burning and looting villages. It was a King's duty to defend his people.

Harold's success in the field had always centred on attack and that was his intention. He was forced to take up a defensive position at Hastings because the Norman advance was more rapid than anticipated.

It appeared to be an excellent position. The enemy would have to fight up hill. Edmund did recall though that his father was troubled by the fact that the deployment area was cramped and a tactical retreat would have been very difficult. Despite this, Edgar had no doubt that they would win the day.

As all these memories flooded his mind, Edmund found it increasingly difficult to bear the Norman's insults. He turned away, pretending that someone else had spoken to him, but his persecutor grabbed hold of his arm roaring, 'Don't you turn away from me Saxon, or I will teach you to mind your manners.'

This was the closest Edmund came to sabotaging his whole plan, but he was rescued by Blanche, who had been watching the situation develop. She glided up beside them and slipping her arm beneath the blustering Norman's elbow she murmured, 'Antoine- I thought I heard your voice.'

The look she gave Edmund plainly said, how could anyone not hear his bellow, but she continued in a honeyed tone, 'Come and talk to me. I hear that your wife is with child again. What a stallion you are!'

Antoine's chest swelled visibly and he allowed himself to be steered away. Edmund smiled at Blanche for the first time that evening. Earlier he was pleased to find that he was indifferent to her beauty, but he would always appreciate the quickness of her wit. He wondered where she was now. She was not beside her brother, bidding farewell to the last of his guests. Perhaps she had retired early, bored with the limited conversation of Roger's friends. He hoped so. In his heart he did not wish her to witness what he was about to do.

He strapped on his sword with a ritualistic deliberation and waited while the last of the guests said their goodbyes. A servant brought in a fresh flagon of wine and was told by his master that he would not be needed anymore that night. Edmund was alone with Roger De Tosny at last.

The Norman thanked him for staying on, assuring him that he would not keep him from his bed too long. He poured some burgundy into a silver goblet, indicating another vessel on the table. The Saxon nodded and he filled that too. Roger sighed with satisfaction.

'I think this evening went very well. Let us drink to many other successful gatherings.' He raised his cup towards Edmund. 'You astounded my visitors tonight.

The ladies were full of your praises. Most Normans know little of the Saxon thegn.

As landlords their most frequent contact is with the villeins with their peasant mentality. You acquitted yourself like some scholar from the court of Charlemagne. Your company will be widely sought after tonight.'

Edmund smiled. 'Oh yes, I am sure it will, after tonight.'

He savoured the burgundy on his palate, watching De Tosny empty his own cup and begin to search amongst the many documents stored in a brass-bound chest on a side table. Edmund studied him. He was neat, impeccable to the point of irritation, everything in place and in control. The Saxon longed to crack that self-possession, to see the nakedness of fear in his eyes.

'You are even more learned than I gave you credit for,' Roger continued as he searched, 'You tend to wear your learning lightly. Do you make use of the monastery library like your brother? Father Robert tells me that he is always borrowing manuscripts. How is Dunstan by the way? I hear he was unwell before Christmas. Remiss of me not to ask sooner. Ah, here it is.'

He drew out a sheet of parchment and spread it on the table. 'You would think with these things stored in strict order, I would find what I wanted quickly, but that never seems to be the case. Well, has the boy recovered?'

He looked up at Edmund who had moved back towards the door.

'Dunstan is fully recovered now. No thanks to you.'

'Me?'

'Yes, you. You and your bastard king with his bastard knights, who killed my kinsmen and almost killed my brother.'

De Tosny had been holding the parchment down at the edges; now he let go and it rolled itself up into a scroll in one smooth movement. There was no surprise on his face at Edmund's sudden bitterness of tone.

'I fail to see what the king or I have to do with Dunstan's state of health.'

'Of course you know. You let him work on the castle when you had no right to keep him there. If Duke William had not laid his greedy hands on this country, Dunstan would have had a decent life. He has known hardship and grief since he was twelve.'

De Tosny seated himself on the edge of the table.

'My dear Edmund'- He offered to pour his adversary another drink. The offer was declined. 'I never insisted that he kept working on the site, only that someone needed to do so. He was there of his own free will, doing an errand of mercy. A foolish gesture in my opinion. You have a penchant for grand gestures in your family. You two are more alike than it would first appear. To prevent him would have breached his free rights. As for your comment about his majesty, I do not think I need answer that.'

'Oh you will answer, Roger De Tosny, with your blood.'

Edmund reached over to the door, turned the key in the lock and taking it from the keyhole, dropped it into his pocket. Roger remained seated as Edmund's sword grated out of its scabbard, but he blinked as the firelight, reflected in the blade, flashed in his face. The Saxon advanced towards him.

'I have so many accusations to throw at you. You badgered my uncle into selling his land, land my ancestors lavished sweat and love on for generations, land never meant for the rank stench of Norman corruption. You took his land, then murdered him and his son. Now you are reaping the benefits of that land which is rightly his grandson's. You Normans with your castles and your knight's fees trying to grind my nation into the dust. A man very like you killed my father at Hastings. So shall it be, cried the King's thegns together, that blood asks for blood, so swear we ever. I doubt if that verse is familiar to you, but it is written on my heart.'

Roger's smile widened.

'It is rather crude and you call us Normans barbarians. Just what is a nation Edmund? Are you sure that you know what you are talking about?'

He made himself more comfortable on the edge of the table, folding his arms, but he kept Edmund's sword hand well in his sights.

'I fought at Hastings too- not because I had a burning desire to destroy Saxons, but like William, I was ambitious. I wanted land. Being a younger brother, I had no inheritance in Normandy. You do not hate us because we are foreigners. You do not consider the peasants when you talk of freedom. You resent us because you are a member of a proud ruling class, which has been ousted by an equally proud, more efficient ruling class. That is all your thegn's creed amounts to. Besides, Harold Godwinson was a usurper, an upstart earl, an oath breaker. The Confessor himself promised the crown to William of Normandy and you Saxons revere the Confessor's name.'

'Edward was a pious, good man. We do honour him for that, but he was weak in many aspects of his rule. His years of exile in Normandy influenced his judgement at first. He had no right to promise the crown to anyone.

He soon changed his mind. He recommended Harold to the Witan before he died. As for oath breaking, Harold was forced to take that oath. William ransomed him from the Count of Ponthieu so he would have a hold over him. He would never have allowed him to return to England if he had not taken such an oath. William hid some holy relics under the table cloth when the oath was administered without Harold's knowledge, to make it more binding and sacred. A typical Norman trick.'

'Saxon fairy tales!' De Tosny said scornfully.

'Indeed? Well, all the official histories since you Normans came here have been written by Frenchmen. Do you tell me that they are all unbiased and factual? Even Duke William, once he was safe on the throne, conceded that King Harold was a worthy opponent. Not at first though- he did not behave with the magnanimity of a victor on the battlefield. What kind of man does not have the grace to allow a mother to claim her son's body? Harold's mother was forced to suffer the humiliation of begging William to ransom the body for gold and even then he would not let her take it away. He told his men to drag it down to the sea shore and bury it so Harold could go on protecting his people from invasion by sea- an unworthy sneer if ever I heard one.'

De Tosny was still smiling. 'Well I doubt if he was in the best of tempers after the fight we had been through that day. Besides as you say, he relented afterwards.'

'Only as a political strategy,' Edmund insisted. 'I doubt if he had any genuine feeling when he had Harold's body buried with dignity and honour at Waltham Abbey and ordered Normans to follow the cortege as well as Saxons.'

'I barely recall that. Your knowledge of the past is far superior to mine. I am more interested in the future.'

'You have no future. I repeat- I am going to kill you.'

'That would serve no purpose. You talk about what Dunstan has suffered. Will it lessen his suffering to see you hung, drawn and quartered for murder? Come now. I thought you to be much more reasonable than this.'

'You miscalculated, my lord of the manor- badly. I never surrendered. Everything I accepted from you served to feed my hatred. But I said that I was going to kill you, not murder you. There is a difference. We will fight on even terms, in an honourable way. Choose what weapon you wish.'

'How noble of you! I fear you will regret it.'

'We shall see.'

Edmund waited while De Tosny decided on his weapon. His sword in its scabbard was hanging on the side of a chair. He took down from the wall, an enormous curtle axe and balanced the weight of it in his hand before saying,

'No, I will use my sword. You Saxons are slashers

and rushers, not skilled with a sword. I will give you a lesson in swordsmanship.'

Edmund acknowledged the Norman's boast with a slight nod of the head and then he lunged at him. A desperate struggle began. They were evenly matched at first, both agile and fast on their feet. But De Tosny's confident, sneering smile began to fade as Edmund stepped up his onslaught.

All the anger, shame and grief accumulated over the years, which the Saxon had struggled to control for so long was now let free and added to his strength. The ferocity of his attack drove De Tosny back. What he had imagined to be his superior skill was negated by Edmund's power.

The ring of steel could be heard all over the manor house. Feet were pattering down the corridors; servants were banging on the locked door. The voice of Roland the steward was calling, 'My lord, my lord, what is happening? Are you in danger my lord?'

As the blows rained down on him, De Tosny edged farther back trying to take a firmer stance. His opponent's sword caught the back of his hand and bright blood sprang from the cut, trickling up his sleeve and down into his palm. He had been driven back right against the table and was trapped. His hand was now slippery with blood and another blow from Edmund knocked Roger's sword right out of his hand, clattering to the floor.

Edmund was chanting in his mind the names of those kin he was avenging, his father, Cenred, Cerdic, trying to keep focused. This was his moment; he moved in for the kill. De Tosny however was quick minded enough to realise that near his feet was a heavy oak stool. He hooked his foot around the leg and propelled the stool hard at Edmund. It crashed into the thegn's legs as he came forward, pushing him off balance. Roger snatched up the curtle axe from the table lightning fast and drove it into Edmund's side. He staggered back with a gasp of pain. Dropping to his knees, he wrenched the axe from the wound and was rising to his feet, when a blow on the side of the head stunned him. De Tosny had struck him with the pommel of his sword.

When Edmund's vision cleared, he realised that he was sprawled on the floor. He knew the wound was bad before he looked at it. The top of his thigh was split open to the bone and the gash in his side was deep. His blood was soaking into the handsome Flemish rug.

Roger was sitting on the edge of the table again, wrapping a napkin around his hand. He had regained his composure, but he was well aware that he was a lucky man. If it had not been for that stool, he would have been dead. The hammering on the door continued. De Tosny spotted the door key that had fallen out of Edmund's pocket on to the floor. He picked it up, tossing it in the air, as if debating whether to open the door and then he shouted,

'All is well, I am perfectly safe. You can stop that noise and go back to work. There is nothing to make a fuss about.'

The sound of reluctant muttering gradually died away, as servants trailed back to their duties, discussing what could have been happening in their master's hall.

'I must hand it to you Edmund. You know how to fight and few men would have got up again after an axe blow like that. You almost had me, but we Normans always come out on top in the end. I think I may have proved that to you at last. You are the one with no future, not me.'

'Are you not going to finish me off, complete your triumph?'

Edmund gritted his teeth in an effort to resist the pain. He would not give De Tosny the satisfaction of hearing him whimper or groan.

'I was trained to put a wounded man out of his misery, but I think I will sit here and watch the fire drain out of you with your blood. I do not much care for attempts on my life. I believe your pride hurts more than your flesh.'

'Are you not afraid that my Saxon blood will ruin your rug?'

'Defiant to the last. I would expect no less. I can afford to buy another rug. You had better prepare yourself for the life to come. You must not go before God thinking such thoughts as you are now, with your heart still full of hatred. What would that brother of yours feel if you refused to be penitent?'

Edmund shifted his knees up towards his stomach, attempting to relieve the searing sensation that ran through the lower part of his body. He did not want to think about the effect on Dunstan. He was not afraid to die .What had he to live for now? He had tried to fulfil his vow, but he had failed, failed his father and the final affirmation that the Normans had indeed conquered was driven home to him.

There was more knocking on the door. De Tosny tossed his head, repeating that he did not wish to be disturbed. He was answered by a woman's voice. Blanche was urging him to let her in. The Norman smiled to himself.

'Ah, my dear sister! I think I will let her in. You will hate her to see you in that state.'

He strolled over to the door and unlocked it, murmuring, 'You are bringing the sadist out in me this evening.'

He was surprised to see Dunstan with his sister, but Blanche did not give him the time to ask questions. She hurried into the room, but stopped at the sight that greeted her. She might have known that her effort was doomed to fail. She gave a weary sigh and turned to Dunstan.

'I am sorry, I tried my best.'

Dunstan ran to Edmund and lifted him forward with his arm around his back.

'Let me see how badly you are hurt'

'No, there is no point.' Edmund was trying to cover the gash in his thigh with the remnants of his tunic and had his other hand pressed over the wound in his side. The hand was red with blood.

'I am sorry Dunstan. I failed. I made an attempt to fulfil my vow, but I was not good enough, just as we were not good enough at Hastings. I have failed father, Cenred, Cerdic and you. There is nothing left for me to live for and

I am not afraid of death.'

Dunstan was still trying to gauge the extent of his brother's wounds as if there might be something he could do.

'I regret lying to you, but I wanted to save you distress while I could. Stop fiddling. There is nothing you can do about this. Shrieve me. I know that will give you some peace of mind.'

Dunstan shook his head, not wanting to admit that Edmund might need the last rights.

'Shrieve me and let me die in peace. I do not need to catalogue all my sins do I? I may run out of breath before I get to the end of such a long list. You know what they are.'

Dunstan made the sign of the cross and began to recite the prayers needed to accompany the final moments of life. De Tosny had lost interest. He poured himself a cup of wine and tossed it back quickly. Blanche moved into a position that shielded Edmund from Roger's view and knelt down beside him. She whispered in his ear, so low that only he could hear, 'Play dead, you splendid madman.'

Then standing up, she said in a clear voice, intended for De Tosny to hear,

'Well, he is dead.'

Dunstan, looking up from his prayers with a puzzled look in his eyes, was about to contradict her, but she lay a finger to her lips to dissuade him.

'Such a waste, so many women over the years to come deprived of your skills my handsome thegn,' she added in her most mocking tone of voice. Roger was walking towards the door. He stopped and smiled.

'You certainly had your money's worth dear sister. I will send someone to clear up the mess.'

He did not doubt her word that Edmund was dead. His confidence was misplaced. If he had considered more fully, he may have realised that in his desperate haste to save himself, his blow with the axe was off target. He had intended to rip open the stomach and spill the Saxon's guts.

His hand was on the door when Blanche called, 'Roger, let me deal with it. You are right; he did dispel my boredom when I was sorely in need of it. I do not want him buried in some ditch in the grounds of the manor house. Grant me the favour of letting his brother take him home.'

'If that is what you wish Blanche. Let the villagers make a martyr out of him. It matters not to me.'

'Thank you. Send Gaston to me. He will sort it out.'

The moment that De Tosny had left the room, she pulled down from the wall a fabric hanging and instructed Dunstan to tear it into strips.

'We must try to slow down this bleeding. You can stop your praying now and start bandaging.'

She was so decisive, so commanding, so unlike the languid Blanche he had met before. She steeled herself to help Dunstan bind the mangled flesh, murmuring, 'Roger is such a butcher.'

Edmund, his head resting against Dunstan's shoulder did not want to make the effort to struggle. He just wanted to die.

'Leave me alone,' he pleaded.

'Be quiet and do what you are told for once. You have done your thegnly duty. Now let your brother do his duty towards you.'

As they shifted his position to tend the wounds, he felt himself drifting away, but he forced himself back to see looming over him the massive frame of Gaston, Blanche's servant. He was as tall as Dunstan and twice as wide, with a bull neck and biceps that bulged from beneath his short-sleeved tunic.

He scooped Edmund up in his arms with ease.

'Remember you are dead,' Blanche reminded him, 'So try your best to look like a corpse, in case any of the servants see us leave.'

Edmund, barely conscious, thought that he would have little trouble playing dead. He just wished that he was.

Blanche went to a small side door in the hall, but before she slid back the bolt and led them into the corridor, she instructed Dunstan to pick up his brother's sword. He was reluctant, but she insisted.

'It was your grandfather's, part of your inheritance. Edmund would wish you to retrieve it. Roger has enough swords. He has no right to claim your family treasures.'

He picked it up, trying to ignore the blood smeared over it, Edmund's own blood. As they walked down the corridor in semi-darkness, he expressed concern about De Tosny discovering his sister's ploy.

'You need not worry about Gaston. He is my

servant, not Roger's. He has served me since I was a child and he answers only to me. If I tell him to say nothing, he will be silent. He would die rather than betray me. But remember, if Edmund lives, you must keep him hidden for a good while. Roger must not find out that he is still alive. He will have him arrested. My brother does not forgive – unlike you.'

They had come out into the yard at the side of the manor house. Blanche's coach was there, the horse still in harness.

She had an instinct that the coach might be needed again. Edmund felt the chill of the air, the sting of the wind and realised that they were outside.

'Dunstan, my horse, where is my horse?'

'You cannot ride like that. We are taking you in the coach.'

'No, you lack-wit, even I am not stupid enough to think I can ride in this state. I do not want De Tosny to have my horse, not my Midnight.'

The effort to speak was painful, but the thought of Roger De Tosny riding his spirited black stallion, the horse he had reared from a foal and ridden for six years was more than he could bear. It seemed vital to him to prevent it happening. 'Hitching rail, by the manor gates.'

'We will pass the rail on the way out,' Dunstan assured him. 'I can tie Midnight to the back of the coach. Do not worry Edmund, I will not let De Tosny get his hands on him.'

The promise lessened Edmund's agitation and Gaston lifted him into the coach. He laid his head against the back of the seat. It was padded and comfortable. He closed his eyes wanting nothing more than to let go and drift away, but Blanche was standing on the step of the vehicle. He heard her voice and opening his eyes saw her face close to his.

'You have done all you can. One man cannot turn the tide. Live my handsome thegn, live. Your brother needs you and if the servants' gossip is true, so does a certain red-haired miller's daughter.' She kissed him on the lips with warmth. 'I shall always keep the memory of you in my bed.'

Dunstan had climbed into the carriage. He was still bewildered by Blanche.

'Why did you do this for us?'

'Edmund was a reckless fool to try what he did, but it was magnificent. Never forget that your brother is magnificent. Now hurry before he bleeds to death.'

She ordered Gaston to go wherever Dunstan bid him.

Before Dunstan pulled down the blinds over the open side of the coach, Edmund could see Blanche standing in the courtyard, the elegant Blanche, her hair dishevelled, blowing in the winter wind, the front of her gown spattered with his blood. He wondered if he was in the midst of some strange dream; nothing seemed real. He was aware of pain, but it was as if it belonged to someone else, or a memory of something long past. Dunstan's arm was around him, holding him close. His brother was murmuring words of encouragement. He could no longer distinguish the words, but the voice was calming and he let his senses slip away.

Dunstan had told Gaston to drive to the mill. Freya was the only local healer that he knew and the mill would also serve as a good hiding place.

The monastery was another option. The monks were also familiar with herbal cures, but as much as he respected Father Robert, he was not certain that the Abbot would keep their secret from De Tosny. He knew that the villagers would not give them away.

He kept talking in an effort to keep Edmund awake and was worried when his brother lost consciousness. He was a ghastly white, as if all his blood was draining away and his breathing was ragged. Dunstan refused to admit to the possibility that Edmund might die. Freya had saved him when he was wounded at Hastings. She could do so again; but he found himself rocking his brother in his arms, repeating like a mantra, 'Don't die Edmund. Please do not die.'

The main road through the village was deserted as the coach clattered along it and drew up outside the mill. Dunstan tumbled out of it, running through the yard and the tent-like structure that served as the Thurkilson's kitchen.

The mill door was closed and he hammered on it. When there was no response, he banged louder, calling the miller's name.

'Alright, alright, there is no need to knock my door down damn it. I'm coming.'

The familiar tones of Alleyn's deep voice came from the other side of the door. There was the sound of a wooden plank being lifted out of place and the door opened to reveal the miller, dressed only in hose and a loose under shirt. He raised the lamp he was carrying, a pottery vessel with a wick floating in oil and peered out into the darkness.

'You must let us in. Edmund is sorely wounded. He will bleed to death.'

Dunstan was desperate, Alleyn could see that well enough. Gaston was standing behind him with the limp form of Edmund in his arms.

'Come in. Freya, Ilsa, get up! Hurry, light the lamps!'

Ilsa knew the moment that she heard the knocking that something had happened to Edmund. When he was with her the previous day, he had been pensive, tender, saying little, but conveying much. His parting kiss was like a goodbye. She realised that the plan he had spoken of that night in the barn was about to come to fruition. She made no attempt to prevent him. She knew it would be useless and if she was honest with herself, she had to admit that she admired his resolution, his steadfast adherence to his vow. She was proud of him. He was aware of that and loved her for it. There was no need for words. It was understood between them.

She had been on edge all day, expecting to hear some excited villager come rushing in with dreadful news. She went to bed in her overdress in case she needed to deal with an emergency during the night and now it had come.

She pulled back the curtain that closed off her sleeping area. Her first thought when she saw Edmund lying on the floor so still, covered in blood, was that he was dead. A chill spread all over her, down her back, through her chest and to the very pit of her stomach. Then she heard her mother talking of washing and binding wounds, so he must be alive. She ran over to him, dropped down on the floor beside him and rested his head in her lap, stroking his hair and kissing it. Her mother gave her a sharp look.

'Twould be more use my girl if you fetched fresh water and washing cloths, while I get the salves.'

Alleyn was more sympathetic to his daughter's distress.

'Leave the girl alone. You know how she loves him. She will help you soon enough. I will fetch the water.'

'You always did spoil that girl,' was Freya's response.

Her father had noticed how nervous Ilsa had been all day, how she did not finish her meals and was abstracted at her work. Did she know something was going to happen he wondered? As he went out into the yard to fetch water from the rain barrel, he walked into the huge form of Gaston, who was leading Edmund's horse into the yard. He called for Dunstan, uncertain how to react to this giant stranger with his impassive face. Gaston asked Dunstan in heavily accented English, what he should do with the horse.

'I will take him now. Go back to the manor and tell your mistress that Edmund is in good hands. Thank you for your help.'

Gaston bowed his head in acknowledgement and turned away. Alleyn advised Dunstan to put Midnight in the storehouse with the two carthorses, in case he was recognised.

'He might think it beneath his dignity being a thegn's mount, to share quarters with two work horses, but I doubt if he will distain some fodder.'

It was only now, as they both carried buckets of water back into the mill, that Alleyn asked Dunstan, 'How did this happen?'

'Edmund tried to kill De Tosny after his New Year feast was over.'

'In the Norman's own manor house? The mad fool!'

Dunstan's own grasp of what had happened was sketchy, but he outlined what details he knew. Freya scolded them for taking so long with the water. She had peeled away the remnants of clothing from both wounds. Alleyn sucked in his breath. 'Jesu, what a mess! Looks like the work of an axe to me.'

Dunstan shuddered, forcing himself to look at the damage.

Freya was cleaning the wounds now, swabbing them with water from the buckets and layering salve from a jar deep inside them.

Ilsa still sat with his head in her lap, refusing to move. She had taken a damp cloth and was bathing his face.

'These will need stitching,' Freya was saying. 'This thigh will never heal together unless tis stitched. Husband, strand some twine and grease it with this salve and bring me a needle, the big one for stitching leather.'

She had been considering like Alleyn that Ilsa knew something about this. Alleyn handed her the needle, already threaded with twine and she began to compress the damaged flesh as firmly as she could and draw the flaps of skin together with the twine. As she worked away she said to her daughter,

'You knew this was going to happen. He told you, didn't he?'

'Not in so many words.'

'But you knew.'

'Yes.'

'Then why did you not try to stop him?' Edmund stirred a little and sighed. ''Tis not helpful girl, to bring him to his senses now. Twere best he did not feel this. Stop that bathing and hold him still.'

Ilsa was looking at Dunstan, wondering if he was disappointed that she had made no attempt to prevent Edmund's venture, nor warned him what his brother intended. 'It would have been useless to try to stop him. He was determined to do it. He had made a vow.'

Dunstan was holding Edmund's hand. It was like ice and he rubbed it in an effort to bring some life back into it.

'No Ilsa, he did not have to do it. Look at the result.'

'The result is not the point. It was the action that counted. He had to make an attempt to avenge Cenred and Cerdic, honour his vow. You love him so much Dunstan, but you will never understand him fully. There are some things that you cannot forgive.'

Alleyn nodded his head in approval. He saw some of the old Viking spirit in his daughter, but practical considerations were also in his mind.

'We must find a comfortable place for him out of sight. Twould be best for now for folks to think he had died at the hands of De Tosny, in case any word gets back to the manor. I doubt if the villagers would betray him, but De Tosny's agents do visit the mill and Gilbert calls regularly.'

They decided to carry him up to the third story of the mill, the floor above the grain shute, where they made a bed on a thick pile of straw, covering it over with blankets to make it less prickly. Alleyn and Dunstan dragged filled corn sacks around him to make a protective screen, which could be raised higher to hide him completely if necessary.

Carrying Edmund up the steeply angled ladder and through the trap door into the top story was difficult. Freya was anxious that they did not tear open her careful stitching.

'Do you think he has a chance to live mother?' Ilsa asked as she placed a rolled bolt of cloth under his head for a pillow.

Freya looked at Dunstan, who dared not ask the question in words, but whose eyes were begging her for a favourable answer.

'How can I answer that? Only God knows that. His body is strong and healthy. When he was wounded before, when the Normans first came, his wounds healed quickly. Twas the fever that almost killed him. If we can prevent fever rising, all may be well. But these wounds are much worse than he suffered then. He has lost so much blood. I will do all I can, but he will need your prayers Master Dunstan.'

Ilsa was concerned that this unheated room, even with the warmth that straw could generate, would be too cold for a man so drained of blood. Her mother pointed out that it would be too dangerous to attempt to make a fire so near straw.

'Not if it was in a brazier,' Alleyn said.

His wife reminded him that they did not possess a brazier.

'Ah, but Oswin does, in the forge.'

'You can't tell Oswin that Master Edmund is here. Twould be all over the village by midday tomorrow.'

'I do not intend to tell him. They are all in bed now. I will sneak into the forge and borrow it. He will think that he has been robbed- give him something to relay round the village for weeks. We are fortunate that we are in the season when Oswin's lads are not working for me. If they were at work on the sack floor and noticed us going up to the top floor often, they would suspect that something was going on and creep up to take a look. I will not be long.'

True to his word Alleyn soon returned lugging a brazier and an iron plate to stand it on to catch falling embers. The miller and his wife then went back to bed, whilst Ilsa and Dunstan kept watch over Edmund.

They sat in silence, their faces strange in the light of the brazier and the flame from the wick in the oil lamp. Ilsa rubbed Edmund's cheeks and forehead in an effort to restore some colour to his face. The cold whiteness frightened her. 'Why did Blanche do it?' she asked. 'He was trying to kill her brother.'

'I think she loves Edmund in her way. She said that she had some finer feelings left and he had awakened them. Then when we left the manor she told me always to remember that he was magnificent.'

'A good word, perhaps she does love him. Dunstan, you know that De Tosny will claim your land now. What are you going to do?'

'I do not care about the land. All I care about is Edmund. I shall go to the monastery. Father Robert will let me live in one of the guest rooms, perhaps the same one I had when I stayed there for a while as a child. I can help the monks with their livestock and gardens. I will go home tomorrow and start packing up a few things that I need- my books, some things handed down in the family.'

He glanced at his grandfather's sword lying on the floor beside the corn sacks. He had no idea why he had brought it up into the top storey.

Perhaps it was an instinct to conceal it. He felt an urgent impulse to clean off the blood that still stained it and taking a handful of straw, he began to scrub away at it as hard as he could.

'And Edmund's clothes. He will need his clothes.' To hear himself make such a positive statement cheered him, bolstered his belief that his brother would not die.

It was not a foregone conclusion. For three days Edmund lay like a dead man, deeply unconscious, still and pallid. Only the rise and fall of his shallow breathing testified that he was still alive and they had to concentrate hard to see even that. Thankfully there was no fever, but the signs were not good.

De Tosny did not waste any time claiming what he now considered rightfully his own. Four days after the incident, he had notices nailed around the village declaring that the lands of Edmund and Dunstan, sons of Edgar the thegn were forfeited to the lord of the manor due to the criminal attempt of the elder brother to assassinate his lord, for which he had paid with his life.

Those villagers who could read passed the news on to those who could not. They were shocked and angry. Their anger was not directed at Edmund. It was a desperate thing to do, but they sympathised with the intent, saw courage and honour in it. As De Tosny predicted, they saw him as a martyr.

The Norman was the brunt of their anger. They could not believe that their thegn was overcome in a fair fight. De Tosny must have outnumbered him with his knights and cut him down.

Gilbert the reeve was genuinely sorry when he was sent to give Dunstan notice to quit the land. He always knew that Edmund's temper would get him into trouble one day, but he was grieved none the less. He had good memories of his friendship with Edgar, how the thegn was so proud of his sons, Edmund in particular. The last thing he wished to see was a family with such distinguished lineage driven from their land.

Dunstan appreciated his sympathy. He told him that he would much rather hear it from a friend and he had always considered Gilbert a friend.

'That night when he chased me off the farm,' Gilbert said. 'I was truly afraid, but I never held it against

Edmund- firebrand just like his father. I grieve at his death. I would have paid my respects at his funeral had I known earlier.'

Dunstan nodded. He knew that he was a poor liar, but it was vital to keep Edmund's survival a secret, at least until he was on his feet. He had confided in one other person only, Steven the priest. It was essential to give the impression that there had been a funeral and Steven was key to this. He offered his help willingly.

All Dunstan required of him was that should anyone inquire, he must say that Edmund was buried swiftly in a favourite spot on the downs, with just his brother and the miller's family present. The villagers would not expect him to be buried on land that De Tosny was about to acquire and Steven could explain that the Norman objected to his burial in the churchyard on the grounds that he had attempted murder.

Gilbert conveyed his master's instructions that Dunstan should be off the land by the end of the week. All the livestock was forfeit, but he was allowed personal possessions and his horse. He had taken his books to the monastery already. Edmund's clothes and both their personal possessions, along with Mankel and the cat were transferred to the mill, so he was willing to leave the day after Gilbert called, arranging for a cottar to tend the animals until new tenants moved in. He took one last look round, but found his heart surprisingly light, freed of responsibility. He hoped the new occupants would look after the stock and the land as well as they had, but he could now concentrate on helping Edmund get well and on life at the monastery. It pricked his conscience sorely to withhold the truth from Father Robert.

The Abbot had welcomed him with open arms. He prayed with him for Edmund's soul and Dunstan was not sure how long he could keep up the pretence.

On the same day that Gilbert called at the farm, Edmund son of Edgar stirred and opened his eyes. He felt himself struggling out of a profound darkness and had no notion where he was. His vision was blurred and he saw odd shapes around him that he could not recognise. A spasm of fear passed through him. Was he in purgatory? He could hear his own breathing and distant voices below him. His sight gradually cleared and he realised that the odd shapes were corn sacks. Even in his confusion, his mind was clear enough to work out that he was unlikely to find rows of corn sacks in purgatory.

He tried to sit up, but did not have the strength and became aware of a sharp pain in his side and thigh. He called out the only name that came into his head.

'Dunstan! Dunstan!' His own voice sounded strange, unfamiliar to him and lacking its usual power. 'In Christ's name where is this?'

There was no answer and he lacked the energy to shout again. Then there was a creaking noise and Ilsa's face appeared through the trap door. She pulled herself up through the opening and hurried over, sitting down on the floor beside him.

'You have come back to us at last Edmund.' Her voice was full of relief.

'Where is this? Where's Dunstan?' He was

disorientated and anxious.

'Be calm my love,' she soothed. 'You are safe in the mill, right up on the top floor. Dunstan will be here soon.'

'Ilsa?' It was Ilsa, telling him that he was in the mill, but why? At one moment nothing would come and then in the next it all flooded back in a series of sounds and images. De Tosny's mocking smile, servants hammering on the door, Blanche standing in the yard with his blood on her gown. So much blood and very little of it De Tosny's. A feeling of bitter humiliation and failure came with the memory; frustration that he was still alive.

Ilsa was advising him to save his strength and not try to talk.

'My throat is dry,' he said.

As she turned to dip a cup into the bucket of fresh water in the corner, he realised that he had a pressing need to pass water. He felt so helpless. Ilsa lifted the cup to his lips.

'I have a sore need to piss first,' he confessed, embarrassed by his predicament.

'That presents no problem. I have a jug here for that very purpose.'

She pulled back the blanket that covered him. Her mother had redressed his wounds the previous night and Ilsa was pleased to see that the bandages were still clean. No blood was seeping into them. Freya's stitching had done its job. They had put a fresh tunic on him, but left the lower half of his body unclothed to make access to his wounds easier. It was an easy task for her to take hold of his member and place it inside the jug. She sympathised with his embarrassment but decided to be brisk and cheerful.

'You need not feel ashamed because you must rely on others for a while. You will need to be nursed for some time to get well again and will have to bear a few indignities at first. Do not forget, I am familiar with your member.'

She hoped that would make him smile, but it did not. After he had relieved himself and taken a drink, he closed his eyes not wishing to communicate anymore.

His progress was slow. The severe loss of blood had left him very weak. Moving and speaking exhausted him and he slept most of the day, happy to take refuge in oblivion rather than dwell on his failure. He made matters worse by refusing to eat for several days. When Dunstan or Ilsa tried to feed him nourishing broth or porridge, he would turn his head away, saying that the smell made him feel sick. Dunstan feared that his brother had made up his mind not to recover.

He was sitting beside him one afternoon with a bowl of savoury porridge in one hand and a full spoon, which Edmund had refused as usual, in the other.

'Edmund,' he said, 'You must stop this. If you do not eat you will die. Perhaps that is what you want. If so, it is selfish. I can be happy at the monastery, very happy, but only if I have you to support me. I have always needed you. I love you more than anyone in this world. Ilsa needs you too. Do not throw all our love and care back in our faces.'

Edmund stared at his brother. He had made Dunstan suffer enough already. It was true that it took very little to make him happy; his life at least could mean something.

'Spoon the damn stuff in then.' It was an ungracious growl, but it lifted Dunstan's heart. Edmund tolerated four spoonsful and then thought he truly would be sick, but the feeling passed and that evening he managed a whole portion of broth.

On a cold February morning Ilsa was in the mill yard washing clothes. The frost was hard. Icicles hung from the side of the mill and from the blades of the water wheel; the surface of the pond was frozen.

It warmed her fingers for a short while when she dipped the garments into the warmed water, but they felt even colder than before once she withdrew them and began to beat the dirt out of the clothing over a washboard. It was never her favourite duty, not even on summer days.

She left the work to gaze through the palisade and up the road, her breath materialising in front of her in gauzy clouds. She could hear Oswin hammering away in the forge. Poor Oswin, he was so offended that some vagabond had stolen his brazier and tray. They would be able to tell him the truth soon.

She saw Steven making his way down to the church, stepping gingerly for fear of slipping on the icy road. Some children had made a slide. They were laughing and skidding around.

One of them almost slid into Steven and he warned them to behave. They sniggered behind his back, no doubt hoping that he would lose his footing and make an undignified landing. In the distance she could see a vehicle approaching. As it came closer she saw it was a small coach, pulled by a single horse and driven by a muscular middle-aged man with the insignia of Roger De Tosny on his surcoat. When the coach drew level with the boys on the slide, the oldest of them snatched up a handful of mud and stones and hurled them at the coach, shouting obscenities. Feeling against De Tosny still ran high in the village. Ilsa stepped back instinctively as the coach pulled level with the palisade.

The blind at the window opening rolled up and she found herself staring into the dark mystery of Blanche's eyes. The woman was appraising her. She had much to thank Blanche for, but she could not prevent a feeling of triumph over someone she had once seen as a rival, particularly now that she was sure Edmund's child was growing inside her. He did not know yet. She was waiting for the right moment to tell him, when he was stronger.

'I am sorry the children threw mud at your coach. The villagers still believe that Edmund is dead and they bitterly resent your brother for it.'

'He is alive then?'

Ilsa nodded.

'Good, then he will have need of this.'

She leaned out of the coach and handed Ilsa a cloak, Edmund's cloak, the one he had worn that night. Perhaps it was just her imagination, but Ilsa thought Blanche was loathe to part with it.

'I recall that he had a fondness for that cloak. He wore it well. How is he?'

'He has a long road to travel yet. He can get up

without help now and walk a little, but he tires quickly and his wounds pain him. The thigh wound grew sore and infected at one end when he started to move around more and was weeping puss, but my mother's salves have overcome that now. Not that he complains. He says very little at all. The most difficult thing to heal will be his wounded spirit.'

'Ah yes, Edmund's pride. He got the better of Roger in that fight you know. It was a fortunately placed stool and Roger's quick-wittedness that saved him, not his knight's skills. I managed to tease that out of him. He was unnerved. He hid it well, but I know he was. It is very rare that Roger is unnerved. Edmund might like to know that. Your thegn is a natural fighter. His spirit will revive in time. But I must go. It would be unwise to linger. Roger might hear of it and question my purpose.

I will tell Gaston to drive faster and avoid Saxon missiles.'

'Do you have a message for Edmund?'

'No, I gave him my message when we parted last. Drive on Gaston!'- with that call to her servant she pulled down the blind and the coach drove on through the village. Ilsa watched it out of sight before she took the cloak inside and returned to her washing. She knew now why Edmund had been attracted to Blanche.

The weather in mid-March turned soft and mild, promising an early spring. Edmund's wounds were healing well but he showed little interest in anything. He replied when he was spoken to, but rarely initiated a full-blown conversation. He spent much of his time sitting in a corner of the mill, staring into space, absently stroking Mankel's head, as the dog sat beside him. Now the weather had improved Ilsa encouraged him to go outside. He had grown a beard and lost weight; if he pulled a hood up over his head when he was out in the yard, none of De Tosny's agents would recognise him at a quick glance. He hated the thought of skulking around. It was timid and base. Was his future life to be spent hiding under a hood? That afternoon he limped outside and wandered around the yard. He found that the cramped, tight feeling down one side that caused him to limp eased the farther he walked. He discovered the shed where the horses were stabled. After that he visited the horses every day, grooming Midnight, walking him around behind the mill, talking to the stallion and the two carthorses in a way he could not to his fellow human beings, not even to Dunstan.

The time had now come to tell the villagers the truth. Dunstan and Steven the priest called on Eadwig, as it would have been discourteous not to inform the village headman first. Gradually the news spread around the village. They were jubilant to discover that Edmund was alive and had outsmarted De Tosny. Eadwig required each one of them to take an oath never to betray their thegn and they were all eager to comply.

Steven rose in their estimation for being trusted with the secret and keeping it so faithfully. Oswin, though hurt at first that Alleyn chose not to trust him, was proud that the iron brazier he had forged with his own hand had helped to keep Edmund alive in the bitter weather. Instead of a dead martyr, the villagers had a live hero.

Edmund dreaded seeing them, afraid they would heap praises on him which would taste bitter as gall. In his mind he relived the fight with De Tosny over and over again, castigating himself for not being aware of that wretched stool that proved to be his downfall. He apologised to his father for failing him, sometimes aloud when he was alone.

His sleep was fitful for he was constantly woken by strange dreams full of shifting shapes, feelings of dread and the smell of death. He was confused about Blanche, not sure if she saved his life out of genuine respect for him or if it was just a whim to confound her brother. She was often in his dreams too, soothing him one minute and tormenting him the next. The villagers could never have imagined how little like a hero their thegn felt.

Dunstan could now confess to Father Robert. It troubled his conscience that he had withheld the truth for ten long weeks. He sat outside the Abbot's room waiting for an audience, hoping Robert would understand. As he waited he was also thinking about Dervorgil.

He had decided to teach her to read, at least to give her a basic grasp of the skill and had asked her parents if she might be allowed to come to the mill for two hours a week for that purpose. Her mother could not see the value of it, but Geraint was more than willing. Dunstan chose the mill because he was not sure that the monks would welcome visits by a lively fifteen year old girl, whose curiosity often prompted her to ask awkward questions.

Now the weather had improved, they could sit outside in the mill yard. Freya agreed as long as they remained outside.

'I have nothing against the slaves, but I don't want her fleas in my house and come summer I will put her in the horse trough and scrub her clean'

That was not a prospect that appealed to Dervorgil, but she tried hard to concentrate on her first lesson. She was easily distracted. Villagers kept arriving at the mill to speak to Alleyn and congratulate Dunstan with pats on the back and knowing looks. She was puzzled.

'What have that lot got to be so happy about?' she inquired and Dunstan was pleased to reveal the secret to her.

'My brother Edmund did not die back in January. He was wounded, but I managed to get him away from the manor house with the help of Lady Blanche and her servant. De Tosny thinks he is dead and must continue to think so. That is why we have kept it a secret for so long and at first we were not sure if he would survive because he was so badly hurt.'

Dervorgil's eyes were shining. She had gone home the night of Blanche's visit to the farm delighted with her treasures but worried about what had happened. When she heard the news of Edmund's death, she had wept, for him and for Dunstan. She wore her cross constantly and at night she would take out the silver pin with a heavy heart because she had not thanked Master Edmund for it. This news was almost too good to be true.

Dunstan stood up and began to walk across the yard, beckoning her to follow.

'Come and look.'

He led her to the store house behind the mill where the horses were stabled. Mankel came out to greet them and Dunstan directed her gaze inside to where a man was grooming a black stallion. The man was bearded and gaunter than when she had seen him last, but she recognised him instantly. Before Dunstan could prevent her, she had hurtled into the stable. He had only intended her to look and be convinced that Edmund was alive. He had with the help of the Thurkilsons, shielded Edmund from all the villagers who were keen to pay their respects to him in person because Dunstan knew that he did not want to see them.

He was not sure what his reaction to Dervorgil would be. 'Master Edmund,' she was saying as she exploded into his self-enclosed world, 'It is so good to see you. It broke my heart to think you had gone to heaven like Master Cerdic.'

He turned slowly and stared at her, then replied with a wry twist to his mouth that could hardly be described as a smile, 'I doubt if that is where I would be.'

She did not stop to consider the meaning of his comment, but rattled on.

'I was sad for Master Dunstan because he told me you were the best brother a man could wish for and I was sad too because I never thanked you for the warm blanket and the silver pin. I may be a slave but I know my manners. I can thank you now.'

He did not respond and because he was silent she wondered if he regretted giving her the pin. Hoping it was not so, she offered, 'You can have the pin back if you wish sir.'

He shook his head. 'No child, what use have I for a silver pin? You keep it.'

He turned his attention back to Midnight, drawing the brush lightly along the horse's glossy back. She waited for a few moments in case he had more to say, but he seemed to have forgotten that she was there and Dunstan was signalling her to come away. They walked back to the chopping block in the yard that they were using as a table.

'Master Edmund said I could keep the silver pin,' she told him with relief in her voice. 'I think he is very sad though. Do his wounds pain him?'

Dunstan did not try to explain what truly ailed his brother, but just said,

'His wounds were very severe. It will take him a long time to come back to himself.'

As he sat outside the Abbot's room, waiting for Father Robert to finish his business with a visiting merchant, he hoped that once Robert knew the truth, he could enlist his aid to coax Edmund out of his emotional torpor, the profound melancholy into which he had fallen. He had not heard his brother laugh since the day of De Tosny's New Year gathering. That afternoon Edmund had related to him some nonsense of Oswin's about fire spirits lurking beneath his forge, giving an accurate impersonation of Oswin's querulous voice and manner. They had both laughed heartily over it. Now even a smile from Edmund was rare. It was as if everything within him was frozen, suspended and nothing had any savour.

That morning Dunstan had called at the mill early.

Edmund was not sitting inside staring into space as he often did, nor was he in the stables with the horses. Dunstan eventually found his brother at the back of the mill watching the water wheel turn, spraying water from the ends of its paddle-shaped spokes. The sunlight striking through them transformed the droplets into transient flashes of colour before they fell back into the pond and were extinguished. Edmund reached out towards one iridescent gleam as it passed near him, cupping it in his hand, but it dissolved the moment it touched his skin and he shook his head in a resigned way. Wandering back into the shadows of the grinding shed he ran his hand over the apparatus that attached the mill stones to the water wheel. It was complicated and clumsy and was vibrating dangerously as the mill stones did their work, making the flimsy lean-to shake.

Alleyn was feeding the grain into the hopper up in the sack room and the convex shaped runner stone spun around, grinding it on to the stationary bed stone beneath. The image struck a chord with Edmund. He felt ground down to the consistency of flour. Oswin's son Centwine was collecting the flour as it was pushed to the outer edges of the stone and sifting it into sacks. Edmund took a handful of flour and let it trickle through his fingers back into the sack.

'Tis good quality Master Edmund,' Centwine assured him with enthusiasm, 'My father says you will find no better for miles around.'

Edmund nodded, but did not reply. He had not noticed Dunstan standing just outside the grinding shed watching him, wondering what he was thinking.

His younger brother stepped forward now saying, 'There you are. I have been looking for you. I am going back to the monastery now and I thought you might like to come with me. Where's Mankel? He would enjoy the walk.'

It was unusual for the dog not to be in attendance on Edmund.

'Oh he is chasing rabbits and why would I wish to visit the monastery?'

'Well it would be exercise for you and perhaps Father Robert-'

Edmund held up his hand palm outwards to prevent Dunstan from finishing the sentence. 'No, I have no need of Father Robert. I shall help Centwine load these sacks on to the platform. That will be exercise enough.'

He turned away and began to heave one of the full sacks up onto the storage platform. Dunstan was obliged to walk back to the monastery alone. He told himself it would take time and he must be patient, but he longed to have the real Edmund back again.

The interview with Father Robert was less painful than he had feared. The Abbot understood the necessity of keeping Roger ignorant of Edmund's survival. He took no offence because Dunstan had not trusted him with so vital a secret and listened with sympathy as he poured out his anxiety concerning Edmund's state of mind. He had comforted men shattered by the experience of battle and knew that severe wounds affected the mind and spirit as well as the body. This failure to accomplish his vow had revived in Edmund all the half buried shock of the loss at Hastings, the upheaval of his whole world and he had not yet built up enough strength to bear it. Sealing himself off from the world was his only defence. He could not see a place for himself in his society any more.

Two days later Father Robert accompanied Dunstan to the mill. Freya was flustered by the presence of the Abbot in her makeshift kitchen. He was intrigued by her collection of herbs. He took the stoppers out of the jars of salves and mixtures, sniffing the aromas and asking well-informed questions about the contents and how they were prepared. Alleyn came around from the side of the mill to greet him, wiping his hands on his apron.

Dunstan walked on into the main room, where Ilsa was sweeping at the dust and trying to stop Mankel from biting the broom. Edmund sat in his usual chair. His eyes were closed, but he was not asleep.

'Father Robert is here to see you Edmund,' Dunstan said, touching his brother's arm.

'You have brought reinforcements have you?' Edmund murmured without opening his eyes.

'Well you must listen to someone. You don't pay any attention to what I say.'

Father Robert came into the room, the hem of his habit disturbing the pile of floor sweepings that Ilsa had brushed towards the door. He greeted Edmund warmly. The thegn opened his eyes, but he did not rise from the chair.

'Have you come to castigate me for my blood lust Father? Before you do, let me say in my defence that I had no intention of murdering him in cold blood. I gave him the chance to defend himself and he got the better of me.'

Father Robert smiled. 'I gather from Blanche that it was quite the reverse. You got the better of him. He escaped by a very lucky chance, the luck of the devil perhaps. That luck will run out one day. He will answer to a higher authority when that day comes. Leave judgement to God. While I cannot condone your actions, I have not come to chide you my son. I hope I can offer solace.'

He sat down on a stool opposite Edmund, tucking the skirt of his habit underneath him with meticulous care and took hold of one of the thegn's hands in both his own.

'Edmund, society must always change and ours will go on changing. I can foresee a time when we will not speak of Saxon and Norman, but simply the English. The villeins and freemen, the ones who toil, they are the backbone of the country and their blood is Saxon. This is still your country. The language spoken is your language. I know the royal court, the Norman aristocracy speak French and official documents are written in either Latin or French, but that too will change- not in our lifetime- but one day, everyone from the highest to the lowest will speak English and all communications will be written in English- the language of the Saxons- with some French admixture no doubt, but surely you will allow us poor Frenchmen a little influence. We have brought a few good ideas over with us as well as bad ones.'

The pressure of his hands was strong and encouraging. Edmund was looking directly at him now, as if the words had begun to penetrate his defences.

'All these people who so rejoice in your recovery and those closest to you who have given so much time and care to make you well have done so because they love you, but also because they believe you have an important part to play in the future. You can help the people of these four villages. They have looked up to your family for generations and they respect you. You are an educated man. You can help to settle their disputes, teach them more economic ways of farming, how to better their conditions by working together more closely, devise ways to blunt Roger's exactions. This has always been a part of a thegn's duties. Take your rightful place among them.

There are other ways to protect those for whom you are responsible than with the sword.'

'He is right,' Dunstan urged. 'There is so much good you can do; so many projects you could organise, because the villagers will take your advice and not squabble so much with you to guide them. We could do things together. We have always worked together. I miss you Edmund.'

Ilsa felt the atmosphere of secrecy that had bound them since January was lifting. She had listened to the Abbot's persuasive plea and was moved by it. She still held a secret of her own however. She had told no one yet that she was pregnant. That right moment had not presented itself, but she would not be able to hide it much longer, especially from her mother. This was now the time to add weight to Father Robert's argument. She opened her mouth to speak, but Alleyn spoke first.

'I have been thinking for some time that I needed a partner to run this mill, one who is good with figures, can balance the books, make sure that the money coming in tallies with the loads going out and that everything is sent to the right place. When I agreed on a contract with Gilbert, while he was still the royal reeve and not De Tosny's dogsbody, there was a clause which gave me the right to build a house on that piece of land near the fisheries. I have never found the time, but with a reliable partner to help me —well, we could build a fair sized house with a proper roof over Freya's kitchen instead of a tent. Room for expansion.'

Edmund's face was coming alive now, as if he had woken from a trance and was attempting to get his bearings and his eyes filled with tears.

Ilsa was sure that this was her moment.

'Viking and Saxon blood is a very strong mix Edmund. I am with child.'

'My child?'

'For certain yours, dull wit. Do you think any other man has laid hands on me? We will teach our son or daughter all your family traditions and all mine too, so it will grow up doubly strong.'

Edmund felt the sheet of ice inside him cracking down the middle and thawing at a pace beyond his ability to cope. He began to weep. Ilsa stood beside his chair and putting her arms around his head, held it to her breast, as he sobbed like a child, unable to control the multitude of conflicting emotions that were set free now that his defences had been breached.

'Let go of it my love,' she soothed. 'Let go of all the pain, the loss, the hatred. Let it all go. We will have a future. We will have a fine future.

CHAPTER EIGHT

The eldest members of the village community declared that they could never remember such a wet spring. It rained all through April and the first two weeks of May. All the streams overflowed and soaked the meadow land; the earth was soggy underfoot, water oozing out beneath the pressure of feet or hooves. Rivulets ran down the side of the road and into the houses. The persistent rain found all the weak spots in the roofs, all the cracks in the walls. The shelter that the family of Geraint the hurdle maker called home was washed away in one deluge. They were living now in a lean-to abutting on Steven the priest's small glebe cottage. They were slaves, but they were still part of his flock and he could not leave them without a refuge. The church roof was leaking above the altar and Steven had removed the cross and altar cloth for fear of staining. Geraint promised to help him repair the roof when the weather improved, to repay the priest for his charity

The common land beside the River Avon had turned into a lake making it impossible for the Melksham folk to graze their cattle. Alleyn the miller feared that the fisheries pond would overflow into the house that he and his son-in-law had only just completed before the rains began. The meadow did flood, but they had built the house on a raised platform, three feet above ground level and although the water ran under the platform, it did not penetrate the house.

The villagers had one consolation. Roger De Tosny's

castle was built. They need divide their labour between working their fields and hauling masonry no longer. It had taken two years of hard toil and now it loomed over them, dark and forbidding in the rain. It had been completed six months past, but they still found it hard to get used to the threatening presence of it. Constructed on a mound, it was surrounded by a ten foot wide moat crossed by a drawbridge. The imposing keep made the castle look larger than it was in fact, for the walls built in a perfect circle just fitted the circumference of the mound. Although he referred to it as 'my castle' with some pride, De Tosny never intended to live in it, so the quarters for the knights were basic and Spartan. It served its purpose as a statement of Roger's power and his ability to defend his own rights, as well as those of the king.

King William, with a large retinue, visited De Tosny the previous October to inspect the castle and congratulate Roger on its completion. Now it was occupied by a small contingent of Roger's knights.

The villagers were wary of these men, who were violent and arrogant with the habit of descending on them without warning, to demand their fattest pig or tender lamb for a feast they were planning.

De Tosny and his sister were in Normandy. Soon after the king's visit, they had left the manor in the charge of the stewards and taken ship at Southampton, sailing to La Havre and travelling on from there to the family estates near Liseux. His brother Ralph had died after a fall from his horse and Roger was eager to secure his lands in Normandy for himself. Ralph's sons were not old enough to inherit and Roger needed to claim wardship.

The responsibility of caring for the business of the estate in Wiltshire fell to Gilbert the reeve, who was instructed to call on the services of the knights from the castle if he needed any muscle. He was determined that such a call would be the very last resort. Gilbert was a loyal servant to his Norman master, but he was still a Saxon. He felt loyalty to the villagers also and always dealt with them in a reasonable manner, giving as much leeway as he dare.

It was the 16th day of May. The late morning sun was warm. It had not rained for two days and the heat of the sun caused the damp earth to steam with vapour. Edmund the thegn stood on the bank of the river with his arm around his wife's waist, looking at the remnants of the bridge. Ceawlin said it had been shattered in a heavy storm over a week past.

Edmund and Ilsa visited Ceawlin that morning bringing a cartload of provisions to relieve his family's distress. The cottar lived on the very edge of De Tosny's estate in an isolated hollow, near a copse. A nearby pond had overflowed and brackish water had saturated the inside of his house, ruining his food store. He had six young children and appealed to the council of the four villages for help. Edmund, who presided over the meetings of the council, organised a collection of supplies from those who could spare them. The bulk of it came from the mill and the monastery.

That May morning they loaded the goods into one of Alleyn's carts and harnessed up Toiler, the cart horse.

Ilsa took charge of the cart whilst Edmund rode beside her on Midnight. They left their nineteen month old son Edgar, named after his grandfather, in the care of his Uncle Dunstan, who was holding the boy up to wave to his parents as they drove out of the yard. Edgar had hoped to go too, sitting in front of his father on the big, black horse, as he often did. He cried for a while, but Dunstan soon diverted his attention.

Ilsa, as she stood with her husband watching the fast swirling current of the river, was thinking how lucky they were. The flood from the fisheries pond might have damaged their own house if it had risen another foot or so.

Ceawlin's small cottage had smelt sour with the damp and part of one wall was crumbling away. Edmund assured him that he would get help to repair it.

Now the weather had turned, a group of volunteers from the villages would assist those in most need to put their houses back in order. The cottar was grateful for any support he could get and he knew he could rely on Master Edmund to keep his word. He told him that the wooden bridge across the river, several miles from the villages, had been swept away and Edmund decided to take a look.

The support posts on both banks were still in place, but the main body of the bridge had collapsed into the river. Pieces of jagged plank were trapped in the vegetation along the banks, but most of it had been washed away downstream. This bridge was the access for all the traffic to and from De Tosny's estate. It was the shortest route to Bradford and Bath beyond it. The next bridge was more than eight miles downstream.

'We must get this repaired quickly,' Edmund mused. 'If there is no more heavy rain, the river level will drop and the current slacken. Using the other bridge will double the time it takes to reach Bradford. Your father will not be happy about that. I think this is Bradford borough land though. I must ask Gilbert to talk to the borough reeve.'

Gilbert the reeve discovered that Edmund was still alive on the day the thegn's son was born. In the May of that year, he was told by Eadwig that Ilsa Thurkilson had married a distant cousin of the miller's from Bristol. James was the son of a merchant and had decided to stay on in the village and work with his father-in-law in the mill. Gilbert knew how attached Ilsa had been to Edmund and thought it wise of her father to marry her off as soon as he could. Ilsa's burgeoning stomach soon bore witness that her marriage had been consummated. He was frustrated though because whenever he called at the mill, he never managed to find James there. He was always off on an errand for Alleyn or taking a load of corn somewhere.

Gilbert was pleased to see the miller start building a house on the meadow by the fisheries and assumed that James put much of his time into that; but again, he was never working there when Gilbert strolled over to check on the progress of the building.

One day in late September, aware that Ilsa was near her time, he called at the mill to see if all was well. The door into the miller's living quarters was open and the reeve heard the sound of a baby crying.

Delighted, he walked straight in. The curtain was pulled back from Ilsa's bed and he saw the miller's daughter propped up with pillows, surrounded by her parents, her husband and Dunstan. Freya took a small bundle from beside Ilsa and handed it to the man Gilbert assumed was James. He would meet him at last.

He called out his congratulations and walked towards them, but when they all turned to look at him, instead of joy at the new arrival, their faces registered dismay.

'I am sorry to intrude on a family celebration,' Gilbert said, puzzled by their reaction, 'I hope it was an easy birth. I am happy to be the first to congratulate you.'

'Thank you Gilbert.' It was James who answered.

The reeve stopped. That voice seemed very familiar to him. He took a closer look at the man cradling his new born son and the shock caused him to step back several paces. He looked so much like his father with that beard. Gilbert was staring into the dark eyes of Edmund, son of Edgar. The reeve leaned against the table behind him for support. His senses were confirming something that could not be true.

'But how, how?' he stammered.

Dunstan took his arm and inviting him to sit down, told him a concise version of Edmund's escape that night. Gilbert sat there shaking his head.

'You mean to tell me that the whole village has known this for months and managed to keep it from me- even Oswin. That truly is a miracle. I wondered why Ilsa's husband was never around when I called.'

Edmund kissed the baby on the head, smiling at the pink, wrinkled face and placed him tenderly back into

Ilsa's arms, before he turned to Gilbert saying.

'Well now you know the truth and our safety is in your hands. It is your duty to tell your master and if you do, Ilsa, my son and I must find a refuge elsewhere. You had best tell me what you intend to do, so we can prepare for it. At least give us the chance to do that.'

'Edmund, do you think I rejoiced at the news of your death? I was sorely grieved and turning Dunstan out of the farm was one of the hardest things I have had to do as a reeve. I have always valued the memory of my friendship with your father and I would never betray his son.'

Edmund was convinced that Gilbert's avowal was genuine. He thanked him.

'That night I lost my temper and waved a sword under your nose. It was hot-headed of me. I called you some vile names I remember and I take them back. You did not deserve that. I hope you will not hold it against me.'

He was offering his hand and Gilbert gripped it willingly his brown face creased with pleasure.

'As you are indeed the first to congratulate us on the birth of my son, who by the way will be named Edgar in honour of my father, stay and take a cup of ale with us to celebrate.'

'The second one will be named after someone in my family,' Alleyn announced, pouring the reeve a drink and slapping him on the back.

Standing on the river bank, surveying the shattered bridge, Edmund recalled the wave of relief that had washed over everyone in the room when Gilbert had agreed to keep their secret. The simultaneous release of breath was audible. Gilbert's support made life easier. On several occasions Edmund stood up to knights from the castle when they attempted to take stock from the villagers without paying for it. Rather than complain to De Tosny, they filtered their irritation with James, the miller's son-in-law through the reeve, who promised to lay the matter before his master, but never did. Edmund was able to walk around more openly now that he did not have to dodge Gilbert. He could not appear at the shire court, but he used Eadwig, the village headman as his mouthpiece to present ideas or complaints and Eadwig enjoyed the respect he attained for his sagacity.

Edmund was wondering now how he could have been such a fool as to think that his life had no meaning because he failed to kill Roger De Tosny, but it had been a hard struggle to regain a sense of self-worth even after he had begun to believe there was some hope for the future. His unsettling dreams had continued for months. Even now there were times when he could feel a dark cloud descending around him and he would go off on his own to wrestle with it. He could not forgive like Dunstan; the best he could manage was a militant acceptance, a determination to preserve his culture and customs from erosion and protect the rights of the villagers where possible. He had to admit that he rarely lingered for long near the family lands. They stirred up too many memories and feelings that he had vowed to put behind him.

Dunstan walked through the woods from time

to time and reported back to his brother that both farm houses were in good repair, the fields and copse well maintained and the livestock thriving.

On one such reconnaissance, Dunstan saw Roger De Tosny in what was once their yard, talking to the tenants. It was not a friendly discussion. The Norman had not dismounted and he appeared to be giving orders in a peremptory manner. Dunstan walked away into the woods. He had no desire to come face to face with the lord of the manor.

Edmund was so lost in thought that Ilsa stretched up and kissed his cheek to break his reverie.

'We must be getting home my love. Dunstan will be growing very weary of amusing Edgar by now. You know what a little demon he can be.'

Her husband laughed. 'Oh Dunstan has the measure of him. I am sure they have enjoyed their morning.'

Mankel, who had been following the scent of an otter upstream, came running back down, growling, his sharp ears picking up the sound of horses in the distance. Within minutes a carriage came into view, heading at a fast pace towards the river, accompanied by a rider on a large bay horse.

Expecting to drive straight across the bridge, the driver had to rein back hard to stop the horse plunging into the river.

The driver was a powerful man with the build of a wrestler. The couple on the opposite bank knew him well – Blanche's servant Gaston. The rider who dismounted, cursing at the broken bridge was Roger De Tosny.

'Christ,' muttered Edmund through clenched teeth, pulling up the hood of his jerkin, 'He is the last person I wished to see today.'

De Tosny was fuming. He had settled his business in Normandy to his satisfaction, but it had taken much longer than he planned. The voyage back across the Channel was stormy and Roger was a poor sailor. He staggered off the boat at Southampton feeling as if he had no insides left. What made it worse was the fact that the choppy seas had no effect on Blanche at all. She continued to look unruffled and elegant throughout the voyage. He was in a hurry to get home. He had designs on Ralph's estate at Tetbury, but had received a message informing him that his sister-in-law's family had anticipated his move. Eleanor's father was influential, a confidant of the king. Ralph's eldest son was twelve and his grandfather intended to protect his interests. Roger had agreed to meet with his representatives at his earliest convenience. The floods held them up on their journey from Southampton and the sight of the broken bridge was the last straw.

'Drive on through it,' he ordered Gaston.

Instead of obeying, the servant jumped down from the coach.

'No, my lord.'

Roger could scarce believe his ears.

'What did you say?'

'No my lord, I am sorry but it is too dangerous. My lady cannot swim and nor can I'

'You will have no need to swim. How dare you defy me! Get back up there.'

Gaston stood defiant. Blanche stepped down out of the coach. Edmund had not seen her since the night she saved his life.

She was as fashionable as ever in a deep purple cloak edged with silver braid, the dress showing beneath it a shimmering summer blue. She registered distaste as her feet sunk into the spongy grass. The unexpected sight of Blanche stirred memories in Edmund that he thought he had buried long since; the sensation of her smooth skin under his fingers, the dazzling sheen of her black hair lying across her naked breast. He stole a quick glance at Ilsa. His wife was so attuned to his feelings, he feared she would sense his reaction to Blanche, but at that moment Ilsa was too concerned over the possibility of being recognised.

Blanche was defending her servant.

'Roger, you know full well that he saw his mother drown in a river when he was a child. He is terrified of water. That is why I lodged him at Southampton instead of taking him to Normandy with us. Besides,' she looked into the fast flowing water, 'I think he is right. It must be seven feet deep. We cannot drive across that.'

'Just here it is not so deep. The river bed rises up much higher at this point. It is not much more than four foot deep here. I will drive myself if Gaston is so lily-livered.'

'Why can we not go down to the next bridge?'

'It must be ten miles downstream. Then we would have to head back up again- 20 miles out of our way. I am late enough already. I have documents to prepare.'

'All this haste so you can cheat your nephew out of his inheritance.'

'I do not intend to cheat him out of his inheritance dear sister. I merely wish to enjoy the profits of the estate while he is still a minor and I need to stake my claim before Eleanor's father and that tribe of brothers of hers get too far ahead of me.'

'But the water will leak into my coach.'

'It will dry out soon enough. You can sit up on the driver's seat with me and keep your clothes dry.'

He stepped forward to clamber up on to the seat, but Gaston barred his way.

'Get out of the way damn you!' Roger pushed him, but it had no effect on the man, who was as solid as a stone wall.

'I cannot let you my lord. You must not endanger the life of the Lady Blanche.'

'You cannot let me? Who are you to tell me what I can or cannot do?' De Tosny drew his sword. 'I have a mind to teach you a lesson.'

Blanche moved between them, resting a hand on the broad expanse of Gaston's chest.

'Let him pass my faithful Gaston. He is angry enough to kill you and that would be a great misfortune. I will perch on the driver's seat with my bad tempered brother and be sprayed with water. There is nothing to worry about.'

Gaston moved aside with reluctance and glowering at him, Roger climbed up on to the seat, holding out a hand to assist Blanche to join him. Ilsa tugged at Edmund's sleeve. 'Let's get away from here. He will recognise you.'

'They have not even noticed us. To them we are just

a couple of peasants with a cart, gawping at our betters.'

Edmund was eager to follow the outcome of Roger's impatience, even at the risk of discovery.

'Do you think he will get across?' his wife asked.

'He is right about that stretch of river being shallower because of the raised bed. They may make it if the current is not too strong.'

De Tosny was urging the horse into the water, calling back over his shoulder,

'You ride my horse down to the next bridge if you are afraid to follow. I will have some harsh words to say to you when you get back to the manor. Do not imagine your mistress will always be able to protect you.'

The coach horse was strong and splashed on without fear while its hooves still touched the river bottom. The water came up to the traces and as Blanche had predicted, into the coach itself. They had almost reached the other side, when the bed of the river dropped down steeply and the horse found itself swimming. It jerked in the harness, afraid of being pulled down, causing the coach to lurch sideways, throwing both Roger and Blanche into the river. De Tosny was thrown right out into mid- stream, but his sister landed near the struggling horse and clung on to the wheel of the coach, which was now tipped over on its side close to the bank.

Edmund did not hesitate. He pulled the knife from his belt and waded into the river, taking hold of the nearest wheel to steady himself. The vehicle was stuck in the mud of the river bed, but the angry current was pushing at it with relentless force and he feared it would break away before he reached Blanche. Avoiding the horse's flailing hooves, he cut through the leather traces that bound it to the coach, enabling the frightened creature to scramble up the bank. Mankel was running up and down, barking in a frenzy of excitement as Ilsa encouraged the horse away from the river's edge.

Edmund, using the remnant of the traces still attached to the coach, hauled himself over to Blanche and taking her around the waist, pulled them both to the bank with the harness. Ilsa helped them to claw their way up the crumbling bank on to drier land.

Blanche sat coughing and spitting out water. While struggling in the river she had little time to study her rescuer. She had not looked him full in the face. It was only when he spoke that she looked at him properly.

'I will try to help Roger.' He was running downstream with Mankel in pursuit.

Blanche recognised Ilsa now, as her thick rope of auburn hair swung across her shoulder. The irony of the situation was not lost on her, but she said nothing, allowing Ilsa to help her up. They both followed Edmund downstream.

Gaston was sprinting along the opposite bank, watching De Tosny pulled along by the swirling current. He went under once, but managed to struggle to the surface. Edmund was almost abreast of him, but the Norman was in the middle of the river, too far for either Gaston or Edmund to reach out to him. About fifty yards further down, a tree uprooted in the storms had fallen towards the river, part of the trunk and the branches projecting into the water. Roger made a desperate grab for the longest branch and clung on. His hold was tenuous and he feared to put pressure on the branch to pull himself towards the trunk in case it snapped off.

Edmund reached the spot and stopped. His pulse was throbbing, but it was more than the running that made the heat rise in his face. He saw Roger De Tosny, the man he had failed to kill, the man he hated so much, clinging to that slender branch, helpless, buffeted by the current. When the thegn lay on Roger's Flemish rug, bleeding from axe wounds, De Tosny had mocked him, refused to finish him off, so he could watch him bleed to death. This was the man who was responsible for the deaths of Cenred and Cerdic and had caused Dunstan so much sorrow. All Edmund need do was stand on the bank and watch until the river washed him away, like so much flotsam and he would be requited.

De Tosny could see a man on the bank and shouted for help. He could feel his fingers, numbed by the cold water, slipping off the branch.

Edmund was aware of Ilsa and Blanche running towards him and Gaston on the opposite bank, his face still impassive, but the tension showing in his body, as he jerked his hands up and down. Another thought struck Edmund, that should he succeed in rescuing Roger, the Norman must recognise him for certain and was unlikely to be grateful enough to forget the past.

But he knew that this was no way to settle scores; to watch an enemy drown was no part of the thegn's creed. He straddled the tree trunk as if it was a horse and edged along it until Roger was within reach. He put his hand over the Norman's.

'Let go of the branch and I will pull you up.'

Roger looked up into the face of his saviour. The Saxon's hood had fallen back from his head. It was not a face De Tosny was ever likely to forget. He stared into Edmund's eyes in disbelief. The thegn was urging him to grasp his hand, but in that moment of astonished recognition, Roger relaxed his fingers and it was fatal. He was caught in an eddy of water, his hand slipped out of Edmund's grasp and he was pulled back into mid-stream, to disappear from sight as he was hit by a large piece of driftwood and sunk below the surface.

Edmund was a strong swimmer and contemplated diving in, but he was restrained by Ilsa and Blanche.

'No Edmund,' Blanche said. 'Do not risk your life. It would be too ironical to see you saved from death after you had tried to kill my brother, only to lose your life trying to save him.'

She was calm; there were no tears, but her face was pale and strained.

'Strange, Roger rarely took risks – all this because he was so eager to lay hands on another piece of property. How will we find him?'

'If he is drowned,' Edmund replied, knowing an alternative was unlikely, but feeling obliged to offer her the possibility, 'the body will be swept on downstream until something stops it – a fisherman's net, wreckage in the river, some reeds- Gaston should take your brother's horse and ride on down to see if he can locate where he comes to rest.'

Blanche nodded. When she called to Gaston her voice was firm, but as she watched her servant running back upstream to retrieve De Tosny's horse, she began to shiver and realised that her legs were shaking. She swayed a little and was grateful when Edmund put his arm around her shoulders. She leaned against him as he steered her gently towards their cart.

'We must take you home,' Ilsa said, 'The sun will help to warm you. Sit beside me on the cart, more humble than your coach I fear, but it will get you home.'

Blanche was surprised that she could not find the strength to clamber on to the cart beside Ilsa. Edmund picked her up and lifted her on to the seat. Ilsa was leaning back, searching around in the cart behind her and produced the two empty sacks in which they had carried the provisions for Ceawlin's family.

She handed them to Edmund, who slit them both open with his knife. One sack they wrapped around Blanche's shoulders and the other they placed across her lap. He apologised for their roughness. 'But they will help to keep you warm.'

The coach horse, no worse for its ordeal, was grazing beside Edmund's black stallion, whose reins were looped over a sapling. Edmund twisted a make-shift halter from a length of rope coiled inside the cart and tied the coach horse to the back of the vehicle. The coach itself was still on its side, stuck fast in the river bed, too heavy for the current to shift.

'You can send some of those bully boys from the

castle to retrieve that,' Edmund said, as he swung himself into the saddle. 'It's about time they did something useful instead of intimidating the villagers for sport.'

His words sounded more aggressive than he intended and he was sorry he had spoken them, for he did not wish to add to Blanche's distress by displaying his antagonism towards her brother's failure to control his knights.

It was not appropriate in this situation. He had never seen her so vulnerable and in need of kindness.

Any villager going about his business that afternoon stood and gawped to see Edmund the thegn and his wife returning to their new house beyond the mill. The last thing they expected to see was the Lady Blanche, wrapped in hessian corn sacks, sitting beside Ilsa in one of the miller's carts.

They had heard gossip that the lord of the manor and his sister were returning, but this was a strange homecoming indeed. Oswin was gazing out from the forge when they passed by and called out to his wife to confirm that his eyes did not deceive him. Then he hurried out to tell his neighbours. Soon the news was all over the village.

Edmund rode on ahead, past the mill, towards the capacious house that he and Dunstan had helped Alleyn to build. They had invited Dunstan to live with them; there was room enough, but he was happy at the monastery and declined. However, hardly a day went by when he did not visit his brother and spend time with his nephew. Edmund could see him now, in front of the house with Edgar on his back, galloping along with his clumsy, loping run. Edgar from his elevated position saw them coming and shouted, 'Father is coming!'

Edmund laughed at himself for the pleasure he felt every time he heard his son call him father, particularly as he recalled that he had once told Dunstan that he did not want any children. Edgar was not yet two years old, but his grasp of words was well beyond many children his age and he spoke them clearly.

Dunstan trotted up to his brother, still pretending to be a horse and Edmund lifted the boy from his back and on to the saddle of the real horse, where Edgar loved to be. When Dunstan saw Blanche sitting beside Ilsa, he looked inquiringly into Edmund's face and walked along beside Midnight while his brother related the dramatic events of the morning.

'I had hold of his hand Dunstan. I could have pulled him up, but he relaxed his grip. I do not know if it was just the shock of recognising me or whether he was too proud to accept my help.'

'But you chose to save him.'

'I must confess that I did ponder over it for a short while. I was tempted to leave him to his own devices, but I had to help him in the end, no matter what the consequences.'

'I know why.'

'Yes, because I am a fool.'

'No because you are magnificent.' Edmund raised his eyebrows.

'Blanche's words Edmund. She told me that night, when I asked her why she was helping us. She said that I must remember that you were magnificent and you are.'

'Tis not a word I would choose brother. Now go in and get the fire going. She is chilled to the bone.'

Dunstan was amused that he had surprised and somewhat embarrassed his brother.

Blanche sat by the fire in a dress borrowed from Ilsa, watching her own garments spread around the hearth to dry. The dress hung loosely on her slender frame and did not smell of the perfumes that her maid sprinkled on her mistress's clothes. In ordinary circumstances this would have troubled Blanche, but not today. All she thought about was the image of Roger disappearing beneath the surface of the water. Edmund once asked her if she loved her brother. Her answer was equivocal then. She was not sure even now, but she felt his loss more than she ever imagined. She and Ralph were both older than Roger, she by six years and Ralph by four. When they were children Ralph had bullied him constantly, but he never whined or complained, nor did he come to Blanche for comfort. He always shied away from any attempts at sisterly affection. He was self-possessed and knew what he wanted at a very tender age. Well aware that his mind worked twice the speed of Ralph's, he was content to bide his time and get the better of him in other ways. He did not seem to feel the need for love or companionship in the way most children did.

Now she had lost both her brothers within a short space of time. She would not miss Ralph but life would be strange without Roger.

Looking up, she saw another child staring at her

with unabashed curiosity. Edgar was standing beside her, wondering who this woman with the olive skin, wearing his mother's dress, might be. She was different from the village folk. Ilsa scooped him up in her arms, scolding him for staring so openly.

'No, do not chide him. He is puzzled about where such a strange creature has come from. His gaze is steady. He has Edmund's eyes.'

The room relapsed back into silence until Blanche murmured, 'I wonder if Gaston has found him yet.'

Dunstan assured her that he would be found, although it might take a while.

'I am going to walk back to the monastery now and tell Father Robert. I am sure he will come to you at the manor as soon as he can. We will all pray for Roger's soul.'

Blanche wanted to make a cynical remark about how little religious devotions comforted her, but she did not have the heart.

She exchanged glances with Edmund who knew well what she was thinking, and then she said to Dunstan, 'You still have all that thatch of hair- no tonsure I see. You have not become a monk then?'

'No, I did not see the need. I suppose I am a kind of lay brother, but I am free to come and go as I please. I work in the monastery fields and tend the animals. I love the gardens. Brother Samuel, who runs the dispensary, is teaching me about herbal cures and I have learned much about them from Ilsa's mother too. Also I am beginning to catalogue the manuscripts in the monastery library. But I could never cut myself off from my family and the village.

I come here most days and help out where I can.'

'He has never been happier,' Edmund affirmed, as his brother took leave of them and set off for the monastery to tell the Abbot the grave news.

When Blanche's clothes were dry enough to wear, she changed back into them and declared herself ready to go to the manor house. She felt strong enough to ride, so Edmund saddled up the coach horse. Blanche embraced Ilsa with a warmth that the miller's daughter did not expect. Edmund had told her that he suspected Blanche to be a lonely woman beneath her sophisticated façade; a woman who had been married off twice to rough, uncaring soldier husbands, who had given her little affection.

Ilsa was sure now that it was true and felt compassion for the woman who had once caused her so much jealousy.

Her sympathy was genuine, but as she watched the solicitous way Edmund helped her into the saddle, she knew she did not want him to spend much more time with Blanche, for fear the compassion would turn back to jealousy again. Blanche had saved her husband's life because she loved him; Edmund must surely feel the attraction of that. There was a spark between him and Blanche still. Ilsa was determined to make sure that it did not ignite into a fire once more.

Edmund and Blanche rode together through the village without speaking.

They were both aware of the eyes that followed their progress, as villagers peered at them from various vantage points. Edmund smiled to himself, imagining the pairs of feet that would tread the path to the mill, their owners hoping to pump Alleyn for information.

They reached the Manor House just as the sun was setting in a blaze of red/gold. Blanche reined in her horse at the gates gilded by the last rays of the sun.

'You need come no further Edmund. I must not get used to relying on you. It is too much of a pleasure and would not be wise. Roger's stewards are both trustworthy, practical men who will give me the advice and support I need. I will send your saddle back to you.'

He shrugged to indicate that the fate of his saddle had not crossed his mind. He was more concerned with her situation.

'What will you do?' he asked.

'Do not worry about me. I can look after myself. I am a survivor; you know that. I shall no doubt come to some arrangement with Eleanor's family that will be advantageous to me. I have choices.'

'Have you family or friends in Normandy?'

'A few, but none I would care to live with.'

He admired her courage for he feared that she faced a lonely future and knew there was little he could do about it.

'I have never thanked you for what you did for me and for Dunstan that night Blanche.'

'You have repaid me in full by your willingness to attempt to save Roger. If you had succeeded, there was no guarantee of his gratitude. I think he would have set his knights on you. He is –was– implacable. Reason on the surface, stone underneath. Poor Roger-'

Her lip trembled and for the first time since the

incident. Edmund thought she might weep, but she did not, continuing, 'It is that noble streak in you which often endangers your own safety. There is one more thing I can do for you. Eleanor's father is a friend of the king.

I will persuade him to arrange an audience for me with William. I believe the king was impressed when he visited the castle and will long remember our hospitality. I will tell him how you rescued me and bravely tried to save Roger at the risk of your own life, despite the fact that your lands were forfeited to him because of a misdemeanour in the past.'

Edmund laughed. 'A misdemeanour you call it! I think attempted murder might be described in far harsher terms. I doubt if William of Normandy would consider it leniently.' He could never bring himself to refer to William as the king.

'I will not give him the details. I cannot get your lands back my thegn, but I will request a pardon from him for any misdemeanour, so you will be free to do your duties at the shire court and beyond. Allow me to do this for you. It is little enough.'

'I would welcome it. I try hard to forget the ancestral lands. It is not easy even now. I was born there, so was Dunstan. In my imagination I often see myself standing in the yard on a golden summer afternoon watching the cows grazing in the pasture beyond or crossing the stream to visit my Uncle Cenred. Yet I do not have the courage to pass too closely there as it is now with strangers in the house. But I have embarked on a new life and I will not squander the chance you gave me to live. I wish there was more I could do for you.'

'You have done more than you know.' She had a strong desire to reach out and stroke his hair, but restrained herself. 'Go home now to your wife and son.'

'I need to visit Gilbert about the broken bridge. I will tell him what has happened. He will be a useful ally for you too. He's a good man.'

He was reluctant to part from her, sensing that it would be final, knowing it was right that it should be so, but feeling a keen regret. 'Do not let any of the contingent at the castle bully you. They are a rough lot. They swagger around the villages helping themselves to whatever takes their fancy. I imagine they will not readily take orders from a woman.'

'I can handle them. Besides the future of the manor and the castle will lie in the hands of the king now. He will decide who becomes the new lord. The knights will be given the choice to offer their services to him or find another master. They are not my responsibility; I shall be free of it all. The only servants I need are my maid Gisella and the faithful Gaston. He is worth his considerable weight in gold. Go home now, but be advised by me.

When you take your rightful place at the shire court and come up against the new lord or challenge his knights in the village, keep a tight rein on that high temper of yours. I shall not be here to rescue you again.'

He smiled remembering how much he enjoyed that teasing tone in her voice when they had been together. He wondered if she had missed him these two years. Her manner suggested that she had. He was sure that he had not troubled her dreams as she had disturbed his, but sensed that a desire for him still remained and it was not just his vanity wishing it to be so. He gazed at her for a moment longer and then turned his horse.

'Edmund, wait!' She rode up close to him. 'When Gaston put you in the coach that night, I kissed you. I thought that to be the very last kiss we would share. In truth I doubted if you would live and now look at you; a father with a fine son and loyal wife, fulfilling your thegnly duties in all manner of ways. Let this be the last kiss in these happier circumstances for you.'

She leaned from the saddle and kissed him. It was a full, lingering kiss, but one that truly meant farewell. Then she urged her horse into a trot, through the manor yard and out of sight. Edmund sat there for a while, savouring the touch of her lips, as he watched the sun slip below the horizon leaving a smudge of pink light edged with gold.

He thought as he rode off to find Gilbert the reeve that it would be more fitting if Dunstan prayed for her lonely soul while she lived than bother with Roger's that was beyond all aid.

Early the next morning, while the mist still hovered at ground level, the body of Roger De Tosny, lord of the manor, came home slung across the back of his favourite horse. Gaston had found him entangled in the support structure of the bridge that had withstood the recent storms, miles downstream.

A shepherd driving his flock to pasture had already spotted the dark shape beneath the bridge and helped to drag it on to the bank. Gaston took the body to the huddle of cottages nearby and demanded a length of cloth to wrap it in. The mere sight of Gaston was enough to intimidate the occupants into surrendering what was for them a valuable possession. Once the body was wrapped in its winding sheet and secured on the back of the horse, it was evening and the weary servant took a meal with the villeins and rested before riding home through the night.

He had made sure that the baron's dignity was preserved by shielding his body from prying eyes not only with the cloth, but also a cloak of darkness. This he did not so much for Roger's sake, but for his mistress, the Lady Blanche, whom he honoured and loved above all people.

He journeyed in a wide arc, to avoid the four villages and was met eventually by a small party of knights who had come out at first light to search. So Roger was escorted part of the way home, past his brooding castle, to the manor house.

Two weeks later, Gilbert the reeve had the satisfaction of nailing up in all the villages a royal proclamation stating that Edmund the thegn was pardoned for previous misdemeanours and all his rights as a freeman were confirmed. Gilbert took a copy to the shire reeve in person.

Roger De Tosny's funeral was a splendid affair. Everyone of any status in the shire attended. The king sent as a representative his half-brother, Odo of Bayeux, the earl of Kent to demonstrate how much he had valued De Tosny. He was laid to rest in a stone sarcophagus in a side chapel of the church, where he and his sister had attended services. A stone mason was already at work on an effigy for the tomb. Roger's sister, the Lady Blanche was heard to remark that though it was a fitting medium for Roger, she had no wish to be commemorated in stone.

On the day of the funeral, Edmund and Dunstan, the sons of Edgar the thegn, set out with a band of villagers to begin the task of repairing the houses damaged in the spring floods.

The End

AUTHOR'S NOTE

Readers who are familiar with North and West Wiltshire will recognise some of the place names in this book because I have used the current names instead of the variations that were in use in 1076. However Roger De Tosny's manor house and castle and the monastery on the hill are all fictional. The four villages on the manor are only partly fictional because I had in mind early settlements at Broughton Gifford, Norrington, Chalfield and Holt, remembering that the story is set ten years before the Domesday Survey.

The location of Edmund and Dunstan's land is very real though.

About two miles from Melksham is a hamlet of five houses called Challymead, bounded on the one side by the River Avon and the Great Western Railway line on the other. The road divides here. The bottom road goes on to Holt and Bradford on Avon and the higher road crosses over the railway bridge taking you to Broughton Gifford and Chalfield.

The name Challymead is of Old English origin with two possible derivations. It could mean low lying meadow land- shallow meadow or derive from the Saxon word ceald meaning cold- hence cold meadow.

In 1076 the landscape would have looked different

from today, flatter, more wooded and with trackways instead of proper roads.

I was born and lived until I was thirty one at Challymead Farm. I had a wonderfully free childhood playing with my friends, who were all keen to come to my house, where we played in the barns, the paddock, the dried out mill pond and across the fields. We waved at trains like the Railway Children and more dangerously, walked along the railway lines to see how far we could go without falling off.

Those fields doubled for the American Great Plains, the savannahs of Africa, the jungles of South America, the Australian outback and we time travelled to a wealth of different historical periods.

Even at junior school my form teacher used to say that I spoke about characters from history as if they lived next door and for me they did. It was inevitable that history was to be one of my subjects at University. I have always been attracted to the Anglo-Saxon period.

King Alfred is one of my great heroes. I have a Saxon patronymic- Boddington- Boda, a personal name; ingas from the Old English meaning people and ton- a settlement. So my early ancestors were the people from Boda's settlement; Boda's people.

Like most families, there have been other blood lines added over the centuries and I have some Welsh blood of which I am proud, but I like to think that my West Saxon forebears fought under the banner of the golden dragon of Wessex at the Battle of Hastings.

The tone of this novel may strike readers as anti-

Norman because it is written from the point of view of the conquered not the conquerors. It is set only ten years after that devastating change and feelings were still very raw. The conquest had less effect on the peasants than it did on the thegn class. The thegns were aristocrats in their society and they lost wealth, privilege and social position.

They found themselves living in a strange and unfriendly environment, survivors but with no place in society any more, tolerated with a sneery indifference by the men who had replaced them. But to be fair to the Normans, throughout the book I have hinted that there are other valid ways of interpreting the situation. The Normans were a violent, acquisitive race, a society far less civilized than the English, but they brought a vitality with them, a political genius.

Father Robert's vision of a unified nation took a long time to come to fruition. It was not until the reign of Edward III, nearly 300 years later that English was adopted as the official language of the law courts and royal writs and for Parliament to be opened in English. But the peasantry had always spoken the language of their ancestors. The core of the English language today is derived from Old English. It has been calculated that seventy percent of the words in any piece of written text have OE origins and the grammatical structure is basically Anglo-Saxon. It is significant too that the Normans accepted the existing administrative divisions of the country in shires, hundreds and wapentakes in the Danelaw. They did not disturb the ancient customs of the local courts because they perceived that the system worked. So much of our current local government has Anglo-Saxon roots.

On the subject of language I feel that when writing dialogue for a story set far back in time it is important that the conversation flows naturally and is not stilted or archaic, On the other hand modern words, phrases and constructions can sound out of place and jar on the ear. I have attempted to avoid linguistic anachronisms, but forgive me if a few have slipped through.

It is many years now since I roamed with my combative border collie Moss, the area where I have sited my story. I roam other fields now, more slowly than in those far off days and with less ability to climb high gates or squeeze through barbed wire, although I am still accompanied by a collie, my fifth since Moss. I cannot imagine a life without dogs. They feature in all my stories. But in my heart Challymead will always be my true home. Like Edmund with his lost ancestral land, I do not go past that way often and never linger. It is much changed and I prefer the images in my head of how it was then.

I first wrote the outline of this story many years ago when I did not think I would ever leave that home. As I have reworked and expanded it into a novel I have realised that it is in part a tribute to my happy childhood and the place and people that inspired it. It pleases me to imagine that it was once the home of generations of West Saxon thegns.

Sue Boddington
May 2020